A HUNDRED SUPERHUMANS WANTED GOLDEN TO THEMSELVES

"Why are you people so anxious to get the Space Force completely off this planet?" General Lorsch made her voice deliberately casual.

"You should not view us as opponents," said Kedro. "Do you believe that I am human, General Lorsch? Or even something less than that, perhaps?" Kedro's voice was low. But it was no longer soft, or tentative.

Seconds slid away in silence. Lorsch, trying with unexpected difficulty to frame her answer, felt an impression growing on her with the speed and force of nightmare. It was the impression that what sat and spoke with her in her office was not a man in any sense, but rather an elemental force, an alien being. She looked into Kedro's eyes, and her ego cowered and whimpered: *Is this how a pet dog feels, when it looks up at—*

FRED SABERHAGEN

THE GOLDEN PEOPLE

A BAEN BOOK

A Baen Book

Baen Enterprises
8-10 W. 36th Street
New York, N.Y. 10018

First Baen printing, September 1984

ISBN: 0-671-55904-4

Cover art by Alan Gutierrez

Printed in the United States of America

Distributed by
SIMON & SCHUSTER
MASS MERCHANDISE SALES COMPANY
1230 Avenue of the Americas
New York, N.Y. 10020

PART ONE

Chapter One

Fourteen-year-old Ray Kedro was backed up against one of the mural-painted walls in the Middle Boys' recreation yard doing what he could to defend himself, when twelve-year-old Adam Mann first saw him. Adam glanced up from the electronic pages of *Space Force Adventures*, and watched for a few moments with a playground veteran's indifference. Then he realized that the six kids facing Ray had more in mind than the routine taunting and roughing that they were likely to hand out to any newcomer. This time some of the guys were really hot about something.

Most of the angry bunch were a year or two older than Adam, and all but one of them were taller. But he was widely respected on this territory. He folded the comic book, the electronic pictures on the thin plastic pages darkening into lifelessness as he did so, and stuffed it into his pocket. Moving in the slightly swaggering gait that he had recently developed to what he considered near-perfection, he walked toward the group.

"What goes on?" Adam demanded. He had dark eyes that were often, as now, belligerent, medium brown hair with a slight curl in it, and a nose that had not been broken—not yet at least—but looked as if it might have been.

"He's a snooper." Big tough Pete swung out a long arm and slapped the new kid again. "He can read your mind. He's gonna be singin' for the bosses here—"

"I'm not!" The new kid was tall for the age-group of this yard, but thin, with incongruously good clothes that were dusty and rumpled now from his being pushed around. Mussed blond hair fell over blue eyes that looked scared but still didn't blink at being slapped. He had a handsome face, almost delicate, and bleeding now a little along one cheekbone and from the nose. But he didn't look to Adam like a sissy, only like a guy who couldn't understand what it was all about.

"He made them dice move!" another guy standing beside Big Pete put in. The tone made it a deadly accusation.

"You wanted me to play with dice!" the new kid shouted back at them. To Adam he still looked more angry than afraid. "I had to show you first what I can do. If I play dice with you, you'll have to trust me—"

"Play dice, play dice!" Pete mimicked, in a changing, cracking voice. Whenever Pete's voice betrayed him in that way, making him sound funny, he got mad, and now it made him madder than ever. "You goddam fairy!"

The guys were all yelling now, and waving fists. Adam was suddenly scared, in a cold, clear way. Not so much afraid of getting hurt, but that these guys he knew could get so wild over something

like this. Some stupid nonsense that didn't matter.
It didn't sound like the new guy had really done
them any harm.

Adam was beginning to understand, vaguely, or
he thought he was. There were, there had always
been, a few people in the world who could move
dice in more subtle ways than with their fingers,
move dice or other small objects using their minds
alone. The same people, or others with unusual
mental powers, could perform other tricks, equally
unsettling. Parapsych talents, the books in the Home
library called such abilities. Up until only a few
years ago hardly any scientists had believed that
such things existed. And Adam had never to his
knowledge met any of the rare folk who were so
gifted.

The little mob was surging forward, bent on
destruction. On impulse, Adam shoved his own
strong and stocky body in front of the new kid,
and knocked down big Pete's upraised arm. "Let
'im alone!"

Big Pete halted, gaping. "Why?"

"Because I say so!"

Pete gave an angry grunt, and swung. Adam's
reflexes and timing were already superb; his head
moved safely out of harm's way, and his own right
fist was already in a good position to hit back. He
got enough weight behind his counterpunch to flat-
ten Big Pete's nose.

Furious and clumsy, the little mob closed in on
Adam and the new kid. Something hit Adam, hard,
on the side of his head. In a daze, he found himself
flat on his back on the playground's genengineered
grass, looking up at a ring of faces filled with hate
and excitement. In a way, though he knew better,
it seemed to Adam that they were all playacting,

they couldn't be serious about this great stupidity they were engaged in. A part of his mind kept wanting to laugh at the foolishness of it all, even while he kicked and struck up at the lowering faces, and feet kicked back at him.

Then the recreation yard monitors came, running and shouting threats, from wherever they had been goofing off. They were older teenagers, full of strength and energy once they got started, and they arrived just in time to break up the fight before anyone was killed or crippled.

Half an hour later, sitting on a cot in the infirmary, waiting to get his lumps patched up, Adam listened with some satisfaction to the moans and curses coming from the next cubicle. That was where they were working on Big Pete, and from the snatches of the medics' talk that Adam could hear, it sounded like maybe Pete's nose was really broken.

Beside Adam sat the new kid, holding a coldpack to his head. His battered and dirty face was still handsome, but an empty, stunned look occupied it now. He was quivering faintly.

Adam asked him: "What's your name, guy?"

"Ray Kedro." The kid pulled in a deep breath, that helped him regain a measure of steadiness. He looked at Adam. "You may have saved my life today—I won't forget it." He tested a loose tooth gingerly with his fingers. "You're name's Adam? I hope this doesn't mean a lot more trouble for you."

Adam tried to laugh with a split lip. "Hey, they won't do much to us for fighting. Long as nobody got killed. Some extra duty probably is all. I was about due to hang one on Pete anyhow. Hey, was all that true, about you being a parapsych?" It was the first time Adam had ever tried to pronounce that fancy word, but he felt pretty sure that he had it right.

Ray hesitated, looking at him closely, then nodded. "I have—some of those—talents."

"Dice?"

"I could if I tried, I suppose."

"What about reading minds?"

The other shook his head. "You just don't reach into someone else's thoughts, for no good reason. It'd be like ... well, like doing the dirtiest thing you can imagine. I mean, I wouldn't like it any more than the person I was reading would."

"Huh." When Adam heard it put that way, it sounded more intriguing and at the same time more repulsive than before.

As if encouraged by Adam's reaction, or lack of one, Ray went on: "Maybe you *can* do it, but you don't. Of course if the other person wants you to get into their mind, and tells you so, that's different."

"Huh." Adam considered. "Hey, you know, I read somewhere once that any parapsych who could move dice with his mind could kill people too, just as easy. You know, just grab a little valve or something in their heart—"

"No." Ray's voice was flat and certain. "The talents don't work like that, they won't kill."

"They won't, huh?"

"They never have. There've been people who have tried it, but they just make themselves sick. Oh, someone might find a way to do it someday. Someone who was evil enough and worked at it. There are a few very rare cases—but those are spontaneous combustion—" The blond boy broke off, smiling suddenly, wincing as he did. "If I had any kind of a knockout punch, I'd have used it out there today."

"Hey, yeah, I guess."

Adam's prediction about the degree and type of punishment for fighting in the recreation yard was proven accurate. All those who had been involved in the playground brawl were given extra work, beginning the next day after school.

Assigned to work together, using a sonic machine to clean the walls and floor of a long corridor tiled in white and green, Adam and Ray talked again.

Adam asked his new acquaintance: "You know anyone else who's a parapsych?"

"Yes. Ninety-nine of them, to be exact."

"Ninety-nine!"

Ray paused thoughtfully. "Ever hear of a doctor, a medical researcher, named Emiliano Nowell?"

Adam tried to remember the name. He looked through daily news printouts sometimes, on days when he didn't use up all his reading time on library books and adventure comics. And he read news magazines when he could find them. "Emiliano Nowell. Isn't he the guy who bought out an old Space Force installation way out on Ganymede, and set up a place there to do research? Why'd he go way out there?"

"He wanted privacy. Not to be bothered."

Adam could understand that. "And he was raising kids there out of bottles, until the government found out about it, and . . . Hey. Are you—"

Ray was mechanically guiding the cleaning machine along, not really looking where it was going, but not looking at Adam either. "Yes, I'm one of his kids. The law took us all away from him and

Regina—that's his wife—and split us up, put us all in different Homes while they try to figure out what to do with us next. We can still touch minds with each other, now and then."

"You were raised way out on Ganymede? Wow."

"Not for very long. We were all brought to Earth about ten years ago. Doc owns quite a bit of real estate here too."

Adam was fascinated. He stared at Ray. "You look—human, like everyone else."

In the blue eyes deep pain was visible for just a moment. "We came from human seed, from human cells."

"Then what's the difference? I mean . . ." Adam was confused. Somehow he would have expected anyone he met with parapsych talents experts to be around three meters tall, and look like either the hero or the villain of a hologram thriller. Of course if he thought about it, that was crazy.

Adam was still curious, but he didn't know what to say now. He realized that he had just given offense by implying that Ray might not be human, and he was trying not to do so again.

Ray asked him: "Do you know what genes are?"

"No. Oh, wait, maybe . . ."

"They're little parts in the center of a living cell. Of all the human cells that make up your body. They decide everything you inherit from your parents: the way you look, your potential intelligence, and your parapsych potential too. What Doctor Nowell did was find a way to make forcefield manipulators small enough and controllable enough to use them to work on genes directly. Get right in and move the molecules and even the parts of molecules around. He experimented first on animal cells, and then on human. When he thought he had the technique perfected, he rebuilt a hundred fertilized human egg cells. And then he stopped."

"Why?"

"He says he wants to wait a quarter of a century, to see how his first batch turns out—that's us— before he does any more. Meanwhile he's keeping his techniques a secret, and some people are unhappy about that."

"Then you're what they call Jovians, in the news sometimes."

"That's right."

"He rebuilt you to be perfect, huh? You don't sound too happy about it."

"I wouldn't say perfect . . . I don't think Doc tried for that. What does perfect mean? Anyway, if we were, I don't think the world would like it. Whatever he tried for, Adam, we're very lucky. A lot of people are still born crippled."

Adam was silent for a while, working away with the cleaning nozzle, attacking stubborn stains on battered tile. This new kid Ray gave him a lot to think about. Ray talked with fancy words and a kind of accent that Adam supposed meant he had been brought up a long way from public Homes. But that way of talking sounded natural, for him.

Ray too was silent, as if he were thinking something out. Then he suddenly spoke up again. "Look, Adam, if things go right, the way I think they will, and I get out of here pretty soon . . . how'd you like to come to Doc's place for a visit?"

Adam almost dropped the cleaning nozzle. "You mean to Ganymede?" For Adam at twelve the Space Force and its activities were a holy cause; but space travel of any kind seemed to exist only in an alternate universe from the one he really lived in, something to be glimpsed only in stories and dreams.

Ray smiled. "No, no, none of us have been out there for years. I meant come to Doc's place here on Earth. That's where we've been living most of our lives. It's mostly one huge building, a little like an expensive boarding school. There are legal reasons why Doc doesn't want anyone but his own kids to live there permanently, but you'd be a welcome visitor."

"Gee, I'd like to see it. You sound like you're sure he's going to win all this court stuff and get you kids back with him again."

Ray's smile broadened. "I know him pretty well."

Chapter Two

The windows of the big laboratory room were wide, and open, and unbarred, and they framed Virginia mountains blue with distance. The giant chair in the middle of the room looked quite a bit like one that Adam had seen, and occasionally occupied, in the Home's infirmary. In that chair at the Home all the kids were tested once a year, and those with suspected brain damage sometimes received treatment. It, like everything else at the Home, looked worn and scrubbed, while this chair, like all the other equipment here in Doc Emiliano Nowell's laboratory, looked modern and expensive.

There were other and still more drastic differences between the two establishments. Here, the unbarred windows looked out from every room, onto what seemed to Adam like kilometers of green trees and grass and gardens. It was hard to believe that one man owned it all, even though Ray and the other kids had assured Adam that the boundary of the estate fell short of including those blue distant mountains.

At the moment Adam was sitting in the giant chair himself, trying to get comfortable under a huge metal helmet that had been let gently down until the probes it carried inside it sank through his brown hair, just to the point where they began to tickle his scalp.

"Doc, can I ask you something?" he wondered aloud, a little timidly.

"Sure. As long as I don't have to guarantee an answer." Doc—everyone around the place, children, servants, lab technicians, seemed to call him that— was a tall, lean, graying man, presently wearing a laboratory coat. He was seated halfway across the large room, in front of the psych-chair's control panel. He had, with Adam's ready permission, begun to put the young visitor through a series of physical and mental tests. Doc wanted to do this, as he had said, just out of curiosity. The two were alone, for the moment, in the lab.

Adam hesitated once more, then put his question: "About how much money have you got?"

Doc Nowell had a contagious laugh. "I thought you might be getting worried about the machine. Or wondering what position emission tomography meant." A little earlier, Adam had been reading those words aloud, from the equipment used in the last test. "How much money, huh? Well, Adam, let's just say that I'm too rich to be pushed around in court. My wealth is sufficient for my purposes. Which makes me a rarity among scientists . . . or among human beings in general, I suppose."

"That's neat, Doc."

"Yes, it is." Watching the panel in front of him, Doc paused to make a note on paper. "Oh, I haven't earned my money from society by probing for the secrets of life. No. It's mine by inheritance. Candy and chewing gum, mostly, a couple of generations back.''

Halfway down one of the room's long walls, a door slid open, and a girl entered the laboratory. Merit Creston was a year younger than Adam, which made her by about three years the baby of Doc's hundred genengineered children. The ages of most of the others were clustered closely together, and ranged up to seventeen. Adam was, at least by strict chronology, a visiting child among adolescents. But he, who had come as an infant to the public Home, could scarcely remember ever thinking of himself as a child. His teen-age hosts had obviously enjoyed a vastly different upbringing than his, and they impressed him as being mentally more grown-up than any group of adults he had ever encountered. Still, they were all so good at saying and doing the right thing that the visiting twelve-year-old rarely felt out of place.

Merit stood there in the doorway of the psych lab, wearing white shorts and a white blouse and a kind of footgear that Adam had learned were called tennis sandals. Merit's slender figure was developing already. Her face, in Adam's opinion, was—well, beautiful. And her hair had a kind of glint in it that made it really unlike the color of any other girl's hair that Adam had ever seen . . .

He knew that in a year or so he would start wanting girls in a physical way, like the older guys at the Home. What he felt about Merit now wasn't really that. It was something more—or maybe something less, Adam didn't know which. All he knew for sure was that he felt something powerful, and

felt confused and strange whenever he tried to
think about it.

Eleven-year-old Merit greeted him now with a
giggle. "Hi, Ad. You look like you're getting your
hair set."

Adam grunted. The problem was that he wanted
desperately to say something witty, to show he
didn't mind if she teased him a little, but he could
think of no words at all. Suddenly he remembered
there were a hundred telepaths, or at least potential telepaths, within a few hundred meters of him.
Now he could feel his face getting warm. Why in
hell did she have to stand there giggling at him—

"I think you'd better leave, young lady," said
Doc, raising his head from his control panel. "You're
a disturbing influence just now."

"All right, Grouchy Doc," said Merit. She spoke
as if humoring some elderly and harmless relative—
but she didn't argue. "Call me if he's mean to you,
Adam." She winked at the boy in the chair, and
gracefully closed the door behind her.

"So long," Adam called out, lamely, at the last
moment, as the door was already closing. Suddenly he felt angry with Merit, irritated with Doc,
with Doc's wife Regina, with the whole crew of
these people here, who had so damn much more
going for them than any group that Adam had
ever met before.

The lean man in the lab coat sighed, bending
over his control panel again. Then he straightened
up. "Let's try something, Adam." With an air of
decision, almost a theatrical gesture, Doc raised
and let fall a hand, extended finger touching one
of the panel switches. Adam could feel no change.
Doc said: "I want you to close your eyes now, and
imagine a black screen, waiting for a picture."

Adam closed his eyes. "What color is the screen?"

"Make it white. Okay? Got it?"

"I think so."

"Good. Now, just let the screen stay there, and listen to the story."

He was about to ask Doc what story, but there was no need. Right on cue, a recorded voice began to reach Adam's ears, coming to him through the helmet. In soothing tones the voice started telling him about a man named Caesar, who at some time, evidently long ago, had loaded an army onto a fleet of eighty ships, and sailed off with them for Britain.

"Keep your eyes closed, Adam," said Doc's voice, coming through the helmet too, now, as the storyteller paused. "Now, as you listen, try to imagine an ending for the story, and guide the story to that ending. Understand?"

"No sir, I don't think so. How can *I* change the story? Isn't it recorded?"

"You don't have to change it, really. Just give it a try. The effort should make some things happen that I can observe. All right?"

Adam shrugged, the helmet rustling on his scalp. He felt a faint tug. Somehow the probes in the helmet had taken hold of him, and he hadn't even noticed it until now. "Yessir, all right."

The whispering voice resumed its narrative. Caesar and his army poked around Britain, exploring and getting into trouble. They lost some of their ships in a storm, and fought against blue-painted warriors who liked to ride in chariots and hurl javelins. Adam didn't think much of Caesar, whoever he was, or had been. He seemed to have had no good reason for going to Britain and bothering the people who lived there.

Eyes still shut, Adam concentrated on trying to change the story. But, of course, the narrator's recorded voice just droned on. Adam didn't have anything to do with deciding what it said.

By now, the imaginary white screen in Adam's mind had been forgotten. If he *were* telling the story, he would have made up a different course of events, disliking Caesar as he did.

If only . . .

Just suppose . . . that some of the offended Britons could have sneaked into the invaders' camp, bent on revenge. Right into Caesar's tent, why not? Adam could see them clearly now, half a dozen men, not blue-painted but wearing robe-like garments, pulling out their knives suddenly and attacking. And Caesar reeled back and let out a hoarse scream, and his clothing was all blood. And Caesar's eyes closed, then opened, fastening on one of his killers. And . . .

"Kai su teknon!" The shouting voice broke with its emotion.

At the sound of the shout, Adam lurched upright in the giant chair. He was vaguely aware again of Doc Nowell's laboratory around him. But still at the same time, like watching a reflection in a window, he was still able to see the inside of Caesar's tent. Caesar had now disappeared, along with his killers, but something—Adam knew it demanded his full attention—stirred the fabric of the tent flap.

Now the head of a handsome man was thrust inside the tent. The man's forehead was high, under a fringe of dark hair, and his features were noble and impressive. But something about him was very wrong, frighteningly so. Adam knew that before he had the least idea of what the wrong thing was. The head intruded a little farther now into the tent, and now with horror the boy saw that it was borne on a long, scaly, reptilian neck. The body supporting that neck was still blessedly hidden by the flap of fabric making the tent door . . .

. . . and now, all around Adam in the vision, people were gathering. There might have been a hundred of them surrounding him. All of them, women and men alike, were giants, godlike in their beauty and power.

And now a single human figure came pushing its way through that awe-inspiring assembly. It was that of a stocky and powerful man, much more ordinary than the rest, except that he was wearing what might have been some kind of elaborate spacesuit. The face of the man in the spacesuit was clearly visible through the faceplate. It was solemn in its expression now, but Adam thought that there was a habit of humor in the eyes.

"My name is Alexander Golden," the stocky man in the spacesuit said to Adam. Then he turned toward the long-necked creature with the human head, and swung his arm as if to strike at it—

And then, abruptly, Doc Nowell's psych lab, its enclosing walls and equipment-loaded benches, was again the only visible reality. The psych helmet had already been raised from Adam's head, and Doc was standing close beside the great chair, looking at him intently.

"What happened?" they asked each other, speaking simultaneously.

It was Doc who answered first, putting on a faint smile that might not have been quite genuine. "Well, you went to sleep, that's what happened. Sometimes my stories, recorded or otherwise, have been known to have that effect on people. But what did you experience?"

Adam related as well as he could what he had seen and heard. As if it had been a true dream, some of the details were already starting to go.

He concluded: "And then the last man said that his name was—Alec Golding. I think. Something like that."

"It's fading?" Doc's tone was sharp.

"Yeah. Like a dream."

"The face of the man in the suit—you say you saw it plainly. Do you know him? Ever see him before?"

"No. I don't think so." It was hard to be sure. Now that last face was going too.

Doc hesitated, on the brink of saying something else. Then he turned away to shut things down at the control panel.

He turned back. *"Kai su teknon* is Greek—means something like 'you too, my child.' It's what Caesar is supposed to have cried out when he was stabbed, though that didn't happen in Britain—you know who Caesar was?"

"Nossir. When I read it's mostly about the Space Force."

"Damn. Oh, it's not your fault. The Space Force is a worthy subject too, I suppose, but—don't they teach you anything at that Home?"

"They say next year they're gonna reorganize the school."

"I should hope so . . . anyway, Caesar was quite a famous man. He's in the minds of a lot of other people down through the centuries, and his death-scene is one of the classical results we get from this test. Though I must say not one of the more common ones. You picked it up either from me, or directly from the past. Shows you have at least a fair amount of parapsych potential, certainly more than I do myself. If you had begun training very early, you might have become quite adept."

Doc walked back to the great chair in which his subject was still sitting, and rested his hands on one of the padded arms. "Adam, you interest me. Your biological inheritance is—superb. Almost equal to that of my children here. Whoever your parents were—you said you don't know."

"Nossir. They never could find out at the Home. Someone just left me there, when I was a baby."

"An unlucky start, in many ways. I was about to say, whoever your parents were, they at least blessed you with a superb genetic inheritance. One quite good enough to enable you to overcome environmental difficulties. You could, for example, become an outstanding athlete. But I think you have too good a mind to be satisfied with only that. We're going to have to make sure that your schooling is improved. And there is definitely some parapsych potential—but you may be happier with that undeveloped."

Adam didn't know what to say. *Almost equal to that of my children here.* He thought of Ray, backed up against the playground wall.

Out of the hundred Jovian kids, as the news media had christened them, only Merit and Ray ever became anything like close friends to Adam. The others, all of them at least slightly older than Ray, were always pleasant enough to Adam on his visits to Doc Nowell's estate. But when they were out of Adam's sight he sometimes had difficulty in even remembering their names and faces.

*   *   *

. . . and now the physical wanting was over, for the moment. In a way, for Adam, it hadn't been much different from what happened when one of the girls in the Home became available and willing. And in another way it had been very different indeed from that.

Adam lay watching Merit, who at the moment was lying on her back with her eyes closed. It was a summer afternoon, and the two of them were on one of the small, isolated roof-terraces of Doc Nowell's huge house. Their clothing was on the tiles at the foot of the lawn-furniture lounge on which they lay, Adam's garments scattered in savage haste, Merit's folded almost neatly.

"For a minute there," said Adam, and had to pause at that point to find the right words. "It felt like I was in your mind."

"Mm," said Merit, and turned her face a little more toward him. Her lips smiled faintly but her eyes did not open.

"Is that what it's like," Adam asked abstractedly, "when Ray or one of the others—?"

Merit's eyes came open now, but they were looking over Adam's shoulder, not into his face. He turned.

Ray was there. Adam hadn't heard the only door to the terrace open or close, but Ray was there. He didn't laugh, or even stare at the couple on the lounge, the way any of the guys at the Home would have done. He didn't show embarrassment either. Adam couldn't read the expression on his face at all.

Merit was at first alarmed to see Ray. Not because her clothes were off, because her first move wasn't to hide herself. Instead she jumped up halfway from the lounge, getting one foot on the deck,

as if to be ready for anything. Adam watched her for
a moment, then scrambled to do the same.

All Ray said was: "It's all right, you two. Really.
It's all right with me." And there was still that
strange look on his face, that was to stay in Adam's
memory almost as indelibly as the image of Merit's
body did. And Ray turned away and left them
alone again, departing in an ordinarily noisy fashion by the ordinary rooftop door.

On his first encounter with the Jovians in a
group, Adam had noticed that most of them seemed
to look up to Ray in some subtle way, even though
Ray was among the very youngest. Once Adam
thought: Ray's a late model, with all the tested
improvements built in. Then he felt vaguely ashamed
of having such a thought about his friend.

Adam returned to Doc Nowell's estate for at
least a dozen visits, at irregular but gradually in-
creasing intervals, over the next five years. Repeated tests showed Adam's parasych potential to
be fading steadily, and eventually Doc gave a shrug
and announced that he would test him no more.
Such withering away of parapsych abilities was
more common than not, he assured Adam, in normal human subjects. It hadn't set in yet in the
hundred subjects of his genengineering work; whether
it would or not remained to be seen. Parapsych
talents had never been established as dependable
effects in any segment of the general population;
Doc still hoped that with his hundred kids the
story would be different.

Somehow the estate, the school, and the people
who worked there seemed a little less familiar
every time Adam returned; and except for Ray and

Merit, the Jovians, though still friendly, were slightly and subtly more remote.

Adam paid his last visit to Nowell's estate at the age of seventeen, proudly wearing the uniform of a Space Force recruit. On that occasion he opened an unlocked door, one that he had opened often enough before, and walked into a room where he thought he might find Merit. She was there, all right. With Ray. Adam stopped silently in his tracks and stood watching them, without comprehension.

Hand in hand, eyes closed, Ray and Merit were floating together in the air, more than a meter above the floor. Their eyes were closed, and they gave no sign of being aware of Adam's presence. After staring at them for a few more seconds he retreated, from the room, shaken.

He would come back later and talk to Merit. Now he decided to find Doc. The halls of the great building, and the grounds around it, were nearly empty of people now. Most of the hundred unique children were out in the world, making their way as adults. As far as Adam knew, they were having invariable success. And no small part of their success, he thought, was the way in which they were managing to fade gradually out of public attention.

A worker told Adam that Doc was in the laboratory. When Adam slid open the psych-lab door, he saw Doc sitting alone at his desk near the center of the room, just sitting there with his hands folded. There on the desk was a picture of Regina, Doc's wife, killed last year in a pedestrian stampede while she had been visiting New New York.

When Doc realized the door had opened, he looked up and jumped up and came over quickly to shake hands. "Well, Adam!" His eyes lighted when he took note of Adam's uniform. "So, it's up and out for you! I knew you'd make it."

"Thanks, I guess I always thought I would."

"I don't suppose you're sorry now that your PS talents eroded. From what I've seen of the Space Force psychological tests they seem to weed out almost everyone who *has* such talents, even in rudimentary form; I know that a couple of my own kids tried to enter and were turned down."

After greeting Doc, Adam mentioned the levitation he had just seen.

Doc nodded, without surprise. "I've seen that one. I once saw about twenty of my kids bobbing around in the air at once . . . it apparently requires a trance-like state that keeps them from doing anything else at the same time. And what good it will ever do them I don't know."

"There must be some other . . ." Adam gestured vaguely.

"Applications? Maybe there are. I no longer try to teach them anything, Adam. I just try to keep up with everything they're doing. And I can't." Doc paused.

"I'm sure they'll do great things."

"Yes, well, I hope so. That was the idea. I love them all, Adam, I tend to worry about them like a parent. And now, already, a lot of them are out in the world . . . what kind of lives they're going to have in this world I don't know. And what are their lives going to mean to humanity, after all?"

The aging man and the young one looked at each other, two mere humans, wondering.

"But come in, Adam. Have some coffee? Tell about the Space Force, how it strikes you now."

But he hadn't got far in his relation when Doc, who seemed scarcely to be listening, interrupted:

"Often, I wonder, Adam. Was there some—some force, some universal, natural law, acting through me, when I pushed my microscopic tools into those living cells, and tore down and rebuilt molecules?"

"I don't know." The young man felt sorry for the old one, and puzzled by his evident quiet distress.

"Are these kids of mine really the next step up from humanity?"

"Oh. Is that what's worrying you? I don't know, Doc. You can be damn proud if they are."

Unexpectedly Doc scowled. "Proud of what? Of being used?" He fell silent, making an irritated gesture. "Forces and laws," he said obscurely, with something like disgust. Frowning made his face look more lined, considerably more lined, than Adam remembered it. Adam wondered if possibly the mind developed lines and wrinkles too.

"She was incurably sterile, you know," Doc said. Now he was looking back at the picture on his desk. "We could never have any children biologically our own." Then he looked at Adam again, and brightened, with a visible effort. "Well, enough of that. You're going to the Adacemy, hey? How soon will you have a chance to try to get into planeteering? I remember how you always talked of that."

Chapter Three

The chance to get into planeteering had not come easily, but it had arrived at last, only after Adam had spent four years at the Academy, and three more at other assignments.

Then planeteering school. After that, his second exploration mission took him to the world that was shortly afterward named Killcrazy, by the survivors among the Earth-descended men and women who had been in the first group to land upon it. But Killcrazy was behind Adam now, along with the homeward-bound starships, and the Terraluna transport run, and the shuttle down to New New York. Ahead of him were thirty glorious days of leave, with Alice. Then the two of them were going together out to the enormous Space Force base located in the Antares system. Alice had a job in the science analysis section, and the baby would be born out there, a spacer right from the start.

Adam had met Alice only a year ago, and had married her only a month before he had to start

out on the Killcrazy mission. But Alice understood.
She was Space Force herself, as were her parents
before her.

This time, coming home, it was fun for once to
encounter the roaring confusion of the great city.
At the shuttle port in New New York Adam came
dodging his way nimbly through the crowd, a thick-
limbed, brown-haired, strong young man of average height, swinging a heavy travel bag. He wore a
dress uniform that hadn't seen much use to date
and a new ribbon on his chest. Alice had written
something about his coming home with the decora-
tion on, and so he was wearing the uniform instead of civvies.

As Adam emerged from a pedestrian entrance of
the shuttle port into canyon-like city streets, he
saw a headline flashing on a media kiosk:

JOVIAN SUPERKIDS—WHERE ARE THEY NOW?

The headline was quickly, replaced by a giant
three-dimensional picture. The face of Ray Kedro,
blond and ruggedly handsome, looked down in a
multiplied image from each of the kiosk's panels.
Adam hadn't seen Doc, or Ray, or Merit, or any of
the other kids, for a long time now. For years. He
recalled having read and seen news stories from
time to time, to the effect that most of the Jovians
were intermarrying with each other, that most of
them seemed to be blending quite smoothly into
society, tending to avoid publicity, not making
waves. The suggestion of the stories was that the
hundred born, or decanted, out on Ganymede, were
after all not that much different from the rest of the
world. Very bright and capable people, yes. But . . .

Pushing his way through the crowds, Adam won-

dered now about Merit, what she might be doing
at this moment. There had been a time . . .

With a small start, a sensation almost of guilt,
he recalled that Alice was almost within reach
now, waiting for him. She was certainly no Jovian.
And for that Adam was thankful—though he had
never made the effort to analyze just why.

The heavy travel bag felt feather-light in Adam's
grip as he changed slidewalks for the last time,
stepping onto the one that would take him to their
little sublevel apartment. Going right home this
way was certainly better than trying to meet her
in the spaceport swarm. People had been queued
up there at all the communication booths, so he
hadn't delayed to call her from the shuttle port.
Anyway, Alice knew when his ship was due in.

Adam surveyed the endless hive of tiny dwelling
units through which the slidewalk carried him,
private cells stacked high and wide, their ranks
staggered and their walls insulated in an effort to
grant the occupants some diversity and privacy.
On Antares Six they would have better quarters
than this. There wouldn't be any outdoors there
for the baby, not for some time at least, except for,
as Adam had heard, a little domed-over garden.
But that was really about all the outdoors you got
in New New York.

Adam dialed his private combination to let himself into the tiny apartment. He put the travel bag
down and moved stealthily, hoping against hope
to achieve surprise. Ready to jump at Alice the
moment he spotted her, he tiptoed into the bed-
room, and then the kitchen. No one.

It was in the kitchen that he found the note.

Darling—suddenly I can't wait to see you, so
I'm going to the spaceport. If you find this,

I've missed you, and the joke's on me for being impatient. Sit tight and I'll be home soon.
Love XXXX Me

He sat tight for an hour, savoring his impatient joy. He looked at Alice's clothes, hanging in the small closet, and touched them tenderly.

The phone chimed.

The screen at first showed only an official shield. Then a man's voice spoke: "Spaceport Authority. I'd like to speak to Spaceman Adam Mann, please."

"Speaking."

Then a man's face, the expression that it wore bringing the first cold blow of fear: "Is Alice Dexter-Mann your wife?"

"My wife. Yes."

"I'm sorry to tell you that there's been an accident."

Adam afterward could never remember exactly what else the man on the videophone might have said. He raced in a nightmare through the bright anthill of the city, back to the shuttle port. Traveler's Aid. They told him where to go. In the Portmaster's office, there were sudden grave, guarded looks when Adam gave his name, looks of sympathy and hidden triumph: *It happened to you, not to us.*

After hearing the words several times, from two different people, he began to realize that Alice was dead. The surgeon on duty at the port said that the baby was dead too, though she had ripped it out of Alice's body, trying to save it.

"We did all we could for her, spaceman. Sometimes it still just isn't enough . . ."

A policewoman sat with Adam and talked to him calmly and gently, trying to bring him through the first shock. She tried to answer his questions. It had been a violent and deliberate attack, right in the crowded port. One suspect had been seized, but then the people who might have been witnesses had all melted away without identifying themselves.

"These teenpacks—I don't know what the answer is, spacer. We do all we can. This year the big thing for some of them is to hunt pregnant women. Last year it was something else."

"Who's your suspect?" Adam's stomach had turned sick and his knees weak. But still the truth hadn't really, totally, sunk in.

"I'll show you. He's a real prize."

The policewoman let him look through oneway glass at a young man who sat slouching on a bench. The suspect's body had grown out of adolescence. But the appearance of him, the look in his face and eyes, suggested that his mind and soul had long since ceased to grow, that now they only wriggled, caught like baby worms on some unknown fishhook. Greasy pigtails framed the masklike face. The oddly-styled leather jacket was lipstick-marked with obscene clan symbols.

Adam opened the door of the detention room and stepped through, moving too fast for the cop beside him, who was left reaching after him with one outstretched arm. There were other police, men and women, in the detention room with the suspect, and they looked up at Adam's entrance, wondering.

"This one did it?" Adam's knees were no longer weak.

The sneering young mask-face held out insult like the groping hand of a blind man, trying to touch someone with it. "Sure, fatherman. I must have did whatever it was."

Now a large and gentle cop was standing close beside Adam, soothing him and standing in his way. "Easy now. Maybe it wasn't him at all." The other cops were standing around a communicator, going on with whatever they had been doing. But they each kept an eye out now for the bereaved young spaceman, watching him with pity and calculation, ready to lead him away if he should become violent.

Little they knew. Adam's brain and body had absorbed the Academy training in personal combat as if he had been designed for that purpose and no other. He might have gone on to world class competition in the martial arts, except that his feelings for them had always been mixed. Arm-twisting stuff, he sometimes called that sort of activity, with a certain contempt that proceeded from a blend of distaste and fascination. What he really wanted was to be a planeteer. But before leaving the Academy Adam had acquired the ability to be more effectively violent than almost any of the instructors.

Now the impersonal trained-in combat computer offered one of several feasible plans: three quick strides to the target, then the certian kick with the left foot, a blow with the right fist. Impacts that would break bone and crush nerves. As like as not the shock waves that the target's brain received would be enough to kill. The police were not wearing their stunguns in here; even so, their numbers and positions in the room could make it an interesting technical problem. But Adam doubted that the police would be able to stop him. The target might react to some purpose by the time he reached it. He doubted that a great deal too.

"Come along." The large cop's gentle hand was

resting on Adam's arm. "We'll find out, if it was him. We'll find out."

The pig-tailed youth, looking at Adam, said: "C'mere, fatherman. I got a present for ya." He giggled, and made a gesture that meant nothing whatever to Adam.

Adam waited for whatever spark it would take to set him off. Once before, as a teenager defending himself on a street near the Home, he had killed with his hands. But why had he bothered to defend himself, that time? He didn't understand it now. It had done him no good, for now his life was gone.

He felt no reluctance to kill, but no spark came. His life was gone. His loss was beyond all paying-back, and made all action pointless. He let himself be turned around and led away. He was very tired now. It would be good to get home at last and . . .

It sank in a little more. Alice was dead.

When he did get home, there was her silent note, still waiting for him on the table.

The Space Force looked after its own. Adam had scream-it-out grief therapy, and then for a while tranquilizers, and after that grief therapy again, this time that of a different school.

He went on with the motions of living, and then, one day, he began to go on again with living itself.

After a tour of duty as instructor in personal combat at the Academy, his revised orders finally came through for Antares.

PART TWO

Chapter Four

The footsteps, those of one person hurrying, came to a halt just outside the messroom door. The door slid open, and the face of the courier ship's captain appeared, wearing its usual expression of faint disapproval.

"Antares Base is on alert, gentlemen," the captain informed his two passengers; and then without waiting for an answer or comment he was gone, perpetually hurried footsteps fading.

Adam Mann looked up and across the chess-board at his new boss, Chief Planeteer Colonel Boris Brazil, and asked: "Suppose it's just practice?"

"I suppose." Brazil slouched in his chair, a tall, lean, blond, bony-faced man, unmoved by the news. "Or maybe something scared 'em. Maybe they heard old spit-and-polish was coming." He nodded after the courier's captain, whose way of running his ship had not earned the Colonel's respect during the days of voyaging. "Anyway, we'll soon know. I concede a draw," Brazil added, nodding cheerfully at his hopeless chess position.

*   *   *

One good thing about putting the whole base on
alert, thought General Grodsky, was that it at least
got him up into a ship again, even if it didn't get
him out from behind a desk. Nothing could do
that, it seemed.

His logistics only grew more complex when an
alert was on. He then had to hold most of his
available fleet off-planet, while keeping the emergency repair facilities on the surface of Antares Six
still ready to function at full capacity, as well as
maintaining skeleton crews of people at the other
Space Force installations around the system, all
under his command. But none of this, somehow,
ever cut down on what was still called paperwork.
It seemed to the General that at least as much of
the dataprocessing as before came shuffling its
way inexorably after him, a many-tentacled mon-
ster of information; and Grodsky wound up still
spending most of his time at a desk.

The door of his inner office aboard his flagship
opened now, and his secretary came in, carrying
more things that he was going to have to deal
with.

The first item in his stack was something Grodsky
had been looking for, and he pushed the rest aside.
"Molly," he told his secretary, "get Colonel Brazil
in here to me as soon as he's on board." The
courier with Brazil aboard had begun to transmit
its routine, official messages from Earth as soon as
it appeared in normal space within reasonable radio range of Antares Base. But Grodsky wanted to
hear from the Colonel the unofficial news of atti-
tudes and rumors at home; and he wanted even
more urgently to get Chief Planeteer Brazil briefed
quickly on this new Fakhuri thing.

*   *   *

Spaceman Adam Mann was kept waiting for several minutes in Grodsky's outer office, but the young man remained standing during that time; the fact was that he felt too keyed up to sit down. Then the inner office door, through which Colonel Brazil had already passed, opened again and a young woman in uniform stepped out. "The Colonel asked me to lure you in," she said with a tolerant smile. The impression she conveyed was that she had known the Colonel for some time, and was willing to make allowances.

Adam marched into the inner office, where General Grodsky was sitting appropriately behind a massive desk, while Colonel Brazil meanwhile perched quite inappropriately on a corner of the same piece of furniture. Brazil hardly appeared to notice Adam's entrance; he was staring into space, as if at some new and fascinating vision that he had just been shown.

Adam marched straight to the desk. "Spaceman Mann reporting, sir." He threw the General a sharp salute.

Grodsky returned the gesture carelessly, but gave Adam an intent look. "At ease, Mann. Colonel Brazil thinks you can fill a vacancy in the planeteering crew of this flagship."

"Yes sir." Adam was well aware of that, and it was exactly why he was keyed up. He hadn't thought, still didn't think, that his being given the job was really in doubt. But if the General himself was taking an interest in the matter ... "I hope the Colonel's right, sir."

In the middle of the largest relatively clear area on the General's desktop there was a personnel file; Adam recognized a permapaper copy of his own service record, which Colonel Brazil had been carrying around with him and had somehow managed to dogear slightly. Grodsky picked up the file now and began to study it. Almost immediately the General looked up with a frown. "You've had only two missions, Mann?" He turned to Brazil. "Boris, I don't know . . ."

Brazil, paying attention now, was wearing one of the more subtle forms of what Adam had come to recognize as his I'm-one-up expression. "Read on a little farther, sir. One of those was the rescue job on Killcrazy."

"Oho." The General checked the record again, and looked back at Adam with new respect. "Were you with the party that went into the crater?"

"Yessir."

Grodsky paged his way deeper into the record and read on. "Boris found you teaching hand-to-hand combat at the Academy. Well, that would fit the team's needs. Krishnan—the man you'd be replacing—had a high combat rating. Hm, I see you've married a Space Force lady. Congrat—oh." The general raised his eyes again. "I'm very sorry."

"Sir, I was intending to stay in planeteering before that happened. I'm really eager to get back to it now."

The General nodded, his eyes probing Adam's as before. Then Grodsky gestured to a chair. "Sit down, Mann. I've already told Colonel Brazil the reason for this alert we're on. Now I'm going to show both of you."

Grodsky picked up a small control unit from his desk, and swiveled his chair. The lights dimmed in the office, and a holographic stage slid up in front of the large viewscreen that occupied most of one of the office walls. "This recording," the General announced, "was made about two standard months ago, aboard the *Marco Polo 7*." Adam recognized the name of a deep-space exploration ship.

There were no titles or preliminary information at the start of the three-dimensional video recording, except the routine security classification label. Not so routine in this case—top secret. Adam hadn't yet seen many of those.

The recording itself began with some solid-looking symbols on the stage, which he was able to recognize as representing the astrogational co-ordinates of some star system or other deep-space celestial object, no doubt those of some system that the *Marco* had been sent out to investigate.

More data about the system and its chief components followed, presented in a routine symbolic form. It contained one star, a sun remarkably like Sol, whose light had been blocked from Earth since before the beginning of recorded Earthly history, by a narrow, twisted cloud of opaque interstellar dust. This Sol-like sun and its planets, all of them as yet unnamed, lay on the advancing frontier of Earth-descended humanity, right on the edge of the thirty million cubic light year volume of space which that ambitious race had somehow managed to more or less explore, marking out a small enclave within the end of one arm of the Galaxy's spiraled bulk.

"We're skipping a lot of early details of the survey," said Grodsky in a quiet voice. "Planet Four looked very good, from a distance. Fakhuri went in for a closer investigation, according to standard operating procedure, and—well, you'll see."

The stage now effectively placed the three men watching aboard the control bridge of the *Margo 7*.

The three-dimensional picture, made in the course of routine recording of periods of key activity, was centered on a dark, intense-looking man who sat in the ship commander's acceleration chair.

"That's Fakhuri. A good man," Grodsky commented firmly. The General paused, and then went on: "At this point, Planet Four still looked almost like a moonless twin of Earth. Which it continues to do in many ways, but . . . now they're launching the scoutship. Remember, Fakhuri is following survey SOP and he hasn't used any radar yet."

Explorers going out from Earth and Earth's advanced bases had yet to encounter any aliens technologically sophisticated enough to be able to detect a radar probe. But if any such existed—and it seemed inevitable that there must, somewhere in the Galaxy—there was thought to be no point in warning them prematurely that they were under surveillance.

As if looking over Fakhuri's shoulder aboard the *Marco*, now cruising some four hundred thousand kilometers from Planet Four, Adam Mann and Colonel Boris Brazil watched and listened as the scoutship, piloted by Fakhuri's Chief Planeteer, made one swing around the planet at about a hundred thousand kilometers, and another slower one at about twenty thousand. Both passes were uneventful.

During his swing at two thousand kilometers, the Chief Planeteer who was flying the scout solo reported observing something strange on the land surface below him.

"Like a lunar ringwall, or a half-buried foundation for a building eight or ten kilometers across," said the radio voice. "Lots of clouds there—I couldn't get a very good look."

Fakhuri's image rubbed its dark chin. "Make a lower pass over it."

Six seconds passed, while the finite speed of radio carried the ship commander's order on a tight beam down to the speeding scoutship, and brought the answer back.

"Roger. Descending to six hundred klicks."

The magnification of Fakhuri's screen showed a tiny dark scoutship creeping across the blue and green and brown of a sunlit alien continent. Then the scout almost disappeared against the background of a dark blue ocean.

"I'm jumping forward again in time," said Grodsky. "We'll pick up the recording again—here."

They were still observing the image as if looking over Fakhuri's shoulder. "Coming up toward that ringwall again," said the planeteer's voice from the little scout below. "I'll go right over it, this time. Leveling off at six hundred klicks. Should get a little atmos—"

And that was all. The radio beam from the scout had for some reason been broken off. Fakhuri turned his head, this way and that, looking for a reason. He pressed things on his panel, trying to extract information from one instrument or another.

Seconds later, another watcher on Fakhuri's ship cried out: "He's falling, out of control!" A closeup of another screen showed how the motion of the scout's flight had changed, from a nearly horizontal creeping to the steep curve of a dropped stone.

"Golden! Do you read me?" Fakhuri was shouting.

And yet another voice: "Radio beam's unlocked, sir, we can't reach him."

"Get us right over him," ordered Fakhuri, reaching with one hand for a red stud prominent at one side of the panel before him. At the bottom of the image on Grodsky's holographic stage appeared the words: RED ALERT CALLED ABOARD MARCO POLO 7. There was justification. Scoutship drives did not fail, communications between scout and mothership simply did not break, not by accident, not just like that.

Now, through a low cloud cover, the huge ring-wall formation on the planet's surface became partially visible in the *Marco's* powerful scopes. The ringwall looked like stone, perhaps once splashed molten, perhaps deliberately piled. Details were still obscure, though the starship was accelerating powerfully in normal space, very quickly getting closer to the planet.

The screens on the *Marco's* bridge showed the scoutship as an almost invisible dot, tumbling toward the ringwall formation as if toward the center of a target.

"No sign of his escape capsule."

"Radio still out, sir."

"Radar," Fakhuri snapped. "Track him. Plane-teering, have that standby scout ready. But don't launch yet."

Grodsky said to the onlookers in his office: "Watch now, here it comes."

Fakhuri's image switched its viewscreen to pick up the radar image when the bouncing pulses brought it back. The seconds of unavoidable distance delay crept by.

"Can't pick up any flash of impact optically, sir. Maybe he hasn't cra—"

The echo came. Fakhuri's screen showed only electronic hash for a moment. Then the radar computer gave up its search for a small moving target, and dispassionately showed the waiting humans exactly what it saw, the problem it was having to contend with.

Some watcher on Fakhuri's ship cried out: "Captain!"

The radar picture electronically frozen on Fakhuri's screen held him—and now Adam—frozen in disbelief. Not the expected rough semblance of the Earthlike planet shown by the optical scopes. Nothing like that—here instead was a bright spheroid, looking smooth and opaque as a steel ball, more than a thousand kilometers greater in diameter than the planet it shrouded.

Fakhuri quickly switched his screen back to present the image brought in by the optical telescopes. Planet Four still reflected the radiation of her own sun as naturally as Earth reflected that of hers—again Four appeared innocent and friendly in her bright aura of oxygen atmosphere, plain and ordinary behind a tattered white film of clouds where her spherical shape curved closest to the *Marco*.

"Evasive action!" Fakhuri ordered. "Around the planet!" If this world was shielded from radar, it might well be armed in other unimaginable ways as well. Anything might be about to come up from it.

The brutal acceleration of evasive action was evidently too much for the *Marco's* artificial gravity, for Fakhuri's chair now folded itself protectively around its occupant. The chair also put forth to the control panel a pair of artificial arms, slaved to the captain's motor-nerve impulses.

"Passive detection still blank screen, sir." That meant that the *Marco's* instruments could detect no artificially produced radiation from the planet.

"We lost him in the surface clouds, before we

moved," said an astronomer's shaken voice. "Never got any indication of an impact where he went down."

"Radar gear checks okay, captain, I don't know what—"

"Pulse again, then! give me the whole planet again."

The *Marco* was over nightside now. The planet showed in the optical scopes as a vague dark bulk, embraced by a thin bright crescent. Then that image was gone, as Fakhuri switched his screen to receive the radar image again. The pulses would be hurtling down again toward the planet . . . down . . . down . . . back . . . back . . .

The marvelous thing flashed from the screen again, electrically beautiful. The only difference on this side of the planet was at the point antipodal to that where the scoutship had disappeared. Here, the radar-outlined, metallic-looking, optically invisible surface curved steeply down to meet the planet's land surface, in an amplexicaul depression, like the dimple around the stem of an apple. Fakhuri sat staring at it, as if the wonder of it was stronger than alarm, for him.

But there were standing orders for exploration captains. Any technologically advanced strangers encountered were to be treated with the utmost caution. One starship could carry a weapon capable of destroying a planet in minutes. There was of course a chance that the scoutship pilot might still be alive; but one of the Fakhuri's mechanical slave-hands was already moving, slamming down on a stud marked EMERGENCY FLIGHT.

The flight had been toward Antares, not Earth; no possible trail must be left toward home.

*   *   *

The holostage in Grodsky's inner office went blank momentarily. Then the General said: "This is the planeteer who was lost, Mann. Colonel Brazil knew him."

On the stage there appeared the figure of a heavily-built, cheerful-looking man. It was a picture made outdoors somewhere that showed its subject, walking quickly, wearing a planeteer's groundsuit, carrying his helmet under one arm.

"Alexander Golden, Chief Planeteer," said General Grodsky. His tone was oddly formal, as if he might be wondering what the name and title ultimately meant.

The secretary, who had re-entered the office a few moments earlier carrying some papers, had paused to watch, and now had a question. "Did he leave a family?" she asked, gazing into the stage.

"No." Grodsky rubbed his eyes. "As I recall from his records, he grew up in some institution—like you, Mann. Never married. Very able spaceman."

"And an able planeteer," put in Colonel Brazil. After a moment he added: "Another happy bachelor bit the dust. Not many of us left. I guess I met him two or three times."

Adam was staring at the last frozen frame of Alexander Golden on the little stage. Something about it was bothering him. "I . . . think I might have met him, somewhere." But the vague sense of recognition eluded Adam and vanished when he tried to pin it down. He shrugged.

As the holostage dimmed down completely and the lights in the room came up to normal, Boris shifted around on his desk-top perch to face the General. "Well, boss, what do we do?"

"We go back there," said Grodsky, swiveling his chair back to face his desk, and the two visitors in his office. The General's face was lined and tight-looking. Obviously Fakhuri's discovery was in his lap. The situation could not be managed from the distance of Earth, not when it took forty days by courier ship for a message to be sent and answered. No Earth government would be foolish enough to send more than broad instructions to Antares base, and in this case there was little doubt of what those instructions were going to say.

"Now," said Grodsky, getting down to business. "That forcefield, or whatever it is, around that planet—let's start calling it planet Golden—the field around planet Golden seems to me a flat impossiblity. Consider:

"First, it almost entirely envelops an Earth-sized world. Second, the passive detection crew on the *Marco* were able to pick up no trace of it. Third, it allowed a scoutship to enter, but only as a falling object. It cut off the scout's engines, its radio, and possibly everything else aboard.

"Gentlemen, we've nothing like that, anywhere!"

After a little silence, Brazil spoke up, casually. "Are we taking a fleet when we go back?"

"I think not. I think just three ships. A whole fleet might look like an attack, to—them. Whoever they are." The General shrugged. "If *they* even exist. We have no proof that this—field—is not a natural phenomenon. Golden couldn't see it without his radar on, and he just drove right into it."

"And just accidentally happened to drop right into that ringwall," said Boris. "That was just coincidence, right?" No one answered him, and he went on: "If I ever drive a scout near that thing, I won't be so damn sneaky about it. Next time we go in radiating the whole damn frequency spectrum in every direction. If someone spots me, it won't be by accident."

Adam couldn't tell if the Colonel was serious about his announced plan or not.

"I intend to take a very good look around there before anyone drives near it again," said the General grimly. "Boris, I want you ready for the best job you ever did, if and when we do go down on Golden. You can pick any planeteers you want, from any crews in the fleet."

"If you mean to launch from just one ship, my own people are as good as any."

The General looked at Adam, then back to the Colonel.

"My crew will be up to full strength now," Brazil added casually. Adam felt a sudden surge of pride and loyalty, about which he would never speak.

Grodsky considered a moment, then nodded decisively. "All right. Mann, consider yourself aboard. You can go look up your quarters, or whatever you have to do."

"Yessir!" This time Adam's salute was even sharper than before.

When the doors of the inner and outer offices were both closed after him, he took a quick look up and down the long main corridor of the flagship to make sure that he was unobserved. Then he snapped his body into a flip, a somersault in the air without touching his hands to the deck. He walked away grinning widely.

He was still quite a young man. For a time, in time, even the murdered love could be forgotten.

When the young Spaceman Mann had gone out, leaving the two of them alone, the General said thoughtfully: "Boris, I wonder if we can really function as a military outfit." They both knew, everyone knew, that the Space Force was organized and equipped and trained for exploration, not for conquest. It had never faced a real war, or anything remotely like one. Who knew what would happen if one came?

"I do believe that courier captain thought *me* unmilitary," Brazil answered. "And all I had done was—well, never mind. You really expect we'll get into a fight this time, boss?"

On an impulse, Grodsky flicked on his big viewscreen. The hellish red bulk of nearby Antares seemed to fill the room. Then the slow rotation of the flagship brought into view the tiny green companion star, and then the other multicolored sparks, cloud behind cloud of them, reaching ever farther and dimmer out to infinity.

"This time, or the next," the General said. "Sooner or later."

Chapter Five

General Grodsky's flagship was a big craft, fast and tough, designed for battle as much as any ship could be when battles between ships were virtually unknown. The outer hull of the flagship formed a sphere almost a kilometer in diameter, and like most Space Force ships it bore no permanent name. Its code designation for this mission was Alpha One.

After a couple of days' passage in flightspace from Antares Base, the flagship appeared in normal space near the Golden system, at a couple of astronomical units' distance above the north pole of Golden's sun. After an hour of general observation from that vantage point the flagship began to move again, staying in normal space this time, traversing a curve that in three unhurried days would bring the explorers aboard into the close vicinity of Planet Four.

Alpha Two, also custom designed, was a much smaller ship, built for high interstellar speed and long range observation. It winked into existence near the point in space where Alpha One had previously appeared, just as One began to move sunward. Two would alternate with Three, its twin, in observing the activities of One and in carrying news back to Antares Base.

At a distance of thirty million kilometers General Grodsky ordered his first radar probe of Planet Golden's surface. He found the enveloping forcefield to be exactly as Fakhuri's recordings showed it, covering the world entirely except for an area of a few hundred square kilometers at most, where the field came down in its amplexicaul curve to meet the land surface of one continent. With that verification in hand, Grodsky turned his flagship away from Golden, and spent a standard month in methodical preliminary survey of the system's seven other major planets. On none of them, nor on any of their major satellites, did his teams find any indication of the presence of intelligent life. Or anything at all to suggest an explanation of Planet Golden's unique and mysterious field.

The preliminary system survey completed, Alpha One returned to the near vicinity of Golden. And now the crew of explorers focused their instruments with great interest upon the surface formation that resembled a lunar ringwall.

The Ringwall, as the human observers now began to call it, occupied most of a roughly triangular river island eight kilometers across, at the confluence of two great streams in a country of low, rocky hills and subtropical jungle. The big island seemed always to be at least partially obscured by clouds and low mist. And infra-red observations of the area were perpetually fogged as if by volcanic heat.

For all the observers above the atmosphere were able to tell, the irregular polygon of mountainous walls might be titanic architecture, now partially obscured by jungle growth as well as by mists and clouds. Or it might still have been accepted as an accidental formation. But, if the ambiguous feature were truly accidental, was it only by another accident that it lay exactly at the antipodal point from the place where the Field curved down to planet surface?

And careful study of Fakhuri's optical recordings showed that, of all the planet's area, Golden's scout had apparently fallen directly into the Ringwall, scoring a kind of crazy, inexplicable bullseye. Another accident?

Wherever the scoutship or its wreckage might be now, optical observation from the flagship could detect no trace of it. And the Field continued to prevent all other kinds of observation.

Colonel Boris Brazil, in the first scoutship launched from Grodsky's flagship toward Golden, drove twice around the planet, keeping about fifteen hundred kilometers above the upper surface of the Field as it was outlined for him by his radar. True to his promise, Colonel Brazil had his ship continuously radiating a wide assortment of signals.

There was no response from below.

That evening, ship's time, the Colonel knocked at the door of Adam Mann's tiny cabin, and on hearing a response from inside slid it open. "Alpha Three should be in the system tomorrow, Junior," Brazil announced. "Two will be heading back to Antares; we're sending a robocourier over to her in a couple of hours with mail, if you want to send some."

Adam was seated at the small desk that folded

out of the bulkhead. "Thanks, I was just writing one." He paused. "How did it look today from down there?"

"Everything looked a lot closer. Here, I'll drop that in the mail bag for you." Leaning in the doorway, the Colonel shamelessly inspected the address on the envelope he had just been handed. Then he held it down at his side, snapping it between long nervous fingers. "Tell you what, Junior, you get ready for a little ride tomorrow. I want someone along to make sure that my scout keeps transmitting on all fifty frequencies. Briefing at oh-five-hundred."

"Roger!"

"Don't look so damned happy. It's disgusting. My good planeteers will be driving their own scouts tomorrow." Boris started to close the door, then paused, waving the little envelope. "Say, this Doctor Emiliano Nowell you're writing to—isn't he the one who had that secret biological lab on Ganymede years ago? The geneticist who started all that Jovian superkid business?"

"Yeah. I used to be invited to visit his estate on Earth a couple of times a year. Got to know some of them. Tell you about it sometime."

Boris's brows rose over his innocent blue eyes. "You move in exalted circles," he whispered, and made his exit.

In the morning, Colonel Brazil was all business from the start. "This reminds me a little bit of a mousetrap," he was muttering, as he sat strapped and cushioned in the left seat of the scoutship's little control room, staring at the radar screen in front of him. Alpha One was now something more than a million airless kilometers above the scout;

the fair true surface of Planet Golden was only a few hundred klicks below.

The radar showed the smooth hump of the Field rising high above the scout on all sides, rising higher and higher as Brazil drove the small ship down in a slow descending spiral. It was as if they were dropping into the vortex of a whirlpool, a solid maelstrom carved into some fluid invisible to human eyes. The walls of the funnel around them constricted gradually as they descended into it. Below them, a circle of planet surface some fifty kilometers in diameter was shown by radar as free of the Field, and to all appearances this comparatively small area was open to normal landings and exploration. The free area was mixed-looking countryside, to the eye indistinguishable from the land immediately surrounding it.

"I don't see any bait," said Adam. He was buttoned into the right seat, alertly watching a multitude of screens and indicators. "But we're here, aren't we? Maybe an obvious trap is bait enough for the curious."

"Now's a fine time to propound that theory," Brazil growled. "How d'ya read me, Alpha One?"

The distance delay. Then: "We read you loud and clear. Good picture."

Adam had an excellent imagination, which in his line of work was not always an asset. Right now he could readily imagine the Field-funnel around them closing in on the little scoutship with a sudden snap, dropping the ship rocklike with them inside it to share Alexander Golden's fate. But the Field did did not snap shut. The Field did not move at all. No change of any kind had been observed in it since Fakhuri's first recorded sighting.

A few hours ago, long probes with loops of

current-carrying wires attached to them had been lowered into the Field from a hovering scoutship. On the wires' first contact with the Field the electrical currents in them had instantly ceased. But mice and other small forms of life, lowered into the Field in sealed boxes, had survived the mysterious condition for several minutes without any apparent ill effect. If Golden had survived the crash of his ship—that seemed a vanishingly faint hope —he might still be alive.

The field-free area of the surface, that the explorers from Earth were now beginning to refer to as the Stem, lay in the low north temperature zone, on Planet Golden's second largest continent. Below the scoutship now, Adam's viewscreens showed rolling, open plains, covered with a probably grass-like plant. The main themes of biology were repeated, sometimes with startling fidelity, from one world to the next, all across the explored Galaxy, wherever closely similar environments obtained in terms of gravity and chemistry, pressure and radiation. Here, patches of deciduous-looking forest were scattered over a line of hills that grew into a range of mountains some kilometers north of the Stem. One of the wide, winding rivers of this continent ran in several places briefly congruent with the intersection of Field and planet surface. But this, again, seemed accidental.

"Enough for today," said Brazil abruptly, when they had cruised for ten minutes at about two hundred kilometers' altitude. "Let's ease up out of this hole."

On a sunny afternoon a few days later, Adam and Boris were scouting again, cruising within a kilometer of the surface, now with the feeling of being part of the world below. The starship overhead was of course invisible to them beyond the sky.

Early summer was warming and brightening Golden's northern hemisphere. The screens showed a view of green plains and forests that made the scoutship cabin feel stuffy.

"Makes me feel like I want to get out and go camping," Adam commented.

Brazil only grunted. He was easing the scout still lower, losing altitude at a rate of a few meters per second. The small ship slid forward through the clear summer sky at a couple of hundred kilometers per hour.

"Looks like a herd of large herbivores over there." Brazil was pointing to a scattering of animate dots on the plain ahead. Under moderate magnification these became deerlike creatures—another major interplanetary evolutionary theme identified on Golden. As the scout drew closer the lenses showed that the deer-like creatures had developed their own variation on the theme, in the form of stretchable necks. In a few minutes the scout passed directly over the herd, gliding on the invisible force of its silent engines, still too high for its presence to alarm the animals.

Adam continued to sweep the landscape below the scout, and the air around it, with his instruments. He even scanned nearby birds suspiciously several times. "I don't see any Field-generating superbeings."

"Maybe they've all dried up and blown away. Are you keeping one eye on the Field, Junior? I have most of my attention on it."

"Ah, roger. I have one screen on radar."

But the Field only waited indifferently, whether

they watched it or not. The smooth cliff of it rising up around them on all sides, as motionless as stone.

Boris drove the scout steadily lower. Inside another hour they were circling the Stem area just off the deck, dipping below hilltops and nearly brushing trees with the bottom of the scout's nearly-spherical metal hull. Some of the flora below them stood fifteen meters tall and closely resembled the hardwood trees of Earth.

As their altitude decreased, Boris slowed their speed as well. Now the scoutship was moving not much faster than a man might run. Birds, singly and in squawking flights, fluttered out of its path, their cries coming plainly into the cabin through the outside microphones. On the ground an occasional animal fled, or crouched snarling in the scoutship's moving shadow.

Brazil said: "Looks like a big trail over there, going down that ravine toward the river."

"Animals only?"

"Maybe." Boris turned the scout, and drove it down the ravine, going lower and slower than ever; and there was the little village, no more than a cluster of teepees whose colors blended with the muddy earth. The themes of Galactic life extended to humanity on many worlds, and that the native humans on a planet as Earthlike as this one should morphologically resemble their cousins from Earth came as no real surprise.

But the native dwellers on Golden, or this sampling of them at least, were less sophisticated. For a long second, naked humanoid figures stood about their village in frozen poses, gaping up at the approaching scoutship, a gigantic mass of bright metal drifting silently through thin air; then the people below dropped fishnets and cooking pots and exploded into frenzied motion.

"Wow—get all those cameras going!" Boris ordered as he turned the scout again, taking it out over the river and there backing it slowly away from the village. "We'll disappear for a while—starting a major panic isn't going to do us any good."

And now the delayed voices from Alpha One began to gabble in the ears of the two planeteers in the scout, urging them to turn viewscreens on this or that detail in the fast-emptying village.

Joined by other scoutships carrying other planeteering teams, Colonel Brazil and Spaceman Mann made one approach after another to the Stem area during the next few days. There were interesting discoveries, but no truly surprising ones, and none that appeared to have any direct connection with the Field. Nor were there any observable changes in that mysterious phenomenon. Whatever unknown powers there might be on Golden appeared to be still indifferent to the presence of the explorers from Earth.

There arrived a morning when Colonel Boris Brazil, with Spaceman Adam Mann aboard, launched early from Alpha One, and drove his scoutship down early into the Field—free funnel leading to the planet's surface. On this flight the Colonel circled the Stem area only once, to let the red sunrise at surface level catch up with his measured descent. Then he drove toward a grassy hill near the river, a spot that had been carefully selected on an earlier trip.

The scout sank gently; landing struts extended

themselves to touch down in the grass. The little ship settled quietly to rest on the hilltop.

The two men inside it examined the outside environment carefully, with eyes and radar and infrared. Here and there life moved, in the grass, in the tall reeds and bushes along the shore, and under the surface of the river.

Life moved, apparently going about its own business. Still nothing challenged their arrival.

"No reaction, Alpha One," said Brazil finally.

"Roger, proceed as briefed," said the delayed voice.

Brazil turned in his seat, and fixed Adam with what a stranger might have interpreted as an angry stare. "Well, Junior, I need a body outside, to lure these Field-formulating superbeings into my snare. Get your ass moving."

Adam unfastened himself from his chair and stood up, already wearing his groundsuit. He gave his boss a half-smile through his faceplate and moved from the control cabin to the final decontamination chamber, in which he stood with his suited arms raised and legs spread, while poison gas and ultraviolet sterilized the outside of his suit, a last step in the effort to protect native life against possibly dangerous Earthly microorganisms.

Adam was going to be First Out. First Out, on *this* planet, where Total Investigation was a certainty. He had to remind himself that such an assignment didn't necessarily mean that he was the best planeteer around. Without argument, it meant he was expected to be one of the best.

A hatch opened in the seamless-looking hull near the base of the landed scoutship, and a short ramp extended itself to the ground. A human figure, anonymous in an armored groundsuit, appeared in the opening. The morning sun glinted on its faceplate as the figure walked slowly down the ramp and into the kneehigh grass. A representative of Earth—descended humanity had set foot upon the soil of yet another planet.

Adam's boots left a dark trail in the dew-silvered grass as he walked a slow circle, going completely around the scout. The sun was well clear of the horizon now, and he could see for kilometers in every direction. There was not another human being in sight, or, at the moment, even an animal, with the exception of a few birds high and far away to the south. The looming amplexicaul curve of the Field was of course still invisible to his eyes. The Field appeared to make no difference at all to anything that he could see. There was hardly a cloud in all the kindly blue vastness of Golden's sky.

He had a sense that the whole planet was—not exactly watching him, maybe, but still aware of him, even if only in the back of its collective mind. Aware and waiting for what he might do.

"How's it going, Mann?" asked General Grodsky's voice. A majority of the hundreds of people aboard Alpha One, all of them who had the chance, were probably watching the video relay, sent to them through the scoutship from the tiny camera in Adam's helmet.

"Fine, sir," he answered. "It just looks good." The words were of course inadequate, but at the moment, with no new facts to report, such words were the best he could come up with.

According to plan, Adam now turned his back on the parked scoutship, and walked about fifty meters to a place from which he could look downhill to a bend of the river. A heavy growth of short trees and tall reed-like plants lined both banks closely. On worlds where native human beings existed, rivers were considered good places to spot them, traveling, fishing, or just getting a drink. In his mind Adam quickly ran through the basic procedures for first contact with Apparent Primitives. But at the moment there were no Apparent Primitives in sight.

As Adam turned and started to walk away, a small creature sprang away out of the long grass near his feet, giving him a start. More startled than its human discoverer, the thing went bounding away from him like a jackrabbit, down the slope toward the river. By all appearances it was an inoffensive herbivore. After the first few meters of its darting flight it began to tumble clownishly, leaping and playing with the exuberance of an otter. Near the heavy bush by the river the small animal stopped, looking back uphill at Adam with apparent good cheer.

Adam returned the look, grinning downhill. Then he gazed around him again at the peaceful river and hills and sky. He surprised himself, with a wish to—well, to pray. He was not ordinarily a consciously religious man. But now he felt a wish to pray, maybe to Whom it May Concern, that this world, new to its discoverers, could be treated right by them, that good would come from their discovery. It was a strange moment for Adam, one in which he felt himself in communion with—with the powers of the universe, perhaps. He had rarely had a similar feeling in his life, and never since Alice—

Something huge was moving, very quietly, down in the thick bush by the river. Then it burst into the open, a massive, bloated-looking quadruped that pounced with startling speed. The rabbit-thing was taken by surprise. One heavy clawed foot caught it in the middle of its first frightened leap, and crushed it down into the grass and dirt, where it wriggled helplessly and let out shrill faint screams.

Its prey secured, the big animal paused, speed leaving its movements as if a switch had been opened. The predator was a little smaller, Adam thought, than an adult hippopotamus, but just as graceless.

Adam thought that he had seen this large species before, or one very closely related to it. But those sightings had been distant ones, to which he had paid little attention amid the superabundance of new things to be observed. He had really seen nothing of the species but its gross overall shape, until now.

Now, when this specimen turned its head and looked up the hill at Adam from only fifty meters away, he felt a chill, even armed and armored as he was. Because the face of the gross beast was human. Not just a close resemblance. Almost exactly Earth-descended human in all its features, enlarged though they were to fit the massive head.

Adam could hear Brazil muttering something; his own shock was shared. Adam dialed magnification into his faceplate. Now, inspecting the beast's face at an effectively closer range, he could see that it was covered with very short pale fur, from a distance resembling light-colored human skin. The red-rimmed yellow eyes of the animal were human in configuration, down to the smallest visible details of the lids and lashes. Something about the lids gave the eyes a look of arrogance, and above those haughty human eyes there rose a smooth shield of some horny substance, in a shape that in a man might very well have been described as a noble forehead. But behind this frontal shield the skull sloped off sharply into a dark and matted mane—there was no room for a proportional brain behind that mask-like face.

There was nothing like an animal's snout on that flat face, but a human nose instead. Not even the great width of the mouth, the heavy jaw, or even the size of the omnivorous teeth—bared now in a sudden yawn—could destroy the impression, the illusion, of man-larger-than-life. Nor could the ears, half-hidden by the mane, and curving along the head in a shape that looked neither human nor animal. Only when the eye reached the longish scaly neck did the illusion fail.

Over most of its body the big animal wore the hide of an elephant, gray and wrinkled, scantily clothed with a thin coat of greenish-black hair. The feet were obviously weapons, half-adapted for gripping and clawing as well as for locomotion. Mud was beginning to cake dry now on the thick legs of this specimen, and a trickle of green slime drooled from a corner of the frowning mouth. Omnivore, thought Adam. It must have been feeding on some river plants, and then it decided to go for a morsel of meat.

With his right hand on the butt of his holstered sidearm, he stared back at the creature. The mask-like face, taken by itself, would have to be called handsome—there was no other word for it. But when Adam saw it on the beast, the total effect was so hideous that he half wished, perhaps more than half, that the thing would charge him, that he might have a good reason to kill it.

"Ugly thing there," said a fascinated voice in Adam's helmet. "What's that it's caught?"

"Rabbit-theme," he answered, without taking his eyes from the bigger creature's face. "I think probably mammalian."

The big animal now turned its full attention back to its victim, bent its long neck slowly and chewed with delicacy. The faint screams went to a higher frequency. Adam thought: *Like an Earth housecat, playing with a victim.* But on a deeper, stronger level, he was thinking also: *Come on, you obscenity, come up where and try that on me. Come on.*

But he was a damned fool, to be upset by the sight of one animal eating another one. He watched a little longer, answering a few more questions from above, then turned his back and went on with his job.

An hour later, when Adam had finished the rest of the scheduled First Out procedures, and was back in the control room of the scoutship, he found Brazil looking at him with an oddly fascinated expression. The first thing the Colonel said was: "I wonder why your big playmate out there didn't have wings."

Adam let himself sink into the right-hand seat with a tired sigh. "Wings? Why?"

"The original did; Geryon was his name. Remember? Or don't you like to read?"

"Jur—who?" But something in Adam's memory stirred faintly. Was it something he had read? Or something else?

But what?

"G-e-r-y-o-n." The Colonel spelled it out. "A thing Dante met when he was visiting the Inferno. It had the face of a just and kindly man. And wings. Among other attributes."

Adam gave a half-laugh. "He encountered it in a likely place, I think. Kind of took me by surprise, out there."

Chapter Six

By the third standard day after First Landing, scoutships were shuttling in an almost continuous pattern between Alpha One and the tiny accessible area of Golden's surface that the explorers had come to call the Stem. As everyone had expected, General Grodsky had decreed Total Investigation here; that meant that eventually everything within reach on Planet Golden was to be sampled and studied. Planeteer teams had already begun analyzing the air, the water, the soil, and many of the smaller forms of life. As yet no attempts had been made to obtain specimens of the larger animals. For one thing, the human natives might be inconvenienced or outraged by such activity, and for another, until more had been learned by observation there was at least a theoretical chance of getting an intelligent, non-primate-theme human being in the game bag by mistake. A very few such races were known to exist in the Galaxy, of intelligent beings therefore classified as human, but with no more physical resemblance to Earth-descended humans than to marigolds or mollusks.

The indications so far on Golden were that life here held at least fairly closely to the commonest Galactic theme patterns for Earth-type planets. Beside the natives who were obviously intelligent beings in the primate theme, there were deer-types and giraffe-types to be seen grazing on the green plains. Species of large animals strongly centered in the cat-theme of Galactic evolution had been observed, preying as might be expected upon the larger herbivores. And here on Golden, as on every habitable world that explorers from Earth had yet examined, there were also apparent exceptions to the standard Galactic themes—here, most notably so far, the species of large omnivores that were already being called geryons.

Day and night the radar equipment of the Earth-descended explorers never ceased for a millisecond to scan the Field. But still the Field was never observed to move or change. Every attempt to measure or analyze it had so far proven fruitless, as every technologically advanced instrument brought into contact with it died on contact. The Field simply existed, as it had since Fakhuri's first sighting, shrouding the planet completely except for the tiny Stem area of the surface.

On the third day after First Landing—Golden's rotation was only very slightly slower than that of Earth—a small group of women and men in protective groudsuits approached on foot the invisible but very sharply defined line where the Field came down in a nearly vertical wall to meet the soil of Golden.

These planeteers carried with them long wired probes, similar to the ones that had earlier been lowered into the Field from a scoutship. It was soon discovered that at ground level the result was the same. Electrical currents died as soon as any part of the wire carrying them was introduced into the Field. The surface of the Field was soon found to be very smooth in every region tested, and very sharply defined. The anomalous condition—now a favorite term of description—was soon shown to extend, in the same plane as aboveground, for at least a few meters below ground level. Plans were begun for deeper exploratory excavations.

Electrical devices of any kind invariably went dead when they were shoved across the invisible boundary. Yet the boundary appeared to mean nothing to birds and animals, or to the native people who like the birds and animals were observed passing in and out of the Field at will, with the bioelectric activities of their bodies presumably unaffected by it.

"Do you know what the word is on Golden?" asked Adam through his groundsuit's airspeaker. He was sighting carefully into a radar instrument as he spoke, and a moment later he began to drive another marking pole into the soft ground, just inside the newly charted boundary of the Stem.

Kwame Chun Li, the only planeteer on this mission who was less of a veteran than Adam, moved his electrical probe a little further on, positioning it in accordance with Adam's gestures. " 'Presumably'?" Chun Lui offered. "I hear the physicists are having it programmed into their writers on a single key."

" 'Apparently' is the one I had in mind," said Adam.

Small Earth animals, pushed into the Field inside a wheeled cage, showed no immediate effects from the exposure, and gave no sign that they were even aware of a change in their environment. But the second time the experiment was tried, and on a number of tries thereafter, the small padlock securing the door of the animals' cage fell open. On examination the locks showed no sign of damage, nor could they ever be made to repeat their bizarre behavior outside the Field. A whole new set of experiments, having to do with the behavior of mechanism inside the Field, was launched.

Levers, screws, and other simple machines, when not part of any complex system, were always observed to perform normally inside the Field. But anymore complex mechanical combinations or systems tended to display wildly erratic behavior. A fine antique chronometer, put at risk by the devoted scientist who owned it, was almost—but not quite—certain to run at the wrong speed, or even backwards, when it was pushed across the border.

No pattern was apparent. Within the Field, the law of complex machines was Chaos. Hope for the life of Chief Planeteer Golden, never bright, faded again; it seemed that the complicated mechanism of his ejection capsule could never have carried him free of his falling scoutship.

Any forcefields that the explorers from Earth were capable of generating simply ceased to exist at the boundary of the Field. And beyond that border, many non-biological chemical reactions, especially the more complex ones, could not be induced to conduct themselves properly.

Over there, atomic clocks and power supplies failed quite dependably, as if their impelling isotopes had been turned to lead. Over there, a fusion power lamp flared out like a cheap candle—someone wrote that as a note and then deleted it. On the contrary, a cheap candle over there burned perfectly well. Yet the high-tech devices could always be made to resume proper operation again as soon as they were pulled out of the Field; and counters in the Stem picked up faint normal background radiation, probably from natural sources, coming from across the border.

Over there, fire burned as always, when kindled in wood or grass by lightning or by human hands, employing primitive means. Over there, animals and plants and people lived, and lightning darted when a rainstorm came. Nature and primitive invention alike appeared to be quite unperturbed by the Field's presence. Only the advanced technology of the explorers from Earth was affected.

Some of those explorers concentrated their observations on the native branch of humanity. Men, women, and children were seen at a distance, repeatedly moving from Stem to Field and back again, without the least visible awareness of any change, or even of the fact that any boundary at all existed. Of course the native humans wore no groundsuits, complex with valves and circuits, and depended upon no machines more advanced than the knife or the bow.

The local people fled at every tentative approach of an explorer. The explorers did not try at all to press the issue. Brazil and his people had plenty to do as it was. Diplomacy, for the time being, could wait.

No objection was offered to the presence of the explorers; the hypothetical Field-builders failed to materialize. After several days Grodsky brought down his flagship to a mere fifty thousand kilometers or so above the Stem, and the distance lag in communication between the flagship and its people on the surface practically disappeared.

The odd Ringwall structure around on the other side of the planet, antipodal to the Stem, remained a mystery. New photos of the Ringwall taken from just above the Field at that point showed essentially no more than the first pictures of it had shown. The Ringwall was an irregular polygon of mountainous cliffs, several kilometers across, above which the lower atmosphere seemed always to be hazy enough to blur detail. If it was indeed to be classified as architecture, there was no other building on Golden anywhere near its size. Neither were there sizable cities anywhere on the planet, or large ocean-going ships, or cities big enough to make space-farers' beacons in the night.

There came at last a lull in the explorers' efforts to gather still more data, a pause while human brains and computers tried to digest the mass of detailed information they had so far accumulated. Brazil and almost his entire planeteering crew went up to attend a meeting on Alpha One, leaving just Adam Mann and Kwame Chun Lui, with a single scoutship, on the surface of the planet.

"You're the boss until I get back this afternoon," Colonel Brazil told Adam on departure. The Colonel glowered. "May the mighty spirits protect our cause on Golden."

Adam and Chun Lui were not to remain idle. They began hopping in the scout around the perimeter of the Stem, following a circular path more than a hundred and fifty kilometers in diameter, repeating earlier tests with probes and meters to see if anything about the Field had changed since the tests began. There was no sign that it had.

Shortly after midday, Adam looked up from his drudgery with marker poles and electric probes, and commented: "More of the damned things."

A hundred meters away, on the other side of the boundary, three geryons had just come over a hilltop. Now another of the beasts appeared on the hill, and presently two more came into view at one side of it.

"They're after something," said Adam. "That's how they hunt anything bigger than a rabbit—in a pack." He had been watching them whenever he could, beyond his normal duties of observation; he felt a kind of private fascination.

"After us, maybe?" Chun Lui wondered. The geryons' dead-looking yellow eyes were turned down the hill in the general direction of the two men.

"Maybe they are. All right, let's go back to the ship for a while. I wouldn't care to start messing around with weapons right here at the edge of the Field."

"Roger." Chun Lui pulled firmly on the rope that he was holding. The rope's other end was tied around the ankle of a humanoid robot, and the robot lay fallen on its face just beyond the line of marking poles that defined the Stem-Field border. One of the routine tests now used was to send the robot walking into the Field and haul it out after the inevitable collapse. Someone in one of the departments on the flagship had evidently thought it would be an informative procedure. Now, as soon as Chun Lui had dragged the heavy metal body back into the Stem, animation returned to it. The man-shaped thing climbed to its feet and took an unsteady step back toward the boundary.

"Halt, Otto," Chun Lui ordered in a crisp voice. The machine stopped in its tracks obediently. Its lenses, halfway eyelike projections on the front of its head, moved slightly, watching the animals on the hill.

"Carry this back to the scout, Otto." Adam told it. "And these things." The robot turned, picked up the indicated equipment, and strode purposefully toward the scoutship, which waited about forty meters inside the Stem.

Adam and Chun Lui followed, carrying the rest of the gear and looking back over their shoulders. The geryons were now moving slowly toward them in a spread-out line.

"Hey, it's not us they're after," said Chun Lui when the walking men had almost reached the scoutship. "Looks like they've caught—" His eyes went wide behind his faceplate, and he stopped so suddenly that Adam almost walked into him.

Adam spun around, just as the machine called Otto hurtled past him, running faster than any man could run, accelerating like a racing motorcycle back toward the boundary of the Field. Fifty meters beyond that boundary the geryons were now ringed around a native child who danced in panic, looking too terrified to scream. The robot's programmed compulsion to protect human life drove it toward the animals, into the Field. At the boundary it instantly collapsed again, tumbling forward in the grass with its momentum.

Adam was only vaguely aware of hearing the first excited comments from Alpha One. Already he had turned and barked to Chun Lui: "Get in the scout and man the turret!" Then he took off running back toward the animals on the hill, the servo-powered legs of the groundsuit churning him forward as fast as any unburdened human sprinter.

He stopped only a couple of paces before he

reached the Field. The heavy machine pistol, as if by itself, had already come out of the holster and into his armored hand. Fifty meters up the slope the child—looked like a little girl—was trying to dodge out of the geryons' circle, but the gray bodies moved with graceless, efficient speed to block her in. Adam could see the irregular white teeth in the girl's open mouth, and hear her thin wailing cry.

He thumbed the pistol's safety off and locked the optical sight onto the largest geryon as it moved. He fired a burst that should have torn its backbone out. The tracers snuffed out when they hit the Field, and thin trails of smoke curved down into the grass not far beyond the boundary. There was a faint pattering disturbance on the far side of the line, as if he had tossed a handful of gravel over.

The geryons ignored the demonstration. The largest of them had caught the child's arm in its teeth now, and Adam could see the blood. The others hovered ponderously, as if impatiently waiting their turns to bite.

"Fire the turret!" Adam shouted. "For effect!" It occurred to him that main turret fire might kill the child, too, if indeed the beams managed to break through the Field at all. But to try it looked like the only chance.

"What's going on?" General Grodsky's voice asked loudly in Adam's helmet. Then that voice was drowned in a burst of noise, as the sharp, nearly invisible beams stabbed out from the scoutship's main turret. The air thundered around Adam, and his armor glowed in the mighty splash of heat that billowed up and down the Field's surface from the point where the beams struck it. On the Stem side, the grass at Adam's feet went up in smoke, while centimeters away, across the invisible barrier, the blades stood green and fresh.

Several of the animals on the hillside turned their heads and looked toward the scoutship, as if the sound of the blast had annoyed them.

"The siren!" Adam shouted. "Turn the siren on!"

Another geryon had caught the child in its teeth now, and was nibbling at her delicately. Her rising scream was drowned with all other sounds when the scoutship's siren climbed to a full-volume howl. Adam turned off his air mikes, and realized that Grodsky was shouting questions at him.

"Native attacked by animals, inside the Field," he called back. "We're trying to help."

Adam did not really hear what the General said next. The effort to help was not succeeding. The siren did not greatly distract the beasts. Now Chun Lui was trying an optical laser in their eyes, but the beam began to diffuse as soon as it hit the Field. The geryons snarled and squinted and turned their heads away from the glaring light. They kept on with what they were doing, like starving animals at food.

But it was not food they wanted, only bloody sport. Adam caught another glimpse, between massive gray bodies, of the child, and could see only too well that she still lived.

If he entered the Field in his groundsuit, valves would malfunction and he would collapse at once, unable to breathe. He brought an arm in from its groundsuit sleeve and had two fasteners loose inside his helmet when the General's voice blasted at him: "Mann, what are you doing?"

"Going up there."

"No! That's an order! Fasten your helmet!"

A third fastener fell loose. "There's nothing else left to try."

"Chun Lui, stop him! Stun him!"

Adam dashed toward the Field, which he expected would protect him from stunbeams. Once across the border, he would have to get his helmet off very quickly, to let himself breathe, then run up the hill and distract the animals. And get the girl to the scout. There might be some chance yet—

The paralyzing beam from the scoutship struck him before he could reach the line of marker poles, and the grassy ground swung heavily up to hit his faceplate. His groundsuit was poor protection against the scout's heavy projector at this close range. But somehow he rolled on one side, reached out an arm. If he could drag himself across . . . it was surprising that he could move at all . . .

The beam struck him again, and his body went dead as ice. The last thing Adam saw before darkness came was a geryon looking down the hill at him, frowning haughtily, displaying red-stained teeth.

Chapter Seven

Alice was holding out her arms toward him, crying for his help. But Adam could not reach her, because the terrible fight in the playground was still going on and he was still trapped in it, pinned up against the wall that was covered with painted murals, unable to break free. Then he was flat on his back. Strangers with hate-filled faces had surrounded him; they were looking down at Adam and shouting hate, for he was somehow odd or different. They kicked at Adam and he tried to hit back at them, but his arms had gone heavy and numb and useless. Then the faces were gone, all of them except one—

—the face of Kwame Chun Lui, who was bending over him. Adam was lying on his back in his bunk in the scoutship. His helmet and groundsuit had been removed. He could tell from the way the ship felt around him, and from the quality of background sounds, that the ship was still parked on the surface.

"Wha—" He sat up with a grunt, and then almost toppled over sideways before he discovered that he was still half-paralyzed. "Uh. How long—?"

"You've been out about an hour," said Chun Lui. Standing back a pace from the bunk now, components from the scoutship's medical kit in hand, he looked relieved and at the same time a bit wary. "I had to do it, Ad. Good thing Otto still had that line tied to his ankle; I reeled him in, and he carried you in through decontamination."

Adam said something vulgar, and let himself flop back on the bunk. He added an obscenity, and repeated it several times. "Why didn't you use that damned thing on *them* instead of on me?"

Chun Lui's voice was quiet. "Well, I tried it on them, Ad. It did no more good than the main burner."

Adam swore aimlessly once more, and then made another effort to sit up, this time with somewhat better success. He sat there on the edge of his bunk, stamping his feet, trying to rub and flex the woodenness out of his thick arms. There had been a chance, some kind of a chance, to help the kid, and they had stopped him. It was all he could think of.

The large communication screen on the bulkhead lit up, with General Grodsky's image glaring sourly out of it at him. "Well, Mann. Since you disobey orders, I presume you possess some information about the conditions there that you didn't have time to explain to me. Let's have it."

Adam stared back doggedly. "Sir. I just wanted to help that kid."

"You think I didn't want to help her?" The screen seemed to vibrate slightly with the volume of the General's voice. Then the volume dropped, but the hardness grew. "What was your next step going to be, exactly?"

"I was . . . going to go on up the hill, sir. To do what I could."

"What you could." Grodsky almost smiled, projecting mock satisfaction now. "Would you outline for me, please, just what that was going to be?"

All right, he was in trouble. Adam told himself that he didn't give a damn. Yet he did, but what else could he have done?

He replied to the General: "Distract the animals. Try and get the little girl away from them. Try to get her downhill to the scout again. Where we could give her medical attention."

"How many of those animals were there?"

"Half a dozen, maybe. Sir."

"And you were going up there unarmed, to take their prey away from them." The General made it sound totally insane. Well, maybe it had been insane. No doubt it had. All Adam knew was that he had been unable to keep from trying. If the situation came up again, he'd have to try again.

The volume of Grodsky's transmitted voice had decreased now by another level, but the tone had become if anything more vicious. "That Field you were so eager to enter, that air you were so anxious to breathe, are still completely unknown in terms of what their effects on an Earth-descended human being will be. Did you learn nothing at all on Killcrazy? Wasn't everything there innocent and peaceful in the first days of exploration? Are you utterly stupid, Mann? We've already lost one planeteer here, and I don't—"

"How about that little girl?" Adam heard himself shouting back. "Does she fit on your scorecard anywhere?"

Violence appeared behind Grodsky's angry eyes. The possibility loomed suddenly, real as a brandished club, that a commanding General's awesome authority in the field was about to be invoked with crushing impact. Adam was suddenly afraid. He knew that the General would have been legally justified in ordering him shot, for disobedience in the field. He wouldn't be shot now, of course; the emergency was over, the situation stabilized. But he might be tried and imprisoned. He might be kicked out of the Space Force. He might be sent back to Earth to some meaningless desk job. Damn it, he had done what was right, and would do it again. But the girl was dead by now, and he wasn't, and he was getting a little scared.

But the General's club of authority—though it had been figuratively lifted from his shoulder—did not strike. Grodsky, as though with the purpose of impressing everyone with the need for caution and control, made his own anger disappear. Adam had observed before, with a touch of envy, how the high brass all seemed to be able to do that.

General Grodsky, his own intentions now as well hidden as a poker hand, asked Adam in a controlled voice: "Have you got anything more to say?"

Adam drew a deep breath. "Sir, apart from humanitarian considerations, it could help us to get on with the natives, to have pulled one of them out of trouble."

"Sure it could," said Grodsky, not impressed for a moment. "Or, that girl might have been a ritual sacrifice, and saving her might have ruined our chances to get on, as you put it—apart from humanitarian considerations. But that's not the main point. The main point right now is that when I give an order it must be followed."

"Yessir," said Adam, meekly. He was beginning to dare to hope that he might survive. "If I was wrong, I . . . was wrong."

"You were wrong, dammit."

"Yessir . . ."

"But what?"

"But . . . I was left in command down here, General, and there occurred what I judged to be an emergency, and I took what steps I thought were best."

There was a silence, long enough for Chun Lui to put in a few words. "Sir, with the turret firing and all, it's possible we didn't hear all of the General's spoken orders very clearly at the time."

Adam nodded. At the same time, Colonel Brazil, for once no trace of humor in his long, bony face, appeared behind Grodsky on the screen.

The General was considering the situation silently. Then he said: "I'm reserving judgement, for the time being, on the incident that's just happened. We'll carry on from where we are."

There was a little silence. Then after a moment Chun Lui said: "Sir, I think sooner or later we're going to have to fight off those beasts in self-defense. More and more of them keep hanging around, watching us. And they seem to build up their courage in large groups."

Grodsky nodded, confirming that the chewing-out was going to be allowed to turn into a planning session. The tension in the atmosphere drained rapidly as the General turned around. "Boris, those animals do seem devilish hard to frighten, don't they? Of course we can defend ourselves against them within the Stem, but I want to hold the killing of any native fauna to a minimum, at least until we know—"

"Seven humans are approaching the scoutship on foot," interrupted Otto's robotic voice.

Chun Lui quickly switched the viewscreen to show the scene outside. Six naked warriors, armed with bows and bone knives, were approaching the landed ship with an air of timid determination. The one woman stumbling along in their midst wore a wrap of cloth about her hips, and was nearly hysterical with grief. The woman bore in her arms what the geryons had left of the little girl, and the woman's body and her legs were stained with the child's blood.

Brazil's voice from the screen said: "I would suggest one of you two down there go out and say hello to the people, since it appears they finally want contact." The Colonel turned away briefly and could be heard exchanging a few muttered words with Grodsky. Then Brazil went on: "Mann, you're still the ranking planeteer down there. Take charge."

And may the mighty spirits aid our cause on Golden, Adam thought. *All right; here we go again.* He stood up. His legs almost betrayed him.

"Damn. Chun, help me up to the left seat, will you? Then you go out and talk to them."

Chun Lui assisted him. "Sorry I had to use that stun beam on you, Ad."

"Dammit, quit saying you're sorry. It's all right. Just shut up and get outside quick."

The seven natives knelt before the groundsuited figure of Chun Lui when he descended to greet them formally.

*   *   *

Dr. Osa Yamaguchi, head of Linguistics, was getting up in years. Whether as a result of her advancing age or not, she sometimes adopted a didactic manner, irrespective of her listeners' rank.

"They're undoubtedly appealing for our help against the geryons," she informed General Grodsky, meanwhile tapping the papers and other records arrayed on the conference table before her. The language of the local people—the Tenoka, they called themselves—was now well on the way to being understood, at least well enough for some practical conversation. The job had taken several weeks of recording and computing and study, since Tenoka was not a simple tongue and the native speakers of it had been dwelling mostly on one subject.

"That's definite?"

"Yes."

Grodsky turned to the head of Anthropology. "How does it look to you?"

"They're not really too surprised at our presence, though they've never seen anything like us before. They accept us as some kind of demigods." The Chief Anthropologist was a small man named Pamon, usually vague of manner and sometimes indeterminate in his appearance. He tended to absorb the behavior of whatever people he was working with; already he was sitting with his hands clasped in the fashion of a Tenoka warrior, though he had not yet seen one of the Golden natives except on a screen.

"So, they ask our help," Pamon went on. "I gather they've had more than the usual trouble with geryons lately. The beasts don't often attack healthy adults, and it seems probable that they can tell when a human is armed. For a child, or even two of them together, to leave the village unescorted is quite dangerous; and yet the children do. I suppose they must, to learn the adult skills."

"Girls too?"

"Perhaps. Or, she might have sneaked out just to watch our planeteering work, just out of curiosity." Pamon sighed.

Grodsky frowned. "Have they any taboo against killing these particular animals? I don't mean to slaughter 'em wholesale, of course; no telling what that might do to the ecology. But if the beasts are cunning enough to avoid armed adults, it occurs to me that we might find a way to teach 'em that from now on attacking children is dangerous also."

"No taboo against killing them, General. But they're doubtless hard to put away with primitive weapons."

"I think we can educate 'em," said Colonel Brazil, breaking a thoughtful silence.

"We have made this magic-doll, in the semblance of a child of your people," Brazil announced a few days later. He spoke in the Tenoka tongue, in which some days of intensive training had made him almost fluent, and he was standing outside his own scoutship on the surface of the planet. "The doll has no spirit of its own. When we wish it, the spirit of one of our warriors will enter into it. Thus we hope that the geryons will come to fear the children of your people."

The Tenoka delegation, twelve or fifteen strong and including both men and women, shifted their feet uncertainly. Strong Breather, who seemed to be the most influential available leader, grunted thoughtfully. Pierced Arms, the local shaman, gave no sign of what he might be thinking, at least no sign that Boris could interpret. Pierced Arms was daubed over most of his gaunt, aged body with colored goo, and the scarred loops of tissue on his arms and shoulders were strung with feathered cords.

The entire Tenoka delegation kept looking at the semblance of a child. A modified small robot, it stood with its back almost against one of the scoutship's extended landing struts. About a meter tall, the robot had been transformed into a tolerably good likeness of a naked native youngster, though if you looked at it closely it was obviously not alive. A breeze now stirred the realistic hair; otherwise the small figure was motionless. When turned on, it answered to the name of Shorty.

"I will tell you now," Brazil resumed, "how we of the far land of Earth plan to help our friends, the Tenoka. As is well known, the Tenoka are fearless warriors; if they see any one of their tribe in danger, they will rush fiercely to help."

Two of the fearless warriors listening to him giggled suddenly, holding sun-darkened hands over their mouths. Strong Breather looked at them sternly, but his own mouth twitched. Wait a moment, thought Boris—did I use the word for 'fiercely' or 'drunkenly'? But in any case it seemed no great harm had been done.

"This magic-doll," he went on, "will not need the help of the great Tenoka warriors. Our magic within the circle of our power is stronger than any number of the geryons. Therefore if you should see this seeming child pursued or attacked by geryons tomorrow, you must make no move to interfere. Will you inform all of your people of this?"

Strong Breather and Pierced Arms exchanged a

look. Then Boris got the chin-thrusts and grunts that meant agreement.

Brazil added: "And tomorrow all of the real children must be kept in the villages, so there will be no mistake."

Again the leaders of the delegation signified that they were willing.

Now came what might well be the most ticklish part of the negotiation. "You have brought the used blankets, and the clothing worn but not washed." Brazil made it a statement and not a question; he could see that they had brought the stuff along as requested, tied into a bundle. But such things were often considered potentially powerful tools of magic against their owners. Pamon had been worried that the Tenoka might refuse at the last moment to turn them over.

The technicians aboard Alpha One had given Shorty no odor of his own, but had provided the robot with a plastic skin that would absorb any smells it came in contact with after activation. The plan was to immerse Shorty in the bundle of Tenoka-redolent cloth for a day. To a geryon, smell might well be a more important sense than sight.

"Take up the cloth things now," Boris instructed the Tenoka, "and wrap the child-doll in them, so it may convey to the geryons the danger of attacking your children. Tomorrow you may take back the things."

After a brief pause, and another exchange of looks with Strong Breather, Pierced Arms stepped forward and delivered a sing-song harangue to Shorty, who received it stoically; then another to Boris, who understood not a word of either speech.

But apparently this did not matter. The old man untied the bundle of laundry and began draping it around Shorty, piece by piece.

"Well, you're the combat expert," Brazil said to Adam in the grounded scoutship that evening. "Ready to go tomorrow?"

"All set." Adam glanced at the puppet chamber that had come down with Shorty from Alpha One, and now filled most of the scoutship's living space.

Right now the puppet chamber resembled an empty shower room, its glass walls enclosing enough space for a man to stand or jump or turn a somersault, but very little more. When the power was turned on, the interior of the chamber was filled by a fine, three-dimensional grid of forcefield lines. The grid recorded every instantaneous position of a human operator inside the chamber, data that could then be passed on by radio to Shorty or any other yesman, allowing a robot to be controlled exactly by the human. There was a return transmission also. Whatever experience presented itself to Shorty's electronic senses would be radioed back to the puppet chamber, and translated there into forcefield effects, with their intensity modified as necessary for the human operator's safety and comfort. A forcefield floor in the chamber acted as a treadmill, and continually modified its shape to imitate whatever terrain was under the yesman.

Shorty was now standing in the scoutship's airlock, still wrapped in the Tenoka bedding and garments. Adam had spent some time in practice with the puppet chamber, marching the small yesman around in the vicinity of the scout. It had not taken long for him, with his reflexes, to regain the walking gait and habits of childhood, with his legs effectively reduced to about half their adult length. Shorty also possessed a kind of autopilot mode, useful for steady travel, in which the robotic brain took over control of legs and balance.

"I'd just like to get started on the job," Adam added. Then abruptly he got up and paced, moving restlessly in the little space that was left outside the puppet chamber.

Since there was scarcely room for two men to walk about, Brazil sat down at the table. The Colonel produced a deck of cards from somewhere, and began in an abstracted way to deal out two hands.

Adam stopped his pacing and watched the fall of cards. "Two-handed poker?"

"Not necessarily. Look, Junior, don't find some new way to go wild tomorrow. Grodsky and I are both sticking our necks out quite a bit by keeping you on the job after what happened."

Mann stared at him for a moment, then said "Thanks" as if he possibly meant it, and spun away with nervous speed to pace again. He came back and stopped. "It's just that I keep thinking about that kid."

"I know." Brazil's own life was not yet very long, as years were counted, but it was crowded with experience. "You'll see a lot of bad things in this job. You can't get too involved."

"But I *was* involved. I was right there."

"You did what you could."

"Yeah."

"Possibly we were wrong to stop you. Maybe Grodsky made a mistake there. He's only human. But maybe you made one, you're only human too."

"Yeah." Mann was looking at him in a new way, as if the Colonel had somehow managed to make a previously unnoticed point. "Yeah, we're stuck with being only human, aren't we?"

Brazil blinked at him. "Right." It was good that he had made *some* point, but . . . the Colonel decided to let it lie. "Now bring back some geryon ears tomorrow, and as a special reward I'll stop calling you Junior."

Adam dozed, on the borderland of sleep. When he got tomorrow's job out of the way, when he had smashed some of those damnable animals and taught the rest a lesson, maybe things in his life would somehow straighten out. Planeteering would once again mean everything to him that it had once meant—or that he had once thought that it was going to mean. Back in the days when there had been more meaning to a lot of things. Before Alice had been . . .

In sleep, Alice's face came again to drift before him. She cried out again for help, only to be replaced by the image of the mangled Tenoka girl.

"Turns out she was an orphan," Pamon had told him. "The woman who carried her to your ship was a widow, acting as a foster parent, supported by the tribe. Interesting institution."

Later there was another dream, this one involving yellow teeth.

Chapter Eight

"Overseer reports another group of five animals, coming this way, bearing about one-two-oh," said Colonel Brazil. He was speaking over the scoutship's intercom system, and referring to an aerial survey of geryons within the chosen area of the Stem. "Range about a klick and a half. That makes twenty-two of the beasties within reasonable walking range. Be nice if you could get 'em all chasing after you."

"I'll walk by and give them the chance," Adam answered, He was standing inside the puppet chamber now, trying to persuade the skin-tight operator's suit to stretch into something like a comfortable fit. "Let's hope they feel like playing."

"Ready for chamber power?"

"Roger."

"Power coming on."

Adam reached up to the top of the chamber, unhooked the operator's helmet from its suspension there and fitted it carefully over his head. The helmet covered his eyes and ears completely, effectively shutting out surrounding sight and sound. Blindly he worked to get the mouth control, that managed certain of the robot's functions, comfortably positioned where his teeth could operate it.

Now Adam let his arms drop to his sides. Color swam and steadied before his eyes, forming shapes and illusory distances, becoming the inside of the closed outer door of the scoutship's airlock. The background noise changed subtly in his ears.

The illusion was well-nigh perfect. Both sight and hearing assured Adam that he was now standing inside the airlock, inside Shorty's metal body, only a meter tall and still wrapped in the Tenoka cloth. He shrugged the stuff away from him, thinking himself probably lucky that the yesman had been provided with no functioning nose.

Adam stepped forward one child-sized stride, and raised one of his/Shorty's little arms. The stiff latch of the airlock door eased open at a touch of Shorty's baby-sized finger, steel-boned, electrically muscled, powered by a tiny hydrogen fusion lamp in Shorty's chest.

Adam-Shorty toddled down the short landing ramp. He was barely able to see over the tallest grass.

"Robot," Adam said, and let his legs relax, as the chamber controls read the code word, and the chamber forcefields tightened to support his human weight. The robot brain had now taken over the routine business of making step after step with the yesman's legs. This might be an all-day job, and there was no point in wearing himself out hiking. Adam steered with the sterile-tasting mouth control, and with a light biting pressure held Shorty's speed to that of a walking child.

Tall grass flowed easily by him, the long blades still bearing traces of morning dew.

"Bear about ten degrees left," said the voice of the aerial observer in his ears. "You're going to find the first group, four beasts, about two hundred meters ahead, moving down a little ravine, very slowly."

Adam bore left as directed. He looked up into kindly blue. After a bit he was able to spot Overseer. If geryons were aware at all of distant scoutships, they ought to be accustomed to the sight of them by now. This one presumably would mean nothing in particular to the animals.

Adam didn't want to run right into the four animals ahead. He preferred to go past them and let them stalk him, if they would. They were cunning creatures, and the lesson was to be spelled out for them precisely and plainly. Death-beams or bullets might not be connected in the geryons' minds with the seeming child they were, Adam hoped, about to attack. Therefore beams and bullets would not be used.

He came to the ravine where he had been directed to go, and toddled along the top of the high bank. Soon he saw the four geryons, all adults, moving slowly along, grazing in sparse cover at the bottom. Adam/Shorty gave no sign that he had seen them. He walked past and let them become aware of him, then turned away from the ravine.

"Where's the next bunch?" Adam whispered into his helmet mike. Then he chuckled at himself for whispering.

Ninety minutes later Adam-Shorty had fourteen of the animals interested enough to follow him. The geryons were moving in a widespread formation that still seemed to be trying to give the impression of aimless drifting. Adam, taking care to keep the little robot well clear of the Field, was headed now toward a certain eroded slope above a bend of the river. There was plenty of rocky ground there to offer the firm support that Shorty's tiny feet might need, and there was a small box canyon that also figured in the plan.

He cast a quick look back over Shorty's shoulder. The geryons, at a distance of a hundred meters or so, were following him a little more obviously now, a slow certainty of intention apparent in their movements. Less frequently now did the omnivorous animals stop to graze, or pretend to graze.

Adam took a quick count—there were fifteen of the animals now, three or four of them only half grown, with scaly-looking bodies and heavily furred legs. The faces of the adult females among the group were those of lovely but unhappy women. The males had men's faces with a look of nobility about them, slight variations on the face of the first geryon that Adam had ever seen.

The illusion was intense of his actual presence out there on the plain, a child small and alone before gigantic predators. How many real children had turned to discover that the things were following them, how many real children had run and tripped and screamed . . .

The illusion was heightened further as Adam took Shorty's legs back under his direct control. Now the rocks of the chosen slope were not far ahead. Out of nervous habit he felt with the yesman's hand for a holster at its side. Then he grinned to himself. Shorty did not carry sidearms. Or need them.

As he neared the stony area, Adam began to run,

imitating the movements of a frightened child. Glancing back at the animals, he saw them drop all pretense of innocence now and give chase. They were probably clever enough to know that a child might be able to find a sheltering crevice among the rocks.

Adam/Shorty toddled into the chosen box canyon only a few seconds ahead of the geryons, then turned and stood as if frozen in despair, near the center of the steep-walled natural trap. His pursuers came crowding after him through the canyon's narrow entrance, snapping and shoving to get ahead of one another. None wanted to be left out. One child was not going to provide much sport for fifteen geryons.

Now Adam continued to stand as if paralyzed by fright, while the huge gray beasts first settled a pecking order among themselves, then waddled to form a ring around him. As soon as the ring was closed, they began to tighten it, moving almost as if in practiced ritual. Some moved toward Shorty with high dainty steps, looking down their human noses at him as if in righteous pride. Some crept forward on their bellies, scummy tongues lolling from their frowning mouths, an effect that ruined the nobility of their fine men's and women's faces.

Adam could feel his breathing quicken and his hands tremble. The sun beat down upon the barren arena. The pack around him gurgled and howled, but only softly.

He made Shorty run to and fro in quick uncertain rushes, as if he were seeking hopelessly to escape. He was no longer entirely pretending; he could feel himself living as a Tenoka child, out there alone in the canyon.

Now the animals' deadly circle was less than

four meters wide. Adam had to fight down genuine panic. He made Shorty spin wildly, and cry out in his high child's voice.

Something struck the yesman from behind. Shorty's legs were now slaved to human reflexes, so he was knocked on his face. Adam felt the impact, scaled down by the feedback system, as a pat between his shoulder blades. He made Shorty roll over on the ground, and stared up at a circle of nightmare-handsome faces. He could feel his living breath sawing in his throat, and could see the kindly sky, the sky remote and indifferent beyond the sinuous gray necks, the clustered evil power.

The thought came flickering through Adam's mind: How many in all the universe, have seen the universe this way—

A massive foot was coming slowly down on Shorty's midsection—not with any weight on it. A dead victim would be no sport at all. Adam had to choke off a scream as one huge head, human-masked, sank toward Shorty's face. The unspeakable mouth was gaping over him. Now, he thought, now, and he thrust up an arm, and the big yellow-brown teeth closed deliberately on Shorty's child-sized fingers.

He closed Shorty's fingers on one big tooth, yanked it out like a thumbtack, and flipped it away.

Adam heard his own near-hysterical laugh at the reaction he saw in the geryon's face as the long neck whipped up and back, away from him. Another similar head loomed over Shorty now, lowering uncertainly. Adam drove an arm up, hard and fast this time. Shorty's fusion-powered arm was slaved to follow Adam's. The metal fingers stabbed through thick neck hide, and drove on spearlike through yielding tissue, until Adam could feel in his fist the greater hardness of the neck vertebrae. He clutched at bone, and squeezed, and had the sensation of crumpling paper in his hand.

He had Shorty out from underneath the thing quickly, before the mountainous convulsions of its death had ceased. Before the other animals could make up their minds that now it was time to run, Adam maneuvered Shorty between them and the narrow entrance to the canyon.

Startled and confused, unable to sense any familiar danger, the geryons ran in circles within the high-walled box, raising clouds of dust in the sunlight. Moving rapidly at last, they jumped and plunged and bellowed. And now the biggest animal turned toward Shorty, looking past the yesman to the one way out of the canyon. Adam/Shorty blocked the path, even as the animal charged him with a snarling howl; in a flash the geryon looked to Adam like the one that had been first to bite the little girl.

He leaned forward, bracing Shorty's feet on firm rock footing beneath him. The geryon did not try to avoid the small figure in its path. The impact that came through to Adam felt like a swat from a pillow, and in it he could distinguish a sudden snapping yielding, that must mean that heavy bone had broken. The geryon fell sideways with a hideous scream, and the pack that had started to follow it halted again, its members colliding with each other in confusion.

Adam/Shorty strode toward them. Most of them scattered before him, not yet in panic, but wary, not knowing what was harming their kind. As one of the bigger geryons dodged past him he caught it by the tail in Shorty's mangling grip, braced his feet on rock again and swung the two-ton squirming mass around hand over hand to face the yesman. The huge head came around biting; Adam swung Shorty's fist with all his strength. Much of the geryon's head vanished in a gory explosion, spattering the other beasts nearby. They howled and turned to frantic flight from Shorty, scrambling in every direction to escape.

Adam pushed his latest victim aside and stamped after the animals on Shorty's tiny feet. With horror he saw that a couple of geryons were already climbing the steep canyon walls, their efforts so fueled by desperation that it looked as if they might succeed.

He grabbed up a loose rock the size of a basketball, and let fly with it at one of the madly scrambling animals. The yesman's throwing arm was slaved to human speed, so the impact was not all that Adam had hoped for, but still the target beast came sliding and rolling down the slope.

Picking up some more rocks, Adam trotted Shorty forward. Something feral and howling took over completely now inside his own skull. The world shrank to a rocky arena where time was hate ...

"Don't forget to bring us a sample for Biology," someone's voice reminded him.

"What? Oh, sure." Adam turned Shorty back to the first beast that he had slain—it was about the least damaged of any—grabbed it by one leg, and began to pull it toward the canyon exit. He noticed that his arms were all red, glistening and slimy. "I need a bath," he muttered.

"Huh? You're still here in the scoutship, remember?"

"Sure—I mean I'm sweating." I'd better pull myself together, he thought, or Psych will be examining me half to death.

The carcass that he was towing caught and tore and abraded on rocks. Shorty could pull the leg right off if the operator wasn't careful, and naturally the biologists wanted a specimen that was in reasonably good condition.

Already the scavenger birds were gathering overhead. They came from kilometers around in no time.

Adam stopped, got Shorty right underneath the hulk, and lifted it. It did not feel heavy to him, but it was an awkward thing to handle. The awkwardness was worse after he got out of the canyon and away from the rocky slope. Now the ground was softer under Shorty's tiny feet, and the burdened yesman kept sinking into the soil. Even when Shorty sank waist deep, almost swimming in the alien earth, Adam could still plow ahead with little physical effort.

The dead beast wobbled repulsively in Adam's grip, the geryon head trailing on the long broken neck, the human face that was no longer handsome abrading away on the ground.

He, Adam Mann, or someone else, would probably have to repeat today's performance, over and over, until every geryon that survived in the Stem had learned to fear and flee from Tenoka children. A good cause, but an unpleasant job.

The "touch" of the dead bulk became suddenly so repellent that he dropped it.

"Pretty tough going here," he said. "Can't you send a scout or a copter?"

Presently a voice from Alpha One reached him. "All right, a couple of biologists are coming down anyway, and they can pick up the specimen right there. They'll be there in a minute or two. Good job, Mann."

As soon as he saw the scout descending, Adam abandoned the dead geryon and began walking Shorty in the direction of his own scoutship. Blood was drying thickly on the yesman and swarms of insects were beginning to follow it. The parallel themes of Galactic insect life were strongly supported here.

He trudged on, a little metal man under the enormous sky of Golden.

PART THREE

Chapter Nine

The man in the canoe, gliding on the tranquil river, lifted the hand-carved wooden paddle out of the water, and a moment later lowered the small outboard motor into operating position at the squared-off stern. The canoe was handmade too, of bark and wood, designed in the native Tenoka style, except for that square stern. Now, as the craft glided from Field to Stem between moss-grown marker poles, the outboard purred smoothly into life, propelling Adam Mann toward the small boat dock at Far Landing.

People from Earth, as it had turned out, could live perfectly well on the surface of Golden without benefit of groundsuits. They could live perfectly well inside the Field, as long as they were willing to leave all high technology behind them. One implication of that was that seven years ago a certain Earthman, if he had been allowed to take the risk and remove his groundsuit's helmet, might have had some small chance of saving a certain

Tenoka child from death at the fangs of timid monsters.

Or, on the other hand he might not.

After seven years, Adam Mann no longer remembered that day's horror very often, or thought about it at all that much.

An Earthman like Adam Mann, who a few years ago had surprised the few friends who thought they knew him well, by resigning from the Space Force, giving up an enviable career to live a mostly primitive life on one particular strange planet—well, such a man with his planeteering experience might have made himself wealthy on a raw world just opened to colonization. In fact, everyone who learned of his decision to resign from the Space Force assumed that that had been his motive.

If it had been, he didn't have a lot of wealth to show for it as yet. Nor any great prospects of much in the foreseeable future. But he was doing all right.

A couple of hours earlier on this mild winter morning, Adam had looked out of the window of his isolated cabin on the Field side of the river, and had seen a shuttle descending to the Stem City spaceport. The civilian starships were coming out to Golden more and more frequently now, bringing with them tourists and adventurers and business people from Earth and a hundred other worlds. Three hundred thousand colonists were now living in Stem City, amid a continual roar of construction. On Earth demand was high for certain exotic products of this world, among them natural furs. Furs like those in the silvery bundle that now rode in the bottom of Adam Mann's canoe.

No road had yet been built between Stem City and the Far Landing dock, but copters had begun

to fly the route on a regular schedule. Adam could
see one such aircraft just landing now on a meadow
behind the dock. The aircraft sat there with its
rotor quietly idling, while a few people dressed
entirely in plain black clothing disembarked from
the passenger compartment. They stretched, and
looked round them, and then got to work unload-
ing from the copter's cargo bay an assortment of
small containers and primitive tools. There were
spades, hoes, and axes. Adam knew some of the
black-clad folk, though these particular individuals were too far away at the moment to identify.
They were religious colonists, who had planted
themselves back in the wilderness, a few kilometers beyond even Adam's cabin.

There was only one traditional-looking tourist
getting off the copter this time, a blond woman
who was wearing jeans and a bulky jacket against
the chill of the mild low-latitude winter day. The
woman separated herself a little from the black-
clad folk, and appeared to be looking round her as
if uncertain what to do next.

Now she raised to her face what Adam supposed
were binoculars, and swept them around until they
were aimed at him. They stayed fixed on him for
half a minute.

All right, girl, he thought. *We'll see about you. Just
as soon as I get these furs checked in.* Lately he had
encountered several examples of an interesting
phenomenon, the attractive female tourist from
Earth or from some other heavily civilized planet,
who was ready to be briefly fascinated by the
half-savage fur hunter and his peculiar world.

The copter landing area passed out of Adam's
sight, behind a rank of riverside brush. The canoe
was nearing the dock now, and Adam swung his

outboard up out of the water and shut it off. There
was only one real building at Far Landing, a lonely
trading shack of log construction. Outside the
shack's door, a couple of Tenoka men were standing,
in their usual costume of almost nothing at all,
arguing about something with the bored-looking
Space Force guard. The Great Council of Tenoka
subtribes had granted their friends from far-off
Earth theoretically limited rights to occupy the Stem
area, and had in exchange accepted a mountain of
trade goods and the permanent right of free medical care for any Tenoka who could reach one of the
new hospitals in the Stem. So far the Tenoka appeared to be generally still satisfied with the bar-
gain they had made.

Adam tied his canoe up beside a new and very
similar Tenoka craft—it had a squared stern and a
motor too—and tossed his bundle of furs up onto
the dock. From the corner of his eye he could see
that the blond woman was approaching, from
around the corner of the trading shack, but he
finished his tying-up before he raised his head to
look at her.

When he raised his head he stood still. Very
still indeed, for a long long moment. "Merit Creston,"
he said then, softly. It had been years, too many
years, but as far as he could see at the moment,
Merit had scarcely changed.

Merit was standing above him, laughing down
at him, laughing very much like a little girl who
has just successfully carried off a joke. Adam hopped
up onto the dock beside her. The smile on his own
face felt strange, as if, somewhere along the line
and without his realizing it, smiling had become
abnormal.

"Adam, it's been so long." She took his hands in

hers. Merit as an adult was just about his own height, her hair as uniquely blond as it had been in girlhood but cut somewhat shorter now. Her body in maturity remained as graceful as ever.

"Too long. Much too long. I wonder that you know me." He took stock of himself: long-haired, bearded, none too clean. He was dressed in hunter's clothes, some of native leather, with a long hunting knife of Earth steel sheathed in Tenoka leather at his belt. "You know I quit the Space Force."

"Yes, I'd heard that." Merit looked out across the wide placid river, where a sky free of human technology arched down to a horizon that was notched only by the trees of the winter-brown forest. "I wondered why—now I think I can see the reason. Or part of it, anyway. It's so beautiful here."

As he remembered, Merit was not one who used that word lightly or often. He asked, seriously: "How are you?"

Merit looked back at him, studying him carefully. Or maybe the impression of care being taken was only a result of her turning her head to free her eyes of a strand of wind-blown hair. "Fine."

"And how are Ray, and all the others?"

Merit smiled faintly. "All well, as far as I know. Ray is fine too, he's here on Golden. We both arrived this morning."

"Welcome to my planet!" In sudden jubilation Adam cried out, and lifted Merit into the air—hey, this was Merit! She squealed, a vulnerable and almost childlike sound, carefulness forgotten. And he kissed her.

Then Merit was resting easily in the circle of Adam's arms, eyes examining eyes at close range. She said: "Someone else was on the ship, traveling with us—my husband."

"Well." It hit him hard. For just a moment, it really hit him hard. He hoped he didn't let it show. He said: "I'll congratulate the lucky man when I meet him. Felicitations for you. Does he beat you frequently?"

Merit gave the little girl's laugh that he remembered. "Hardly at all."

"Would I know him?"

"Oh, I don't suppose so." Merit disentangled herself gently from his embrace, and stood gracefully trying to keep her hair from blowing in her eyes. "I don't know why you should. His name is Vito Ling. He's a physicist, specializing in field theory, and he works for Earth Universities Research Foundation."

"Then he's not one of Doc's kids? I don't remember the name. And tell me, how is Doc?"

"No, Vito's not a Jovian." The remnant of Merit's laughter faded from her face and voice. "Doc's dead, Adam. Suddenly, about a year ago."

After a moment he asked her: "How?"

"A heart defect. Evidently it developed rather rapidly, between his regular checkups. He was alone in the lab when he collapsed. By the time someone found him—it was too late."

"And no one—none of you—sensed—" Adam made a gesture of futility.

"None of us. They're so undependable, our parapsych talents. Usually most undependable just when they would seem to be most valuable. Maybe it was . . ."

"What?"

"I was going to say that maybe the reason we sensed nothing was because Doc felt no fear at dying. No wish to tell us anything. His life with us was a hard one, in some ways, I'm afraid."

Adam squeezed her shoulders. "That was the life Doc chose, the one he wanted." He took Merit's arm and they walked along the dock. "So now tell me about your life, my lady."

Merit's cheerfulness returned. "I'm here partly just to be with Vito. I must admit he's taken up most of my life for the past two years. Now naturally you want to know what he's like. He's tall, and dark, and brilliant, and quick-tempered."

"And not a Jovian."

"No. I said not."

Adam asked it bluntly. "Since he's not a Jovian, does it ever bother him to be left out, when you and the others start with your parapsych tricks?"

"We don't try to make our friends feel that way. Did you ever feel that way?"

"Yeah. I did. I know you don't try. You're right. But even so . . ."

There was pride in Merit's eyes. "And Vito won't let it bother him. His ego is neither small nor fragile. He won't see anything more in Jovians than gifted humans."

"*Are* you anything more? I can remember Doc soul-searching over that."

The question did not seem to surprise her; but she replied to it only with one of her own. "Do you want us to be?"

"I don't know. I've thought about it, and I don't know. I suppose you and Ray and the ninety-eight others are all still just one big happy family, too."

Merit shrugged. "We have our differences. We always have. But in a sense, yes, I think we're definitely like a family, if you can imagine a family of a hundred people. Maybe all the more like a family because we do have differences, and surmount them. I suppose Ray is really the father now."

Their walk had reversed itself where the riverside path began to grow difficult, and now their course brought them back to where the bundle of furs still lay on the dock. Adam scooped the bundle up, and said: "Let me take care of these." Merit came into the trading shack with him, and observed with interest the transaction between Adam and another Earthman behind a counter. The clerk opened the fur bundle and examined each item closely, then wrangled briefly over quality and prices before noting down the amount to be credited to Adam's Stem City bank account.

Adam, folding his paper receipt into a pocket, waited until he was outside again with Merit before he asked her: "Where are Ray and your husband now?"

"They went straight from the spaceport to the physics lab, at some place called Fieldedge. Scientists to the core. I told them I'd rather try to look you up first, and see some of the scenery at the same time. Since Earth people are rather confined here—or most of them choose to be—I thought I could probably find you with a minimum of trouble."

"Glad you did. Very glad." Adam paused. "You said that you were here partly just to be with your husband. What else?"

"For one thing, I have an obvious interest in seeing what had become of you. But there's something else, too. Geryons."

"Geryons. That's right, the last time I saw you you were getting into exobiology, weren't you?"

"Yes, I'm into it, as you say, rather deeply now."

"In fact—wait a minute. There was somebody

named Creston mentioned as a source in a couple of references, last time I was over at Stem City library trying to look something up."

"The accused stands before you. It wasn't geryons you were looking up, I trust, or I couldn't possibly have been quoted as a source. I find the idea of them fascinating—the face, of course—but I've never even seen one outside of a holograph. I'd like to begin a study, though."

"Their faces, yes."

"You see, it's occured to me that their faces might be less a result of chance than an example of interspecies parallelism on different but closely similar worlds."

"I wondered about that too. I had to study some of that evolutionary theme theory, of course, for planeteering ... so, Ray's here taking an interest in the Field. I wonder what he thinks of it. What do you think?"

"About the Field? I don't know what to think." Merit looked out over the river, past the distant line of marker poles, then closed her eyes briefly. "I don't sense it there at all. I haven't been able to sense anything about it, since we arrived. Though I suspect Ray may have ... do you know if anyone with parapsych talents has tried to investigate it?"

"I know of a few civilians who claimed to be making some effort along that line, years ago. As far as I know, they had no success. But of course they weren't Jovians ... what are your plans? I mean right now?"

"Right this moment? I don't really ..."

"Then how about a canoe ride? You can enter the Field directly and experience it first hand. Not that there's really anything to experience."

"Oh, yes. I'd like to!"

They walked back to where Adam's square-sterned canoe was waiting. The Space Force guard on duty in front of the trading shack looked up from his weary debate with the two Tenoka long enough to nod familiarly to Adam.

As they got into the canoe, Merit remarked: "It looks like the Space Force is going to trust me not to start any trouble with the natives."

"You're with me." Adam untied the canoe and shoved off from the dock. "And the Space Force usually humors me, because I'm still something of a privileged character with the Tenoka. They identify me particularly with the help we gave them against geryons, back in the early days. Of course if I ever get far enough from the Stem, well beyond Tenoka territory, things are going to be different. There are quite a number of other tribes out there, who I gather don't much like the Tenoka or their friends." The outboard started purring.

Merit was trailing her fingers in the water. "I presume this is safe to do. Nothing's going to come along and snap some of my fingers off?"

"Don't hear me yelling, do you?"

The Far Landing dock was falling behind. Ahead of them, open wilderness expanded.

"Adam, are Earth-descended people ever going to be able to see much of this planet?"

"Frankly, I don't think so. I don't believe we know any more about the Field today, really, than we did on the first day we ran into it."

"You don't seem unhappy about that situation."

"Actually, I suppose I'm not."

Merit was laughing again. "I can see already that you and Vito are going to hit it off just great. Oh, wow. He's all charged up with theoretical ideas, schemes on how to solve the problems that the

Field poses, in what he still likes to call general field theory. I think he spent most of his time on the ship worrying that someone else would have the Field completely figured out before he got here."

Adam found himself smiling, grinning broadly, and then enjoying a laugh too, for what seemed like the first time in years. "I'd say he may have a few days yet, before someone beats him out. Now hang on, here we go."

Already the canoe was closely approaching the line of marker poles, at a place where that line went marching almost straight across the river, at right angles to the banks. Adam turned off the motor and let the small craft drift on its momentum toward the boundary.

He grinned at Merit. "Look at your timepiece," he suggested. Her expression brought back to him memories of her as an—occasionally—wide-eyed little girl. The flat silvery plate that she was wearing on her wrist went totally blank a moment after the invisible border had been crossed. Then numbers and other symbols reappeared on the small surface, but seemingly at random, flickering on and off erratically.

Adam was on the point of asking Merit why she wore the watch at all; no Jovian in his memory had ever needed an artificial chronometer just to know what time it was, only perhaps for the exact timing of a race or some scientific experiment; and this particular instrument didn't look as if it was intended for such purposes. But the convincing idea at once suggested itself to Adam that the timepiece was a present to Merit from her husband, who when he gave it to her had not known her as well as Adam did. At the thought, Adam felt a moment of superior pride, mixed with an uncertain amount of jealousy.

With a sigh, Merit at last raised her head from contemplation of the confused chronometer and looked around her. "I still can't sense anything different here," she murmured. "Are we bound for anywhere in particular?" She sounded as if she would be satisfied either way.

"If you've got about an hour to spare, I'll show you where I live."

When they were quite near the Field-side shore, Adam spotted something moving in the bushes there, and rested his paddle for a moment, watching alertly. Two Tenoka children, a boy and a girl, came out into the open as soon as they saw that he was aware of them. Then they stood on the shore giggling and dumb with shyness, impressed by the strange woman in the canoe.

"You have a couple of admirers," he told Merit. "Wave to them."

Merit and the two children had a waving good time until the canoe reached Adam's little dock. At that point the kids vanished back into the leafless winter brush, too shy to approach the stranger closely.

He led Merit up along the well-worn narrow path, that wound a hundred meters up the side of a low bluff, to the shelf of land near the top where his cabin stood. The cabin was built mostly of native logs, the chinks between logs filled with local clay and sealed with a little liquid plastic. The small house, hardly more than one room, had a shingled roof that had been sealed with plastic in the same way, and a chimney of clay and stone.

Merit appeared to be enchanted by his home.

But a thought struck her. "How do you lock up when you leave?"

"I left the latchstring hanging out this time. There, see? Any of my local friends who happen to come along can walk in, but animals are kept out."

"Don't the Tenoka ever steal?"

"Rarely from a home. Quite rarely. And anyway I'm something of a privileged character, as I told you. If the tourists get much thicker out this way I may need to devise some more protection." He swung open the stout wooden door, that moved easily and silently on its Earth-fabricated hinges of neat modern metal, and gallantly bowed his visitor in.

Merit, following Earth custom, slipped off her shoes at the door. Once inside, she was instantly fascinated by his hearth and hewn furniture, and by the couple of trophies he had mounted on his walls. The heads were of different species of large carnivores, evidence of Adam's bow-hunting prowess.

A small fire was still burning, to which Adam now added fuel. The cabin was reasonably warm.

Merit was gazing at a mounted head. "Leopard-variant theme, I take it."

"Though it doesn't really look that much like a leopard at first glance. Right. You're the expert."

"But the rug—it isn't real fur." It covered much of the rough wooden floor.

"I bought the rug in Stem City," he said. "Keeps my feet warm, when there's no other way." He was still standing just inside the front door, and now he gently made sure that the door was tightly closed, and pulled the latchstring in, not wanting interruption. Then he went to Merit, and turned her around so they were face to face, and pulled her gently, firmly against him.

She didn't pull back. She didn't argue, or protest, or say anything at all, but after a moment he knew that it was never going to be any good like this, not with her.

He said: "You didn't always say no."

"I wasn't always married."

Adam raised his hands to her shoulders, and held her that way, still very gently. He said: "I guess this husband is pretty important."

Smiling, Merit hugged Adam as if she were his sister, with a kind of tired tenderness. "I'm glad to hear someone say that," she told him.

And so it seemed that someone had said otherwise.

Chapter Ten

The outboard purred faithfully into life as soon as they had re-passed the line of markers in midstream. Adam asked: "Back to Far Landing?" He could be calm; he knew it wasn't over yet between him and Merit.

Her voice was ordinary, and he supposed she knew it too. "Vito and Ray were heading for a place called Fieldedge, and since it's a physics laboratory I've no doubt they're still there. Is it far?"

"Fieldedge. No, not far, just a few kilometers. And we can take the boat right to the door." Adam headed the canoe downstream.

Ahead of them now the river curved deeply into the Stem. Falling behind the canoe now, the line of marker poles marched in their great steady circle toward the river's wild bank, up onto it, and on away from the water, vanishing from sight.

Now the land on both sides of the river bore new roads, a number of new buildings, and a great many enigmatic surveying markers, bright-colored poles and pylons. People and machines were at work at scattered sites on every hand, clearing nature from the land's surface and building what they wanted in its place. Adam sat silently in the stern of the canoe, steering with the motor. Merit occupied the seat ahead of him, her trousered knees aimed at him but her face as often as not turned away, while she took in the sights of the new land around her.

Watching the beauty of her face, the curved grace of her body as she turned from side to side, Adam tried to imagine that they had grown up together in some normal family, that Merit was his sister.

The effort failed totally.

After curving majestically almost two kilometers into the Stem, the river's course bent back to the Field again. The great circle of marker poles reappeared, marching toward the water and into it, here crossing a bend of the river at an acute angle. Just where the line of markers came closest to the Stem bank, a large new building of concrete and glass jutted out over the water, projecting deliberately across the invisible line. The relatively small portion of the laboratory building that extended beyond the markers into the Field had been constructed mainly of simple interlocking plastic slabs, resting on stone piers.

The canoe was still several hundred meters away from the building when Adam saw three men walk out of a door on an upper level of the structure, to stand on an esplanade steeply terraced above the Fieldedge dock.

*   *   *

Vito Ling's mind, energized now by anger, was working with the speed and skill of an acrobat's warmed-up musculature, juggling mathematical equations and shuttling values in and out of them. Every calculation he could make assured him that Kedro had been right: they should have insisted that the time—quanta device be redesigned, before they agreed to leave Earth with it. Now, of course, it was too late for design changes. And in its present form the device was not going to be of the least help to them in understanding the nature of the Field.

What really angered Vito most was the fact that Kedro had been a step ahead of him again. This time they had really been on the same side, arguing against the false economy of the Research Foundation administrators. But he, Vito, keen to come to grips with the Field directly, had been willing to give in to the administrators, for fear that otherwise they might call off his trip to Golden altogether; and Kedro on the other hand had remained firm in his opposition, only yielding at last, gracefully when he did so, to the opinion of Vito Ling who was supposedly the senior scientist.

It was as if Kedro had been using some precognitive talent to foresee their present trouble. Of course with the Jovian Kedro, something of the kind was possible. But looking back, Vito had to admit to himself that parapsych talent would not have been necessary to have predicted the trouble, the blind alley in which they already found themselves with their experiment. Looking back now, melding what he knew of physics with what he knew of the behavior of administrators, he was able to see it himself with perfect clarity. But only Kedro had been as certain of the result when looking forward, not letting himself be blinded by impatience or anything else.

The perfect intellect, thought Vito now, angrily, watching Kedro's massive tapering back as the Jovian man moved ahead of Vito out the door at the side of the Fieldedge lab. The perfect man—or would Kedro perhaps object to being called a man? Would it be better to say the perfect being?

Vito was jealous and angry, and angrier because he knew himself to be thinking unreasonably now.

"Well, we can't be sure today," said the calm voice of little Dr. Shishido, director of the Fieldedge lab, coming outside behind Vito. "Tomorrow, we are certain to learn more."

Vito suppressed an angry answer. They certainly knew enough now to be able to predict total failure for the time-quanta gadget in its present form. And if it failed, after much investment of time and money, what chance did they have of learning anything of importance without it? He might as well turn around and go back to Earth tomorrow.

He wouldn't do that, of course. Having come this far, he would stay on for a while, and try.

Ray Kedro, his fair hair stirring in the faint breeze, was leaning now on a railing overlooking the small dock and the broad river, and had apparently given himself up to staring across the width of moving water. It was as if the Jovian were trying to pierce the mystery of the optically invisible Field with his unaided senses.

The hero posing, Vito thought. Challenging the mystery too great for mere humanity to solve. Well, we'll see. I don't admit a damned thing about your so-called Jovian superiority, and Merit *is* my wife, and she enjoys being my wife, and wouldn't trade her life with me for anything that you could give her. And I bet that fact gripes you yet, for all you act like her older brother.

And I hope you're reading my mind.

Then, for some reason, a recurring question nagged at Vito: Why, really, didn't Merit yet want to have a child? Early on in their relationship they had agreed they would. But now . . .

Little Dr. Shishido, who had been last out of the lab, came to stand between Vito and Ray Kedro, drawing deep breaths of the mild winter air. "Why don't both of you come and have dinner with my wife and me tonight?" the lab director asked. "And bring your, er, sister, of course, Dr. Kedro." No doubt about who Shishido considered the senior scientist to be. "We're looking forward to meeting her. And, ah—"

"Maybe I'll bring my wife, too," said Vito.

Ray turned round, sensing minor difficulty. "Ms. Creston I expect will be glad to attend, in both capacities. You're right, of course, Dr. Shishido, Merit and I do usually consider ourselves as siblings for social purposes."

"Er, yes. That's what I was . . ."

Shishido actually appeared to be made somewhat nervous by the Jovian superman's mere presence. *Damn fool*, thought Vito.

Out loud he said: "I usually consider Merit as my wife. We find it works out well. We'll be glad to come." It took him an effort right now, gritted teeth, to achieve even that modest degree of civility. Temper, if you could only watch your temper, friends sometimes said to him. To hell with them, he'd like to show them what real temper was.

But with another effort he managed now to ease his mental wrestler's grip on the problem of the

Field, and started to take notice of the new world surrounding him.

A stair led down from the open space where the three men stood, down to a small dock where a couple of the indigenous people were sitting, onlookers without any visible purpose. The country on this side of the river looked to Vito like it was only beginning to be settled, and that on the other side was to all appearances utterly wild.

Kedro, still gazing out over the water, said: "Doctor Shishido, I think you're going to meet Merit before this evening."

Only now did Vito really notice the small boat that had been slowly and steadily approaching from upriver, with two figures in it. The two people were still too distant for any certain identification, but one of them was a blond woman wearing a bulky jacket that certainly looked like Merit's. The other appeared to be a man, and not a Golden native.

Had Merit hired a boat? But she had said something about going to look up a childhood friend. Yes, some former planeteer who had lost his wife.

The three men at the railing watched in silence as the boat drew near, heading right for the dock. There was no doubt now that the woman was Merit. She waved up at them cheerfully, said something to the man who was with her, and then hopped out nimbly on the dock. Her companion was a rough-looking character, bearded and dirty, and wearing a knife at his belt. After one glance up at the three men watching, and a quick wave, he busied himself with securing the canoe. Then the two native men came over to him and began a conversation, while Merit started up the stairs.

Vito stood at the top of the stairs, looking down

at her, while she climbed toward him, smiling happily.

"Who the devil is *that?*" It came out rougher than he had intended.

"An old friend." Merit suddenly looked worried. "His name is Adam Mann. I told you about him, darling."

The anger rose up in Vito, a flame finding new fuel. "Didn't lose any time getting cozy with him, did you? He looks like a tramp. Is he another of your parapsych friends?"

"No—no." Merit was shaken. She appeared to be too surprised by his outburst to know how to react to it; somehow that only made him worse.

"So, you got off the ship and went straight to see him." The wrong words, meant to hurt, came out with perverse ease, like lines well-studied for a play, even when Vito knew that they were wrong.

"Yes, Vito, I did that." Merit, as usual, had needed only a moment to regain complete control of herself. Still she was angry too. "And I even went to visit the cabin where he lives. So be angry if you must. If you can't grow up. You could decide to trust me."

"Oh, I could, could I? And what would happen then?" *How good it would be, how really fine, to find some reason to hit someone.* And meanwhile Dr. Shishido, looking more and more worried, was hovering almost beside them, watching the argument. He kept making little fussing starts of movement as if he yearned to interfere. And Kedro still stood at the railing, now looking down at his huge hands clamped onto the wood, determinedly minding his own business.

It was just at this point that the Earthman chatting with the natives on the dock below looked up at them all again and smiled pleasantly. To Vito, at the moment, there was no doubt of what that smile meant: *She came straight to me, and I took her to my cabin, and what are you going to do about it?*

Vito growled in his throat, and started down the stairs. Mann, or whatever his name was down there, was shorter than Vito and a little lighter probably, but the bastard was carrying a knife, and if he wanted to try using his knife Vito right now didn't give a damn.

"Vito, no!" Merit clutched at his arm belatedly as he went by her, and it afforded him minor satisfaction to be able to tear his sleeve free of her grip without a pause. Skipping downstairs with the unthinking balance of the natural athlete, he knew in the back of his mind that he was wrong, dead wrong and going overboard. But this was one of those times when temper just got out of hand, and afterward there could always be apologies.

He heard and ignored Shishido behind him, the little scientist raising his voice in some ineffectual protest. Then Vito hit the bottom of the stairs, and bounced along straight toward the man who owned what must be a very attractive cabin. The two natives saw Vito coming, and the way he looked, and they hastily backed away to stand with folded arms and wooden faces.

At close range, he could see that Man was well built, with a deep chest and strong arms; good. There wouldn't be much difference in weight after all. Mann's pleasant smile had changed to a look of startled caution.

Vito stopped just within his own long reach of the bearded man. "Have a good time with my wife today?" he asked. He felt his lips drawn back, the blood beating in his head, the muscles in his face hurting a little. He felt his fists big and hard, and his feet ready to shift, quickly and lightly.

"Yeah," said Mann, plainly. He was squinting at Vito with his head a little tilted, as if he were trying to understand something.

Vito said a filthy name and shifted his weight and stabbed his left arm out in a well-aimed jab that shot past Mann's instantly moving face. The second jab missed too, and the hard overhand right, thrown without having the range at all, missed so badly that Vito almost fell down.

He lost sight of Mann for just an instant, and spun around with his guard up. But Mann was only shuffling backward away from him. A clumsy-looking man of about average size, his arms down, still puzzled. "What goes on?" he asked, seeming no more than annoyed.

Vito moved after him, with cold precision, and no lessening of the urge to strike and destroy. He shifted and feinted, like the good amateur boxer that he was, but drew no response. He moved in with another left jab that also missed those unblinking elusive eyes, and a long hook that touched only air, and then a looping right that was stopped when his forearm caught on Mann's, which came up with unhurried speed and felt like a wooden club

Vito stood there for a long instant, with his right arm caught and his left out of position, his feet somehow misplaced and his balance failing as Mann's forearm pulled him slightly forward, and he knew he was ripe to be clobbered, by someone who knew how.

But Vito wasn't clobbered. Mann disengaged at once and stepped back again.

"Keep it up, bud, and I'll chuck you in the river," he said in a flat voice. "Pretty cold this time of year."

Vito too stepped back this time. He was breathing heavily. Merit was calling something to him. From the sound of her voice, she was almost in tears. Shishido like an angry schoolmaster was saying: "Here, now! Stop it, you two!"

And now Vito's rage was burning out quickly, not with fear or frustration, though he began to feel both of those, but as if the fuel were being cut off. He backed away carefully from Mann, turned and headed for the stairway.

The draining out of anger left him shaky, going up the stairs. Oh, by all the Laws, he thought, I really popped my circuit breakers that time, He stopped and half-turned once on the stairs, intending to try to say something to Mann; but what was there to say?

Keeping his back turned to the dock, Vito climbed on. At the top of the stair he muttered some futile apology to Shishido, who favored him with a look of sad pity as he went by. Vito plunged right on into the lab; he had to be alone for a minute.

What kind of a damn fool *am* I? he thought. What have I done to Merit now? I never blew up like *that* before in my whole adult life.

He leaned against a generator that was still humming itself down slowly into silence after the day's futile experiment. After a few seconds he heard the door behind him, and then Merit's blessed footsteps.

"Adam, the way you look seems to prove that going native here is healthy. I should have come to try it years ago." It was Ray Kedro who said that, Ray grinning as of old, looking down from his great height and engulfing Adam's right hand in his own, almost crushing it in greeting.

"Seeing you and Merit again was what I needed," said Adam. Ray was looking stronger and handsomer than ever. Somehow he even gave the impression of being still bigger than the last time Adam had seen him, as if he might have kept on growing after the age of twenty or so. But it wasn't really an increase in physical size, Adam decided. In controlled dominance, perhaps.

Adam was introduced to Dr. Shishido, who went through the motions rather blankly, his mind obviously elsewhere. As director of the lab he probably had a lot to think about, when his physicists started trying to pick fights with strangers. Merit had already followed her husband inside.

"Do you suppose we had better postpone our dinner engagement?" the little administrator asked Ray now. Shishido was still looking almost fearfully after Vito and Merit.

Ray told him: "Sorry about the demonstration."

"It's not your fault, Dr. Kedro." Shishido dropped his voice. "Tell me, is he—?" He concluded with a nervous motion of his head toward the closed laboratory door.

Ray puffed out his breath faintly. "Vito really isn't himself just now. There have been problems, some of which you know about . . . I regret to say that I think you're right about the dinner. Should I call you about it tomorrow?—maybe we can arrange to get together then."

"That would be best, I suppose."

"Good." Ray shook his head, as if trying to dismiss a nagging thought. "Right now I'd better start trying to get back to town. I have an appointment in half an hour to see General Lorsch. Ride in with me, Ad?"

"Sure."

While walking beside Ray toward the meadow where the shuttle copter waited, Adam remarked: "Merit's husband is not himself just now, you said. I can believe that. Why would she have married a total madman? What's going on?"

"It's a long story, Ad. Bureaucracy and frustration are only part of it. Among other problems. I didn't want to go into it all in front of Shishido. I'll tell you the whole story, sometime."

They walked the next few paces in silence. Then Adam commented: "So you're going to see the General, not wasting any time. She hasn't too much to do these days. There isn't very much Space Force left on Golden."

"I'm not wasting any time," Ray agreed, looking gently serious. "Not here on Golden. I don't think that there's any time left to waste."

And though he tried fiercely, Adam could not persuade him to elaborate on that.

Chapter Eleven

"Why are you people so anxious to get the Space Force completely off this planet?" General Lorsch made her voice deliberately casual. "I know you're putting pressure on Earth Parliament."

A woman whose rather shapeless body never managed to look well-fitted in any uniform, she still sat with practiced ease behind the huge desk she had inherited some years ago, along with the mysteries of Golden, from General Grodsky. Grodsky was currently serving in a high-placed staff job back on Earth. There were times when General Lorsch would have been quite ready to change places with him.

The only other person in the General's private office at this moment was the Jovian, Ray Kedro, who was sitting in an equally relaxed attitude in the big visitor's chair on the other side of the desk.

"General Lorsch," said Kedro, "I just got off the ship from Earth this morning. I've come to Golden as the representative of several organizations, so I'm not sure what you mean by 'you people'."

Lorsch consulted a scrap of paper on her generally untidy desk. She said offhandedly: "Oh, those organizations, yes ... I have the list here. You represent the Research Foundation, of course, plus a hotel chain, plus a mining corporation. Plus one or two others."

"Is there anything wrong with my representing them?"

"No. Not necessarily. Though *I* wouldn't want to represent them all. Most of the people on this roster, probably all of them, have schemes to get rich quick, and some of them would like a freer hand in trading and dealing with the natives here ... when they've made their profit, of course, they will then pull out, leaving a mess for someone else to worry about."

"You may be right about them, General, in some cases at least. My representation of them on Golden is limited. And it has a purpose."

"I'm sure it does. And I know I'm right. They have put similar schemes into operation on other planets."

"I—we Jovians—have had nothing to do with those schemes. I would only suggest that here, on this planet where we are somewhat involved, you might wait and see if those companies don't manage their affairs somewhat differently. More to the benefit of all concerned."

"If I waited to be sure of the result, it might well be too late."

"Not necessarily, General. It would depend to a great extent on how the contracts were drawn, wouldn't it?"

"Perhaps ... but let that go for the moment. Even that is not my first concern just now."

"Then what is, ma'am?" Kedro, she thought, could find just the right note of politeness.

"I'll tell you what. There's recently been extra heavy pressure on Earth Parliament to get us—the Space Force—to leave Golden. And I don't mean just pressure from the mining corporations and so on that I've just been talking about. That kind of thing we expect, that's routine. This, as I say, is extra. And it comes from you people, always from you, and you know who I mean. Jovians. Now why is that?"

Kedro had been gently nodding his understanding throughout her speech. Now his eyes seemed to be asking her to understand him too. He said: "To me, the concept of 'my people' extends a long way beyond my ninety-nine siblings. I consider that my people are the human race. The whole Earth—descended branch of it, at least."

"I might say the same thing about my own feelings," commented the General drily. She made her chair creak, rocking gently. Sometimes the creak unsettled visitors, and she had an urge to see if Kedro could be unsettled. "But what I have in mind now is a certain sub-class of that large group, the very one you first mentioned. Namely you and your gene-altered friends. Your siblings, if you want to call them that, though I understand there's no direct biological relationship among you. In the popular phrase, the Jovians."

"You should not view us as opponents," said Kedro. His manner was still thoroughly calm, his tone almost reproving. He seemed to be skirting the edge of the attitude of someone who lays down moral rules and then expects to have them followed.

"General, I think that your organization and mine can help each other, to the benefit of the entire human race. And I don't mean just the Earthly branch of it."

"Fine!" Lorsch pushed forward a carved box on her desk, offering Kedro several versions of Antarean cigars, an invitation which was politely declined. The General chose one of the smaller variants for herself, and lit up. Then she leaned back, still rocking and creaking a little. Then she asked again, patiently: "Why do you people want to get the Space Force off this planet?"

Kedro said imperturbably: "I think you are no longer needed here. I think that the Field itself adequately protects most of the natives of this particular world from exploitation. Adequate local laws, and improved contracts in the case of some of the people you mentioned, can protect the rest, here in the Stem area, which is the only place the Space Force can protect them anyway. I also think that the best place for the Space Force is elsewhere, out on the real Galactic frontier, exploring new worlds and in general doing the job that it was created to do."

Lorsch drummed her fingers on the desk. "Golden still is a frontier. What we have here is a small beachhead on an unexplored planet, though Earth people who live here for any length of time tend to get used to having the Field surrounding them and think of it as something natural. I wasn't in favor of opening the place up for colonization so quickly, myself, but . . . that's been done now. You're going to work on the Field at the lab. Do you think there's any hope of our physicists being able to solve the Field, manage it, push it back in the near future?"

Kedro shook his head, a thoughtful but definite negative.

Lorsch went on: "So, we're still very much on the frontier here, even though as you must know we've explored for a dozen parsecs beyond this system in every direction, trying to find more evidence of the Field-builders. So far, no success."

"I don't know that there are any Field-builders," Kedro replied.

The General was surprised. "You say it's a natural phenomenon, then? Why?"

"I don't know that that's the right answer either . . . well, stay on Golden if you like, General. Not that you have to ask my permission. I have not much influence in the matter, whatever you may think. But if this is, as you say, still a frontier, then I wonder why you haven't done more frontier work here over the last few years. Has the Space Force ever made any serious attempt to explore this planet's surface away from the Stem?"

Lorsch's cigar was burning itself out, forgotten in an ashtray. Her chair was still. "There have been a few scouting expeditions, necessarily made on foot—neither horses nor native animals have worked out as well as we had hoped for transportation. We intend to send out more expeditions eventually, probing deeper."

"I'd like to go along on the next one that you do send, General. It might be possible to make some observations away from the Stem that would materially help the physicists' work at Fieldedge."

"Well." Somewhat surprised, Lorsch thought it over. "Maybe something can be arranged along that line." It didn't hurt to say that much, at least. "I'll let you know if a suitable chance should come up while you're still on planet."

"I intend to be on Golden quite a while. Why did you call me in here today, General? Just to ask about my lobbying efforts back on Earth?"

"You weren't forced to come when I called. You're a practicing telepath, aren't you? Do you need to ask me about my motives?"

"I need no special parapsych powers to read your hostility. General Lorsch, you must know something of how telepathy actually works, as opposed to the popular ideas. You must realize that the idea of probing your mind is as distasteful to me as it must be to you. And I can assure you it's not a very reliable way to obtain information."

"You *have* tried it, then."

Kedro ignored the question. "Now why do you think I want you and your people to leave Golden? So I can make myself governor? Dictator? Or enrich myself by smuggling?"

The General shook her head. "No." Her voice was weakening a little, and with a conscious effort she made it stronger. "I don't really think you people want such things, except maybe in an incidental way. You people don't work to become conspicuous rulers, and you're not ostentatious about your wealth. You'd much rather stay behind the scenes, and marry each other, and cooperate with each other to accumulate indirect control over all kinds of human activity."

"I might say the very same things, and just as accurately, about the Space Force, General Lorsch. Are those things evil when we do them, and good—"

"It's not the same thing at all, dammit!" Lorsch, to her own surprise, could feel her self control slipping. "It's simply not true that we try to control all kinds of human activity. And we don't consider ourselves to be more than human!"

Kedro looked down at the floor for a few seconds. His handsome face was sad. When he raised his eyes and spoke, his voice was soft and almost tentative. "Why should you be tempted to consider yourselves more than human, General?"

"Do *you* think *you're* more than human? Homo Superior? I've heard that you do!"

"Do you believe that I am human, General Lorsch? Or even something less than that, perhaps?" Kedro's voice this time was still low. But it was no longer soft, or tentative.

Seconds slid away in silence. Lorsch, trying with unexpected difficulty to frame her answer, felt an impression growing on her with the speed and force of nightmare. It was the impression that what sat and spoke with her in her office was not a man in any sense, but rather an elemental force, a materialized law of the universe that had taken on a slightly larger than human form, and might at any moment take on a different and more disquieting form than that.

While remaining physically calm, the General found herself somehow—unable? unwilling?—to move or to speak. And her inner being froze and screamed silently in fright at the prospect of confronting directly, seeing clearly, the alien being, the god, who sat facing her across her desk.

Part of the General's outer mind was able to say comfortingly: Nonsense, this is just a foolish notion that's taken me. Nothing is really happening. I can move and speak whenever I like. Of course I can.

She looked into Kedro's compassionate blue eyes, and her ego cowered and whimpered: *Is this how a pet feels, a dog, when it looks up at—*

"Well, do you?" Kedro prompted, in an ordinary voice, and the instant he spoke the spell, or whatever it had been, was gone.

"Do I what? Oh. No, I can't admit that you're

more than human." Lorsch moved slightly in her chair, to prove to herself that she could do so. Her uniform adhered to the chair irritatingly. The words of her answer almost stuck in her throat. But still, everything was normal again. Except that she was perspiring. It was only a big man who sat there, across her desk. A big, handsome, and extremely dangerous man.

"Then isn't your fear of us a touch irrational?" Kedro's voice was as reasonable as any voice that she had ever heard. "Really, we have the talent to get what we want by ordinary, legal means. Power? We don't especially want the responsibility of governing, this planet or any other. And even heavy manipulation from behind the scenes, however it might be accomplished, implies responsibility.

"We *do* like to guide the world of Earth-descended humanity just a bit, keep it when we can from making certain catastrophic mistakes. Show it values that it might otherwise miss. We'd like to be able to do a better job of guiding."

Kedro shifted in his chair, leaning his perfectly proportioned bulk forward, resting one elbow on the desk. He was smiling now, his handsome eyes narrowing in friendly, almost irresistable intentness. "Think of the good that we could do if we had, working with us instead of against us, all the wealth and power and organization of the Space Force. Or even a part of it. Say the Wing that you command, here on Golden . . ."

The General could very easily visualize the benevolent giants, golden in their virtue, superior to natural humanity. From their height above the struggling confusion that had given them birth, the Jovians saw far into the future, far and accurately, discerning a thousand dangers and warning their parent race against them all. The godlike powers of the Jovians' superior minds won victory after victory, over ignorance and disease and human misery, victories gladly shared with mere humanity ... and now the golden people turned toward General Lorsch, seeming to plead: *Help us, help us to do these things. For your own sake, help us.*

The dream of glory faded. Of course Kedro had been projecting it somehow into her mind. Lorsch started to say: "Oh how I wish—"

She meant to finish: "—we could do that."

"—I could believe you," was what she said.

Kedro leaned back from the desk. He lowered his face into his hands for a moment and rubbed his eyes. He looked tired when he straightened up in his chair again. Tired, but not diminished.

"I wish you could," he said, and got to his feet. "Was there anything else?"

The General shook her head. She felt that she might commit some spectacular failure if her confrontation with this—visitor—went on any longer.

Kedro towered over the desk. "Let me know about the expedition, please," he said. "Really. If and when it ever gets organized." And he walked out of the office.

It was over. The General sat quietly for a minute, pulling her nerves back together. Trying to pull them back. She was all right, she was functional, but she suspected she would never be quite the same again.

When she got up to check the cameras and recorders hidden in her office she found that all of the machines had unaccountably stopped functioning and that nothing of the interview was preserved.

Chapter Twelve

Adam Mann stood stretching and yawning in the open doorway of his cabin, looking out from inside with a comfortable small fire at his back. He was gazing upon yet another mild winter afternoon with something like contentment—though it was a different sort of contentment than he had enjoyed, or had thought he was enjoying, a few days ago. Satisfaction with cabin life was mixed now with a new restlessness.

Merit was here. Only a few kilometers away.

Ever since he had joined the Space Force, the idea of living on Earth or some other crowded planet had repelled him more and more. Then the Space Force had lost its attraction too.

What Adam really wanted, when he looked at it squarely, was to be a Jovian, to have Merit for his woman and Ray and the others as his peers, as his brothers and sisters in a sense. But he was not going to become a Jovian, no matter what he did. Therefore it was necessary to adopt some other life. Until a few days ago the cabin and the rough, chancy existence of a fur-hunter had been, for the time being at least, quite satisfactory.

Merit was here, only a few kilometers away. But there were other women in the world. Many others, in the plurality of available worlds. Tenoka women, themed close enough to Earth-human for fun, still separate enough for there to be no worries about fertility and responsibility.

Adam stretched again. Tonight he intended to go into Stem City, and enjoy one last little fling before he left to spend a week alone up in the northern mountains. One more good haul of fine furs should be possible before spring.

Someday the tribesmen who lived up there, distant cousins of the Tenoka, might try to kill him, just to steal his marvelous bow, compounded of magical Earth materials. That risk, he thought, was not yet too great. But what was the risk of going into town tonight, to seek out another man's wife and at least spend as much time as possible with her? Because that's what he was intending to do. There was no use trying to lie to himself about it. And in fact he doubted very much whether he was starting for the mountains tomorrow, either. Not while she was here.

Out of all of them, the entire hundred, Merit was the one, the only one so far as Adam knew, who had chosen a non-Jovian to marry. And when she did that, she picked out a man who lived on Earth like an Earth-descended human being, not one who had turned into a hermit on an alien world—

Someone was approaching the cabin. It was a single person, walking quietly but not sneaking. Thin ice in a small shaded puddle crackled underfoot. He or she was coming along the faint path that followed the top of the river bluff, from the direction of the nearby religious colony. Again Adam heard movement, and saw small birds fly up from the brush near the path.

He knew that he had an enemy or two in Stem City, among the hoodlums settling in there on the fringes of the fur business. Then there was Tooth Biter, the Tenoka he had once caught stealing. Without moving from his position in the doorway, Adam reached an arm along the inside cabin wall to take his twenty-five kilo composite bow down from its pegs. He set the bow on end just inside the doorframe, and reached again to slide a broad-bladed hunting arrow out of the hanging quiver.

Then in a few seconds he saw the white robes, marked with the symbol of the cross. Adam put back the weapons, and stepped out in smiling welcome. "Father, glad to see you."

Father Francis Marti was young and small; at first glance, he might have been a theological student lost in the woods. His hobby was studying the native wildlife of Golden, while his work was in a parish in Stem City. There, as he had once told Adam, the geryons' faces were sometimes even more convincingly human than were the faces of the geryons out here in the wilderness.

Now he might have been greeting a favorite parishoner. "Adam. Are you keeping well?"

"Still alive. You trying to convert your religious competition over there?" Adam nodded in the direction from which the priest had come. The colony of black-clad folk were back that way, only a couple of kilometers distant.

Father Marti appeared to consider the question seriously. He said at last: "No. I have been trying to warn them—some of them travel frequently alone

and unarmed in the woods. Maybe their patriarch
would listen to you more readily than to me."

Both men glanced toward the end of the right
sleeve of the priest's white robe, from which no
hand emerged. Father Marti did own quite a good
right hand, but it was complex enough that the
metal and plastic joints of it tended to freeze up or
exhibit other bizarre behavior whenever he wore
it into the Field. He usually, as today, left his right
hand in the city whenever he visited the wilderness.
Father Marti too had once walked in these woods
unarmed. But then had come his wrestling match
with a small geryon. Since then he came with the
sheath of a Bowie knife hanging on his belt, ready
for a left-hand draw.

"I'll talk to them tomorrow," Adam said. *Before
I leave for the mountains*, he thought. *I really had
better go. Then why don't I tell the Father I'm making one more hunting trip this winter? Because I
know I'm not going. I mean to stay here instead and
hang around another man's wife. Being merely
human, I always lie to myself.*

"Father . . ."

"What is it?"

But there was nothing, really, to be said.

In the late afternoon Adam heated some water
and got cleaned up and dressed to go into the city.
He had no very extensive wardrobe, and wore a
modified version of his usual garb. According to
what he could see of himself in his small metal
mirror, he looked like a tourist trying to look like
an old settler. Not, he supposed, that it made any
difference anyway.

By the time he had paddled and motored himself
across the river to Far Landing, darkness was at

hand, the million distant lights of Stem City starting to come on against the night. The shuttle copter rose from the meadow behind Far Landing into the last fading fire-glroy of the sunset. The only other passengers this trip were a tourist couple carrying cameras and wearing tired, vaguely disappointed expressions. Maybe I shouldn't have washed up and changed clothes, Adam thought. He pictured himself boarding the copter in a begrimed hunting shirt, saying to the tourists: "Me half Tenoka. You take picture?" He grinned.

When he was on his way to look for Merit, he could feel good about his life.

The first thing he did on reaching the city was to try to call the Lings at their hotel—she had told him which one they were staying at. But they were out. They might, Adam supposed, be dining tonight at the home of one of the Fieldedge scientists, but he had no way of looking for them there. Stem City's rapidly multiplying places of entertainment were a different matter. He would give some of those a try.

Already the center of the only city on Golden strongly resembled that of a resort town on Earth. If the buildings here were not yet quite as tall as those on more crowded worlds, the money flowed at least as freely. People who traveled this far from Earth or anywhere else to seek amusement had plenty of money to spend.

Adam started on a round of bars, working his way outward from the exact center of town. He actually drank only a small amount. Neither alcohol nor other drugs had ever assumed any great importance in his life.

While smoking an Antarean cigar in a place that

featured the worst music he had heard in at least a year, he happened to glance out through a large bubble window a hundred meters above the street. Kilometers distant, out near the northern perimeter of the Stem, there stood the newest tower on the planet, four hundred vertical meters of steel and stone, bathed at night in searchlights of changing color. A huge sign flashed pictures, first frothy bubbles pouring from a glass, then a couple dancing side by side, then the name of some entertainer blazing out, and then the cycle started over.

Yes, Adam thought, quite likely. It was the newest hotel on planet, advertised as top-status. Built on a hill that was still outside the burgeoning city proper, the tower looked up to the northern mountains in the distance, whence the savage fur hunters could look down at it in wonder. A Fieldedge scientist might well consider such a hotel the ideal place to take off-world visitors. Anyway, Merit would certainly not be here where Adam was now, listening to this subhuman music.

From the center of Stem City an enclosed, multilane slideway stretched all the way out to the new resort. FASTEST WITHIN TEN LIGHT YEARS! advertised the slideway's entrance signs. The dully-gleaming, black-surfaced lanes bore a thin scattering of passengers. Adam stepped from lane to lane, out to the express walk that moved nearest the stationary central divider, and was whistled along at highway speed. People going the other way blurred past him, just on the other side of the air-buffered plastic barrier in the center.

There was clear plastic overhead, too, a shield against weather. Every two hundred meters or so, glass or composite observation platforms had been bubbled out from the slideway's structure, otherwise mostly enclosed tunnel. These platforms were accessible from the slow outer lanes, and gave day or night a good view of the Stem country. Much of the Stem was already lighted at night, sketched in with roads and markers for future development even where there were as yet no buildings. Soon, Adam expected, the city was likely to fill the Stem completely; at which point the developers would be sure to want a new treaty with the Tenoka, and then an expansion of development into Field territory. Which, Adam thought drily, should be fun to watch.

Now a pair of teener boys came hurtling past Adam on the other side of the center divider. With an expertly violent throw, one of them heaved something over the barrier as they came shooting toward him, some object that was caught and spun in the air buffers but still came past Adam's dodging head at sixty or seventy kilometers an hour, to land on the strip that he was riding and make a long streaked splash of something messy. For a second he thought of chasing the kids, but decided that would be a waste of time, whether or not he was able to catch up with them.

As he drew near the outer terminal, the flow of the black solid surface under Adam's feet began to slow and thicken, like water in a deepening river. Soon all the lanes were moving at the same low speed, and he walked forward to the splendid entrance of the Pioneer Hotel.

Ten copied pairs of Ghiberti's gigantic bronze doors opened into nothing that at all resembled the baptistery at Florence. The huge lobby inside was decorated in Imitation Primitive, with fake logs roaring electrically in fake fireplaces, and a few real furs and other trophies on the walls. Adam made a mental note that he might find a good market here after his next hunting trip. There were no geryon heads on display; he had yet to see one mounted anywhere. With the beast's body gone, the look was just too overwhelmingly human. It occured to Adam that Merit would probably have something to say about that, too, when he had another chance to talk to her. It occured to him also that Poe said it once: *Even among the utterly lost, there are matters of which no jest can be made.*

He realized a need: someone that he could talk to.

Tourists moved through the lobby, coming and going.

"Welcome to Golden, sir, we hope you enjoy our world," said a voice near Adam's ear. A pale young man, evidently an employee of the hotel, was standing beside him. "Were you desirous of a room, sir?"

"No." He would have to pick tonight to dress like a tourist, well, if he had come in his ordinary clothes they probably wouldn't have let him in.

"Entertainment and refreshment on the one hundred and first floor, sir, companionship available one hundred and two. High speed lifts to your right. Hope you enjoy your stay on our world."

"I hope so too."

He got off the lift at one hundred one, to find himself just under a crystal roof exhibiting the stars, and walking directly into the restaurant-bar-dance floor-whatever. Anyway it was a vast dim circular area containing people who had come here to be entertained, with fake trees and rocks making divisions everywhere, and pathways that were supposed to look like forest trails winding everywhere among the trees and tables. In places the ceiling was invisible, except for the way it contained rolling clouds of some light vapor, again shot through with multicolored light. There were probably several hundred people scattered about through the enormous room, but still it was not really crowded. It would take some searching to locate anyone here.

Sidestepping robotic waiters in the form of rolling trolleys, and a human hostess who appeared to be entirely naked except for her multicolored body paint, Adam made his way to an observation bubble—Stem City architects never seemed to tire of such constructions—that bulged out over the side of the building. There were several tourists standing and sitting in the bubble, some using the radarscopes that let them see how the funneling sides of the Field hemmed in the Stem on all sides and mounted up above. Three or four hundred meters below, the surface of the Stem was aflame with all the colors that humanity was able to get out of electricity. Rivulets of people and vehicles crawled everywhere, many of them going apparently in circles. *I stand here like Dante on the lip of the Pit, thought Adam. I need a Geryon to fly me down.*

Bah.

Instead of calling for a geryon, Adam went back to the bar, and bought himself a drink, and pinched one of the hostesses, who seemed to be expecting some such attention. Thoughtfully rubbing his fingers together, feeling the slippery body paint they had picked up, he looked around.

There they were, at a table a good distance off. There was Merit, talking and laughing and gay, wearing a kind of gown that Adam hadn't seen on anyone before, that was probably the latest fashion on Earth or somewhere else, or would be the latest fashion there next year. There was little Shishido of the Fieldedge lab, with a woman, her back now turned to Adam, who would doubtless be Shishido's wife. And there of course was Vito Ling, a lean, strong man, a handsome and energetic and restless-looking man, laughing now at something that Merit had just said.

If I go over there, thought Adam, maybe he'll try again to hit me. Probably that would be easier to deal with than some other things that could happen.

"This time I think it's safe," said a magnificent, familiar voice at Adam's elbow.

He turned to see Ray Kedro.

"Well, that's what you were wondering, isn't it?" Ray asked, grinning down at him. "I don't have to probe your subconscious more than six or eight layers down to detect that."

"Hello," said Adam, and relaxed, or tried to relax, leaning on the bar. He experienced, as usual, a sudden wave of mixed feelings on encountering Ray. "Good old Vito Ling didn't give me a chance to say hello, the other day. Damn, he can't always be that touchy, can he?"

"He's not," said Ray, and paused thoughtfully. "Actually he's a pretty good guy." Ray paused again, and a faint smile appeared on his face, evoking old days at Doc's school, old shared pranks and adventures there when Adam visited. "Pretty good for one of you ordinary second-rate human types, that is."

"Yeah, sure." Adam turned back to the bar.

"He is. Merit picked him out, didn't she?"

There was a pause, in which Adam thought he could feel the slight intoxication of his evening's drinking fading prematurely. "Right," he said, not able to think of anything else to say. He wondered if Ray could tell how he, Adam, felt about Merit, and intended to try to do with her. He wondered how Ray felt about her himself. Wondered, and couldn't guess.

"We've already got serious trouble at the lab," said Ray. "And it's been getting Vito down." He ordered a drink from a robotic creature that appeared behind the bar, and Adam got himself another. The area behind the bar was all colored lights and shadows, and music, much better than some that Adam had heard recently, was coming from somewhere.

"What kind of trouble?" Adam asked, sipping.

"Mainly because of an expensive gizmo that the Foundation sent with us from Earth. It was supposed to be just what we needed to unravel the mystery of the Field. But it just flat won't work. Vito and I both told the administrators back on Earth that it should have been constructed differently, but they wouldn't believe us. They were wrong." Ray swallowed half his drink. Suddenly Adam couldn't remember if he had ever seen Ray take alcohol before.

Adam asked him: "So, you haven't much hope of success now with the Field?"

"We might have had a good start on it, if our gadget had been properly designed." Ray appeared to brood. "Now, we'll have to find another way."

"Another way?"

One of the naked hostesses, on the customers' side of the bar, was approaching Ray. When she got close enough to touch him on the arm, and he turned to face her, her professional smile suddenly altered. It was as if she had been awed despite herself by the Jovian man's size and masculine beauty, suddenly confronted at close range.

When the hostess finally opened her mouth to speak, Ray closed it for her with the lift of one massive finger under her chin. "You might come back and look for me again in a couple of hours," he told her. His voice was abstracted, as if his thoughts were elsewhere. The girl backed away, the professional smile almost totally gone, until she bumped into someone and the spell was broken.

There had been music in the background all along, ever since Adam had walked in from the lift. Now the instruments suddenly blared up louder, and more colored lights began to focus upon a wide central stage.

"So." Ray's eyes considered Adam. "Something drew you to settle on this planet—when, about four years ago? Something keeps you here. When I first heard you were living here, that you'd quit the Space Force, I thought it was the Field. But that's not it, is it? Not directly."

"You're right." Adam tasted his drink. "Something. And no, not the Field exactly. I don't know if I can define it. But the Field's what brought you here. Or is it? What does this planet mean to a Jovian?"

"You're as perceptive as ever, Adam." Ray slouched easily, elbows on the bar, leaning there like a crouching lion. "No. The Field isn't really all."

"What else?" asked Adam. Then an answer occured to him. "In your case, because someone built it. That's it, isn't it? It's the Field-builders who are on your mind."

"They are. Increasingly." Ray downed the rest of his drink. "Let's go over to the table. I don't think you'll have to dodge any more punches."

Ray was making fascinating statements, opening topics and then dropping them. That wasn't really his way, as Adam remembered. Adam still leaned on the bar. He wasn't ready to drop this one. "That's it, isn't it? It comes back to the Builders. Why did they create the Field, and where are they now?"

"Why? I think they created it—just to see what would happen when someone else, like—Earth-descended humanity, discovered it. And where are they now? I think that they're not too far away." Abruptly Ray pushed off from the bar. Not really looking to see whether Adam was following him or not, the huge man led the way toward the distant table where the Lings and the Shishidos appeared to be having a genuinely good time, celebrating something. Celebrating what, Adam wondered? Certainly not the laboratory failure he had just heard about. Certainly not the near-fight on the dock.

"Do you think the Field could be a parapsych effect?" Adam wondered aloud, suddenly, as they were skirting the low stage. The stage was occupied by frenetically dancing girls whose skins were covered with colored lights and almost nothing else, and Adam felt a little idiotic walking almost among them, discussing parapsych effects.

Ray turned to answer, the lights playing indirectly on his face. "If it is, it's a damned good one. They've integrated it with effects of the physical sciences. That's a little beyond what we can do. So far." It sounded like that, maybe, was the main point of what he had been thinking about. He turned again and moved on.

Vito Ling was the first person at the table to see them coming; the tall physicist's face took on an anxious look, and he scrambled to his feet and stuck out his hand to Adam. "Sorry about the other day. Really sorry. I had no reason to act that way, no excuse at all." He was obviously sincere.

"It's all right—no harm done."

"I'll say not. I'm just lucky that you're cooler than I am."

The handshake was firm. It might be easy to get to like this character, Adam thought. That was all he needed, that would make things really nice. Oh, yes.

Merit, delighted at the truce, got up to greet Adam with an old friend's kiss. He sat down in the chair Ray pulled up for him, between Merit and Ray. A drink was poured for him. He was introduced to Mrs. Shishido, at close range a nicer-looking woman than he had expected. Mrs. Shishido beamed at him.

"Well, now!" said her small husband, also well pleased to see peace. "Well! Mr. Mann, I understand that you are actually the first human being of Earth to ever set foot on this planet—except perhaps for the unfortunate Golden. And you've been living here for some time now? I wish that I might have been able to meet you sooner."

Shishido was genuinely interested in the planeteering history. The others were too, once the subject had been raised. Adam began to talk of the earliest days of the Space Force exploration of Golden, telling as an eyewitness of the first experiments with the Field. He could speak well when he wanted to put forth the effort, and now he had a willing audience.

Vito Ling and Dr. Shishido listened with complete attention. Ray stared into space, but Adam felt that he was absorbing every word. The eyes of the two women stayed on Adam's face. The noise and visual confusion of the Pioneer Hotel faded into a vague background.

When Adam paused, Vito let out a sighing breath, and shook his head. "I wish I'd been here then!"

"It's still the same planet, outside the Stem," said Adam. "That's what I like about Golden. We haven't been able to ruin it. And it's still the same Field that we saw then."

The physicists began a three-way argument among themselves, each for slightly different reasons damning the theories and activities of the Research Foundation. Meanwhile, dancing was in again this year, and Adam danced with Mrs. Shishido, though he didn't feel much like it.

Then he led Merit out onto the crowded floor. The music was part of an uproar, that was about all you could say for it. Bodies jostled them this way and that.

"How's the geryon research going?" he asked.

"Slowly. I don't know if I can even call it research yet. I've been to your local zoo and library."

"They do a pretty good job, I think. I helped the zoo people collect some of their specimens, last year." Merit dancing beside him was silent, as if her thoughts were wandering. He asked: "What brought you to the Pioneer Hotel?"

"The Shishidos' idea. I really don't mind a place like this—about once a year." She didn't ask Adam what had brought him here tonight; probably she knew. Instead she asked him: "How do you like my husband?"

"I guess I like him."

"I love him, Adam. And he's a good man." Something was definitely worrying her. "And what more important things than those is it possible to say about anyone? About you, or Ray, or anyone else?"

Adam said nothing, important or otherwise. He held Merit gently and chastely in his arms, at the proper times during the dance, or tried to do so, while they were bounced around like fools on the stampeded dance floor. This was what he was going to get from her. This much and no more.

When there was a pause in the dancing, and the two of them got back to the table, Adam looked carefully at Vito for signs of another jealous fit. But Vito only smiled vacantly at both of them and went on with the scientific discussion of the Field.

Adam sat and listened to the scientific argument, meanwhile sipping on another drink. Now the alcohol in his bloodstream was easing him past the level of slight exhilaration, to the point where there seemed to be a certain amount of electronic noise in his brain, and concentration was needed to drive clear signals through.

Ray and Merit. Always his friends, right from the start. More than his friends. And yet at the same time always above him, above the rest of humanity too. Merit and Ray, their ninety-eight . . . siblings, Ray called them sometimes. Kin? Clan members? In Adam's opinion there still wasn't a good word. Maybe that was by design, to make the Jovians appear to outsiders as less of a cohesive group.

Not pretending to be superior. Not pretending anything. Not claiming a birthright above common humanity for the purpose of boosting their own egos, or to maintain themselves somehow in power. Adam might deride, or fear, or feel contempt for people who claimed superiority for such purposes, but he would never envy them.

And the truth was that he did envy the Jovians. They *were* superior, standing together above the world. Suddenly he wondered if there were any little second-generation Jovians as yet. It would be very strange, he thought, if there were not.

Some words caught his ear. The subject of table conversation had shifted, and he broke into the talk of Golden's possible future. "Hold on, this planet may be pretty well populated already."

"Primitive," said Vito. "Oh, I don't mean that we should talk all over 'em. But there must be enormous uninhabited areas out there, hey? Practically whole continents."

Adam said: "I really wouldn't think so. Of course it's hard to tell, from pictures taken from above six or seven hundred kilometers. The Field seems to cause random distortion of detail."

Ray chuckled softly. "I wonder how random it really is."

Chapter Thirteen

Adam got to his feet; he felt a little drunk, maybe more than just a little, and the sensation was unpleasant as well as unfamiliar. "Well, glad to have seen all you people. I feel the urge to move on." Merit looked up at him with an unreadable expression. The other people round the table made their several protests and offered their farewells, and he started away from them. From near the elevators he looked back, across the room's activity. Ray was standing now, resting one giant muscular hand gently on Merit's head, while she sat with her eyes closed and face relaxed, looking as if she might be sound asleep. The others round the table watched the two Jovians, not understanding any more than Adam did. And we never will, thought Adam.

Abruptly Ray left the table and walked toward the stage, which was empty now of dancers and musicians. Adam turned his back and found his way to the wall near the elevators, where in an alcove stood a discreet machine, dispenser of sobering pills. He gulped down a pill, and looked around again. Now Vito and Merit, who was lively again, seemed to be getting ready to leave, and Ray was seated at a piano beside the stage. Adam recalled suddenly that there had almost always been beautiful music, live or recorded, to be heard at any time somewhere in Doc Nowell's enormous house. And it would be like a Jovian, Adam thought, to play fine music now, in a place like this, amid such noise that no one else would be able to hear it.

It struck Adam that the drunken uproar was noticeably diminished. In the vicinity of the stage, a circle of heads were now turning toward the piano. The ring of quiet polarization widened. Now, even where he stood at the wall, Adam could hear some of the piano notes. And now he could hear more.

Ray's music flowed out to where the night sky of Golden was curved around the bubble windows. *I've never heard this*, Adam thought. *What can you call this kind of music? What is it?* He moved forward into the room again, until he stood gripping the back of someone's chair.

He can do this, too, Adam thought. *They can do this.*

Now the vast room, or most of it, was almost quiet, expect for the music that Ray Kedro played. Somewhere at the far side of the room, among the distant trees and rocks, one person sobbed, loudly and drunkenly. Then a door opened in the wall near Adam, and a fat man in evening dress came hurrying out, as if the silence had alarmed him. Then the fat man too stood quietly listening.

Experience this, said the music. *Feel this—you can almost touch it now. This is what life is about.*

No. Adam turned away, heading again toward the elevators. How would you know, Ray, what human life is like?

Adam's mind felt blurred. The alcohol and the sobering pill were fighting it out in his bloodstream.

The elevator door closed on him, shutting him in, cutting off the golden sounds. He was alone in the car going down. I usually am alone, he thought. You stupid drunk, he told himself, why don't you go off somewhere and cry?

There were only a few people in the hotel lobby when he reached it. Adam looked at his timepiece. It was two in the morning. He hadn't realized that it was so late.

He stepped out of the lobby onto the black and dully gleaming slideway. His head was full of vague thoughts, none of which really demanded his attention. The slideway shot him back toward Stem City, carrying him past observation platforms and alcoves. In one of these large recesses eight or ten young people were dancing to some music of their own. They had set up a screen on which the image of some retchsinger was contorting itself in three dimensions and unnatural color. No, at second glance it appeared that the screen was attached to a built-in, coin operated video that they were playing. Something new here every day.

The rest of the observation niches were empty as Adam glided past them. There were only a few people on the slideway, most of them riding in what looked like a grim hurry on the faster center strips.

Far ahead of Adam, going in the same direction as he was but on the slowest outer strip, a man and a woman moved along arm in arm. At a distance they looked like Merit and Vito; they were certainly dressed the same. But how could Merit and Vito possibly have got ahead of him?

Just as the couple were passing one of the observation alcoves, four figures erupted from concealment inside it. Like a pack of wild teeners, swinging fists and weapons, the four charged the couple from behind. The man and woman were both knocked down. Already they were being dragged off the slideway and back into the alcove.

The cold combat computer had flicked on automatically, and Adam was already hurtling forward, running in a curved path over slower and slower strips toward the alcove. He pounded off the slowest strip just in time to see the top of one pigtailed head vanish down through a utility trapdoor at the rear of the bubble-walled enclosure. The attackers were gone.

Vito Ling lay on the deck of the observation platform, twitching, wide-eyed, dead. His face and head were covered with his blood.

A few meters away . . . Merit . . .

Adam turned her over, to lie face up. She was unconscious, but she was alive, with no injury that his frantic examination could discover. A pulse throbbed in her wrist as Adam's shaky fingers held it.

He looked away for a moment, toward the closed trapdoor. Would he have a chance of catching anyone? But no, he had better stay with Merit. He looked back at her.

Adam screamed, as his legs thrust him erect, away from the figure on the deck. His hands came slapping up to hide the world from his eyes.

Instead of Merit, he had seen Alice on the deck, pregnant and butchered and dead.

Behind his closed eyes, his mind scrambled for truth, some kind of truth that he could cling to. Fearfully he uncovered his eyes, looking toward the place where Vito—

Had been. Vito's body was now gone. There were no bloodstains there on the deck now. Nothing.

Numbly Adam looked around. No Merit on the floor. No Alice either, of course not Alice. And no Vito Ling. No pigtailed attackers. Adam Mann was alone in the alcove, breathing hard and trembling.

A couple of people shot by on the fast strip of the slideway, paying him no attention.

Hallucination. Forcing himself to think, to act, Adam walked to the rear of the alcove and examined the trapdoor closely. It was locked shut, and a thin film of unmarked dust lay around it and over it, along with a little windblown litter. It looked as if no one had used the door for days at least.

Hallucination. He stumbled out onto the slideway and resumed his journey. He was shaken, hardly aware of what was going on around him. To think that he sometimes envied others their parapsych powers . . .

But what could have brought on this experience? He had never had anything like it in his life before. Probably his feelings for Merit—relating her to Alice—but of course it *might* have been genuine precognition, which would mean that some time in the future, Merit and Vito would travel this way, and would be attacked.

Shock hit Adam again. Merit had said something like: "I don't mind a place like this—about once a year." It wasn't likely that she and Vito would be on Golden that long. It wasn't likely, Adam thought, that they would return to the Pioneer Hotel before they left. Tonight it was going to be, of course, tonight.

In a slow unthinking way Adam had moved again out to the rapid strip; now he spun around and raced back for the immobile utility walk along the outer edge of the slideway. He had to get back to that alcove—or might the attack be going to take place at a different one?

Looking down the long slideway toward the Pioneer Hotel, he could now see Merit and Vito in the distance, approaching arm in arm, gliding toward him along the slow outer strip.

Adam reached the utility walk and sprinted back toward them. Now his view of them was blocked by vending machines on the walk ahead of him. How far was it to that alcove? God, it mustn't be far, the attack and killing took only a few seconds.

A lone man went by on the slideway, turning his head to watch Adam run, then turning away with determination, minding his own business.

Adam ran.

There was a scuffle and a faint outcry from close ahead. Adam rounded a vending machine and came dashing into the alcove. A figure at the rear was just putting coins into the video machine to turn it on, bringing the retchsinger figure gigantically alive upon the holostage above.

Vito Ling was not dead on the floor, he was still more or less on his feet, but he was being held in that position. One of his arms was being twisted behind his back by a tall powerful young man in teener garb, while another one stood before him with a brassknuckled fist drawn back, holding Vito's bleeding head up by the hair while turning his

own head to look at Adam. The fourth attacker,
who appeared to be more or less directing matters,
was a short, lightly built man with a face lined
well beyond the teenpack age. He looked around
with surprise at the sound of Adam's entrance,
then put a smile on his face and stepped toward
Adam.

And there, behind the short man, Merit was lying
on her face, just as in the vision.

The short man stepped forward. He was a cocky
little character with dangerous eyes. But now he
was going to do his imitation of polite reason-
ableness.

"Friend, we really don't need no help here," said
the short man to Adam in a pleasant voice. The
other three had paused, waiting and watching to
see if there was going to be a real distraction.

Vito looked like he might be going to die.

Adam did not move or speak.

The short man said to Adam: "I mean the lady
had a touch too much to drink, you know, and it's
just a friendly little argument."

Adam leaned forward a little. At the end of his
run he had automatically come to rest with his
feet just the right distance apart for balance and
quick movement. He could feel the strength ready
in his arms, that were hanging loosely in front of
him, and he could feel his chest heaving with the
exertion of the run and with the build-up of
adrenalin.

Alice. And now Merit. Twice in one lifetime. But
now he had them in front of him. He watched the
short man's eyes, and smiled at him.

"I mean," asked the short man, in a new tone,
one meant to frighten, "why be a dead hero?"

When nothing happened, he stepped forward, making his voice friendly again. "Let me explain—"

Adam observed the short man's subtle shift of weight in stride, which meant that the right knee was going to come up for Adam's groin. The combat computer guided Adam's sidestep, and launched his right fist in what would have been a clumsy sucker punch if it had not come with almost invisible speed from a standing start. The blow took the short man on the neck under his left ear, and lifted him onto his toes. He fell, rolled over, and lay face down on the deck without moving.

The retchsinger image tore off its shirt, and jittered in its plastic cage. Its mouth opened and noise came out.

"Get him!" ordered the man who had been feeding the retchsinger coins, the lean figure standing close under the noise and light of the machine.

The two who were holding Vito let him drop and came at Adam, spreading out to get him between them. Their faces also were too old for teeners. Adam defended cautiously when they closed in on him, and in the first blurred second of savage motion and impact he knew they were a professional team. It was all he could do to keep himself alive and spin out from between them.

The lean figure in the rear came forward, cursing impartially at them all. "*Get* him, I said."

Adam had two seconds to look at Merit again. Still she had not moved.

The two big men regarded Adam with awe, and paused before coming at him again. One of them was flexing his wrist, where the edge of Adam's hand had caught it. The man was getting his fingers to work again, but his length of metal pipe had bounced away and was riding the slideway to Stem City.

"Come on!" urged the lean one. "Quick!"

Adam started a move at the biggest man, a subtle feint intended to fool a good fighter. The man jumped back a step as Adam spun round. He caught the lean man moving in, with a side snap kick that hit him in the knee like a swung hammer. One more down.

The giant with the brass knuckles was almost quick enough; Adam felt a scrape across his forehead as he dodged the swing. Then he was stepping in, hitting with backfist, knuckles, elbow. He thought that he had never hit anyone or anything so hard before.

And now the big character who had lost his pipe weapon was the only one besides Adam still on his feet. Still flexing his sore wrist, the big man backed away, no longer a workman going at a job, but a man with the fear in him. Now he was shaking his head a little. This one knew, this one appreciated what was going to happen to him.

The man took a last look into Adam's face, and turned and ran for the slideway. Just at the edge of the alcove Adam caught him from behind. The two went down, with Adam on top; the man beneath him strained and squealed and then his neck was broken.

Adam turned round in a crouch. The lean opponent had overcome the pain of his knee enough to pull out a gun; and Vito, battered almost to death, had got up to throw himself at the enemy and save Adam from a bullet.

Vito had luckily managed to bang the lean man's sore knee, and now the two wounded were struggling feebly against their injuries and against each other. Or, they had been struggling, for by now Adam had crossed the intervening space and kicked the lean man in the head. The head on its lean neck bounced through one vibration like a punching bag on its mount, and then was still.

Bloody and gasping, Vito just stayed sitting on the deck, staring ahead of him. Adam, gasping if not bloody, stood beside Vito looking warily around in all directions, ready to meet the next threat when it came. People were still going by on the slideway, passing the alcove scene and looking in at it, then turning away with a desperate blankness in their faces, eager to not-involve themselves. Adam eyed the passing people cautiously. But it seemed that none of them were going to turn aside into the alcove and try to hurt Merit any more.

In a few moments he had regained a certain relative sanity, and went to look after her. She was just stunned, he thought, just as in the vision. She was undoubtedly breathing, and now she was even turning her head a little from side to side, and her blood was still pulsing safe inside its warm tender vessels. Adam touched her face with one of his terrible hands. A living face. Yes, Merit had to be alive, because the universe still had to be a place in which a man could live.

The jukebox was still playing. Probably less than two minutes had passed since the start of the fight. But suddenly the voice of the retchsinger was silent. Adam looked up to see the image swallowing, drinking from its bottles of colored liquids, meanwhile twisting its body in time to the throbbing music, its sculptured belly muscles writhing.

Then the image raised its arms and the music crashed toward a climax. The imaged body snapped forward, and with a heaving groan projectile-vomited a streaming rainbow of bright color that splattered and filmed the inside of the plastic cage.

Vito Ling lay looking up from his hospital bed. A hundred thin insulated wires led to the helmet in which his head was cradled, but he was aware of his visitors and perhaps he was trying to smile at them. It was hard to be sure.

Adam kept watching Merit as she sat beside the bed holding Vito's hand. Her eyes seldom left her husband's face, and when she spoke to her husband her voice was sometimes not loud enough for Adam to hear it clearly. Vito was unable to speak to answer her, but his eyes kept coming back to her face and he appeared to be listening to what she said.

After a while, Adam got up and left the room.

Ray, his face looking tired, was waiting out in the corridor, where small bubble windows glowed with a wintry dawn.

"Looks like he's going to make it," Adam told him.

Ray nodded. "I've just been talking to the doctor in charge." Then he made a gesture of futility. "You saw it coming, fortunately, but I saw nothing. Nothing. Parapsych talent, the undependable. How can we build on it? And yet we must."

The two of them stood talking there in the corridor for a little while, not really saying much, until Merit, smiling tiredly, came out of Vito's room. She took an arm of each of them. "He seems to be doing as well as we could hope. He's going to make it, I'm sure now. Let's all get some rest."

Two plainclothes detectives met them just as they were passing the waiting room. "Mr. Mann, we'd like another few minutes with you, if you please."

Adam shrugged wearily. The small bandage pulled at the slight cut on his forehead.

"We'll wait downstairs," said Ray exchanging looks with him. He moved away, with Merit leaning on his arm.

The detectives watched them go, then faced Adam. One said: "We checked up on your Space Force background. I guess it is possible that you laid out those four hoods all by yourself."

"I'm glad to hear it. I was worried. Mind if I sit down?" He stepped into the waiting room and took a chair. Physically he felt weary. And he felt a little giddy, lightheaded, almost cheerful. Merit was all right. Merit was all right. Nothing else mattered very much.

The other detective asked Adam: "What do you think those four men wanted?"

"Looked to me like they wanted to kill Vito Ling. But you'd better ask them."

There was a brief pause while the two detectives exchanged glances. "Three of them are dead," one finally informed Adam. "It's not certain that the fourth one is ever going to think straight again. You hammered him pretty good. They say an artery in his brain gave way."

He knew their eyes were probing him to see what he thought of the carnage he had wrought, but he had been looking down at his hands when he heard the words and he just kept looking at them. The fight seemed unreal to Adam now. At last he looked up. "Can't say I'm especially sorry. I guess there are a lot of members of the human race I just don't give a damn about any more."

The two detectives had sat down facing him

across the little waiting room, that was otherwise empty. One of them sighed. "Well, can't say I'm sorry either. They were all professional strong-arm boys. Two just arrived on Golden last month, two have been here for a year. They worked a lot for gamblers."

"We're growing into a big city," Adam said.

"Does Dr. Ling like to gamble a lot, do you know?"

"I couldn't say. I just met him a couple of days ago. But he's only been on Golden a couple of days. I doubt he's had time yet to run up any giant debts and refuse to pay them."

"Yeah." The detective sighed again; it made him sound as if he were surprised and saddened by the kind of things he kept running into in his job. "Know any other reason why anyone would want to kill him?"

Maybe me, thought Adam. *I want his wife.* Or maybe there was something else. His imagination showed him the president of the Research Foundation on Earth, tired beyond endurance of Vito's complaints, calling in the hired killers. He smiled (for Merit was safe, and he could smile) and said: "I have no idea, no."

And something was still worrying Merit, something besides the mere fact of her husband's being nearly killed. Well, he, Adam, intended to find out what it was.

"We understand Mrs. Ling is a Jovian, is that correct? One of those . . ."

"Yes. She's one of those."

"She's a telepath, then, isn't she? But she didn't foresee the attack?"

Adam felt annoyed. "They don't go around reading people's minds right and left. And once the action started she must have been stunned before she knew there was anyone approaching. Any danger."

"Stunned expertly," said a detctive. "Very expertly. The doctors say there's no sign of any damage now."

"Yes?" Well, there were ways in which that could be done. "Meaning what?"

"What do you think that fact means?"

"Someone wanted her husband dead, but not her. Is that all? I'm tired."

Again the police looked at each other. "That's all for now, Mr. Mann," one said. "You're not being charged with anything, of course. In my personal opinion it'll smell a little sweeter here with those four gone."

"There'll be four more—or eight," said Adam, moving wearily away. "Lots of opportunity on Golden."

Chapter Fourteen

"It's this damned Jovian business," said General Lorsch. She was sitting behind her desk and looking at Boris Brazil through tired eyes. "Probably that fight episode on the slideway, with the Jovian woman involved, is somehow tied in with all the rest of it." With one hand she pushed a carven wooden box across her desktop to the Colonel. To Brazil it looked like Grodsky's old desk, but the Colonel wasn't going to try perching on a corner of it today.

He silently accepted the invitation to smoke, and took a little time to get his chosen cigar fired up. Time in which he could also do some thinking.

He was glad to be back on Golden again after a seven year absence, even glad in a way that the Field was still unconquered. But not everyone was so happy, evidently, or he wouldn't have been called back. He hadn't met General Lorsch before today, but he doubted that she normally appeared as worn and harried as she did right now.

"Excuse me, General," Brazil asked, "but is the problem really just these hundred Jovians?"

"Yes, it's basically just the Jovians, even if there still are only a hundred of them." The General, toying with a small cigar of her own but not lighting it, managed a smile. "From your viewpoint, Colonel, maybe I sound like a trifle like a monomaniac—but you don't really know anything about these people, do you?"

"The Jovians? No ma'am."

"I didn't either, until very recently. Now I've been through one interview with Ray Kedro—he's evidently their leader, to the extent that they have a leader—but I can't communicate what happened during that interview as evidence. There are the intelligence reports."

She could, thought Boris, at least have talked to him about that interview, since it sounded so important. Maybe later he would push to hear about it.

As for the intelligence reports, Boris had already read through some of the printouts that were now scattered about on the General's desk. Now the Colonel glanced down again, skimming quickly over certain paragraphs:

"—Jovian organization has penetrated every branch of Earth society, probably including the Space Force. Their economic power like their political influence, is indirect but enormous—"

"—can they be considered subversive? If they would lead or coerce humanity, they have given no real evidence of what direction they would choose."

Subversive. Boris frowned at the word. He knew that there were people, in the Space Force as elsewhere, who could see subversive plotters behind every rock. There were also a few very real people, real terrorists, who for one reason or another plotted violence and destruction of the government. Usually, as far as Boris could see, it was not really because of anything in particular that the government had done, but just because the government was there, and terrorists in love with violence and destruction had to have some target, and big important targets were more fun.

And some of the terrorists might, for all that Boris knew, be Jovians.

The most urgent-looking message on the table read:

—EVIDENCE INDICATES JOVIAN CONSTRUCTION ILLEGAL STARSHIP ON GANYMEDE. GANYMEDE INSTALLATION NOW DESERTED JOVIANS UNFINDABLE IN SOL SYSTEM. PROBABLE SPECS OF SHIP CONSTRUCTED HERE FOLLOW:

The ship appeared to be a big one, and if the specifications given in the report were accurate, it mounted certain generators and other equipment generally reserved for exclusive use in weapon systems. It looked like the Jovians had built for combat.

"Neat trick, putting together a starship in secret," Boris commented. "One like this, especially."

"They're pretty clever people," said the General drily. "The authorities on Sol System didn't realize that the Jovians were up to anything on Ganymede until all the Jovians known to be in the system began to head that way. By the time we really took notice that something was up, they were in their starship and gone."

The situation was a complete dustcloud to Boris. He leaned back in his chair, puffed gently on his cigar, and said: "So, they're all out joyriding in their outlaw bird. I take it you expect them to come here, to Golden, ma'am, since you pulled me off another job and had me brought here and are telling me all this."

"I do expect them to show up at Golden, yes."

"I see, ma'am. What'll they do when they get here?"

"I wish I knew." Lorsch shook her head, and threw her own tormented cigar away, still unlighted. "I have three ships ..." The General let her words trail off, then added: "I've asked Antares for some reinforcement, just in case. Three more ships. Don't know if I'll get them."

"You're expecting a fight, then?"

"I want to be ready for one."

"And just what am I here for, ma'am?"

"You're here because you know something of the planet and the situation, Colonel. And according to the records, you also know this fellow Adam Mann."

Aha. "Adam Mann. Yes ma'am, I remember him. He worked for me as a planeteer at one point. Right here on Golden."

"So the records state. What did you think of him?"

Brazil pondered. "A good man, basically. Not—well, not an ordinary man, even for planeteering, where we tend to get—an assortment."

"Yes," the General responded drily. The reputation enjoyed, or endured, by the planeteering profession was nothing new to her. But she was thinking now of something else, of Adam Mann specifically. "I don't know if he's working for the Jovians now, or just friendly with some of them, or what. In any case he probably knows them at least as well as any non-Jovian alive. I'd like to talk to him, find out if he's disposed to be helpful to us, and, if he is, consult with him. If he isn't—I'd like to know that too. And he's not always an easy man to talk to, or so I've been told."

"So you'd like me to try. All right. I'll talk to him." Boris got up out of his chair and took a quick nervous walk, the length of the office and back. Standing in front of the desk, he said: "It's the Field, of course, that's the special thing about Golden. If the Jovians, or anyone else, could control the Field, obviously they could control the whole planet. And any other planets where a Field could be established."

"Yes, I've thought about that, Colonel. That's an obvious answer. But I'm not sure the truth is that direct and simple. I tell you, every time I think I've figured out what they're up to, something—"

The intercom chimed, with muted elegance. The General answered it. "All right. Have him wait a minute." She raised her eyes. "Colonel, Mann's here now."

Coming into the inner office, not knowing why the General had asked to see him, Adam stopped short at sight of the unexpected face. "Well, I'll be—Boris!"

Pumping his hand, Brazil said: "Look, when I told you to go out and scout, I didn't mean you had to live five years in the woods. You can come in now, there's a settlement here."

The two of them shared a modest laugh, and there was an easing of tension. They had asked each other the usual questions people exchanged during the first stage of a reunion, while the General, smiling benevolently but guardedly, watched from behind her desk. Adam, noting her scrutiny, felt more and more certain that he knew what this meeting was all about.

Brazil had hardly changed, to the eye. He was still planeteering, of course, and Adam suspected he was now in chronic trouble with certain of his superiors, enough trouble at least to have prevented his promotion, while at the same time his reputation for getting results kept getting him what Brazil considered good jobs, interesting assignments. Maybe the Colonel really preferred not to be promoted into dullness.

"There're women chasing me on most of the old planets—the only time I get any rest is on the new ones," said Boris, who would have a lot of new planets behind him now, and a billion and one more ahead of him if he could keep going that long. And Adam was sure that the Colonel would try.

"Where was your last one?" Adam asked, now beginning to feel the old lure again himself.

Boris glanced at the woman who sat patiently observing them from behind her desk. He said: "A good long way from here. I sort of got pulled off the job."

"Oh?"

"To come here. Certain of our leaders"—he wasn't indicating whether General Lorsch was one of them—"think that the human race here has a Jovian problem."

That announcement was, by this time, no real surprise to Adam. He said: "There're only two Jovians on Golden, that I know about. So what—?"

They told Adam about the Jovian starship, built secretly on Ganymede and now departed Sol System for parts unknown. Now Adam was puzzled. He had heard no hint from Ray or Merit of the existence of a Jovian interstellar craft, in Sol System or anywhere else.

"Well, if they built it, they must have had a good reason," Adam said at last. "They wouldn't just break the law . . ." He gestured, trying to find the word he wanted. "Casually. You know, cynically. Not just for their own personal profit."

"They might break it, though," said Boris.

Adam looked at him. "Anyone might, who thought there was enough at stake. I seem to remember that you've bent a rule or two from time to time."

"How long since you've been on Earth, Mann?" General Lorsch asked him.

"I take it you've been looking over my record, General, and you probably know how long. It's been years. Why?"

"People can change, even your Jovians. There's good evidence to indicate that during the past few years they've been behind a number of dirty deals, on Earth and the settled planets. There's more evidence that they're out to weaken the Space Force, reduce our influence. Have a chair, won't you? Want to look at some reports?"

Weaken the Space Force—ah, so that was the capital crime! Adam opened his mouth for an angry answer, but Lorsch looked so tiredly determined that an angry answer seemed certain to bring on an angry argument and that seemed futile, so he forebore. He could argue anytime; right now he wanted to learn more. Silently he accepted the chair the General had indicated.

Boris was waiting, watching him silently.

The General pushed a pile of paperwork on her desk, evidently the reports that she had mentioned, toward Adam slightly. She watched him too.

"I've known Ray Kedro since we were kids,"

Adam finally told them both. "I'd trust him with my life."

Boris asked: "How well have you known him, Ad?"

"Well enough. As well, I suppose, as you can know someone who—you know what they are?"

Boris spread out his hands. "We don't know that, not in the same way you do. Maybe our suspicions are all wrong. Can you explain why?"

"I've never known one of them to do a mean thing." Only at this moment did Adam fully realize that fact himself; and with the realization he could feel his anger growing. "I've known people to beat *them* up, for the crime of being different. That's our way, isn't it, the way of the great human race?"

"Sometimes," said Boris. "But I have to put in a good word for my employers, in spite of all their blunders that I bitch and moan about. As far as I know, the Space Force has never deliberately exploited or injured an alien race."

"We've never before met another race we had to look up to." Adam paused, feeling a little embarrassed by what he was going to say. "Only the Jovians. They're like our children, growing up and getting ahead of us in the world. I think we should be proud of them."

"I see," said General Lorsch, tiredly, after a little while.

Later that day, when Adam entered the hospital room, Vito was sitting up in bed and working at feeding himself, apparently enjoying fair success at the job through the helmet with its hundred wires was still on his head. The tiny probes inside the helmet were keeping his injured brain going, stimulating and guiding a healing process. Some of Vito's cranial bone was still in the hospital's deep freeze, awaiting the right time for replacement.

Merit, sitting at bedside, looked up at Adam's entrance, and reached up a hand to him; he was able to hold her hand while he stood there getting the routine chatter of greeting out of the way. There was a newsprintout open across the patient's knees, and Adam could see one item headed: SEEK MOTIVE IN SLIDEWAY ATTACK. And below: Police Probe Jovian Angle. But as far as Adam knew, no one had really found an angle yet, Jovian or otherwise. In a few days the item would be out of the news, and half-forgotten.

Which would suit Adam fine. He moved a few centimeters closer to Merit and put a hand on her shoulder.

"I'd like to take your lady out on a little sightseeing trip this afternoon," he said to Vito. "Give her a chance to relax."

"You do that," Vito responded instantly. His voice sounded all right, though he obviously still had to be careful about moving his head. "She needs that. Look at her, all worn out, looks worse than me. Bring me back a picture or two, hey Hon? Send me a nice thought, maybe, from out there?"

Merit looked at them both. "I will," she said.

When she had stepped out of the room for a moment, wanting to talk to one of the doctors, Vito said to Adam almost truculently: "She'll be safe with you. Safer than with me. Some good I was for her the other night."

"Hey, you probably saved my life by jumping that last guy, remember? And what could you do, with four of them?"

"You did all right."

"I'm a kind of well-trained freak."

* * *

The most easily reached Tenoka Village was a couple of kilometers inside the Field. Riding the shuttle copter out with Merit on the first leg of the journey, Adam brought up the subject of his own unsuspected parapsych powers.

"There's a mystery for you. Why did I have that precognitive experience? I've never had, seen, done, anything like that in my whole life before."

She had listened to his account of the experience carefully. "I don't know what to tell you, Adam. People throughout human history have occasionally had such experiences. Usually—they don't have any vital effect, either on the person who goes through them, or anyone else."

He sighed. "Everyone says how undependable parapsych powers are. I guess the accepted wisdom is in this case right. You and Ray and the others—it's all fading away for you, right? That's what I've heard."

"We don't do those things as casually as we once did. I'm not sure that the power to do them is fading for all of us. Is that a village, over there, behind those trees?" Now the copter was descending.

From the shuttle landing place Adam and Merit hiked along a trail that he knew well, past the line of marker poles, here placarded with warnings to tourists. Essentially the signs cautioned them that from here on they would be in Field and on their own.

The appearance of the villages near the Stem had changed substantially over the last few years, as had the lives of those who dwelled in them. Now, nearly all of the Tenoka teepees were made from tough Earth fabrics, and nearly every Tenoka fire heated a cook-pot of Earth metal.

The warriors of this particular village greeted Adam warmly, and eyed Merit and her camera with greater toleration than most tourists received, since she was with him.

"There have been signs and omens, Geryon-Slayer," said one of the elders, speaking in his own language. "Even now Pierced Arms lies in trance. We have been expecting you, for he foretold two visitors for today."

"Did you get that?" Adam asked Merit.

She wrinkled her forehead. "Not too well." There was nothing unethical in a telepath's "reading" a message that was available to the ears anyway—and, as Adam understood it, nothing particularly unpleasant to the reader. But thoughts formed in an unknown language were apt to be difficult.

When Adam translated for her, Merit was interested. She asked: "Could we see this medicine man? Do you think it's genuine parapsych or fakery?"

"Probably fakery, if I know old Pierced Arms, and I think I do . . . but then, I thought I knew myself, before I started catching glimpses of the future. Well, we can try."

Adam turned to the elders and addressed them in their own tongue. "How about if we see old Pierced Arms? Would it be possible? Might scare my lady here a bit."

They smiled and took the bait; very little was so sacred to the Tenoka that it could not serve as the basis for a practical joke.

"He speaks messages now," whispered an attendant, as Merit and Adam were ushered into the darkened lodge. This one, consecrated to magic, was made of real skins. Surrounded by a large assortment of magical paraphernalia, with oil lamps burning at his head and feet, Pierced Arms lay tossing on his pallet. The body of the medicine man was daubed with colored clay in intricate patterns, and strings of feathers were laced through the loops in his wrinkled skin. Now his eyes were open, now they were shut. His arms and legs twitched, and he breathed irregularly and jabbered strange words.

"I don't quite get that dialect," Adam whispered.

Merit closed her eyes. "I can get something out of it. Yes. I think—a message from one man to another, here on Golden. They're distant relatives, and they live a long way apart. Congratulations, I think, one is saying to the other ... congratulations on I don't know what. Something will be sent. A present. But both men are surprised at being able to communicate in this way. It doesn't usually—"

Her eyes opened. "And, Adam, wait. There's something else going on, in the background." Merit was excited. Not quite worried; alert.

Then she was silent for a moment, and Adam said: "I think you're right about the messages being passed, somehow." He was fascinated. "I've never seen this before, though I've heard stories."

Merit pressed his hand, urging silence; she was concentrating intensely.

The shaman was beginning a new message now. His voice changed in tone as he did so, and shifted to a language that Adam had never heard before. Neither could Merit really follow it this time. Then quickly there was another shift. More talk followed, more minds were tapped. There were greetings between more people who were surprised to find themselves in mental communication—usually the subjects were not really astonished, though. It was something not unknown to the natives of Golden, this type of communication, but it was something rare. When they found themselves unexpectedly in mental contact, they exchanged greetings, or occasionally threats. Sometimes the exchange consisted of obscure words and ideas that neither Merit nor Adam could understand.

Once, when Pierced Arms paused longer than usual between messages, Adam paused to open the tent flap and look out. He was getting restless. "We'd better start back soon. It's going to be getting dark—"

Merit gripped his hand, suddenly and hard. But it was Pierced Arms whose voice boomed out a second later, louder than before, commanding, uttering perfectly accented words and sentences in the preferred language of Earth's Space Force and most ouf her colonies.

"Raymond Kedro, a message for him," Pierced Arms almost shouted. "My name was Alexander Golden, and I speak to warn the man from Earth called Kedro. He closes his mind against me, but he should hear. If he persists in what he plans for this world, he must fail. People will die, other people will suffer. Kedro himself may die—"

Merit raised fists to her forehead. Her scream was an elemental, primal sound, that had to have been driven out of her by some force greater than the mere shock of the words, of any words. The scream was so loud that it made Pierced Arms awaken, with a start.

Adam held Merit tightly while she recovered. The Tenoka at the door of the lodge were giggling quietly at the joke's excellent though long-delayed success.

"Merit. What was it? Merit—?"

"Adam," she whispered, "Ray was here—his mind— fighting something—"

"Hungry," muttered Pierced Arms, sitting up and scratching his lean old ribs. "Much talking always makes me hungry. Where's my worthless elder wife? Ha, Geryon-Slayer, you bring a woman to hear me speak? No matter, she can help prepare the food. Wife!"

"Merit, brace up," Adam murmured in her ear. "We'll talk later. Right now we'd better be good guests."

And she did brace up, immediately. If an ordinary woman had recovered with such speed from screaming fright, you would think she had been acting.

Chapter Fifteen

The string twanged sharply, and the arrow from Earth went humming away from Ray Kedro's thirty-five kilo bow. After a flight of thirty meters the shaft punched almost exactly into the center of the bright blue bullseye. The target, concentric rings of color on a soft plastic disk, hung from the stump of a branch on a tree at the edge of a clearing. The clearing was no more than about a hundred meters from Adam's cabin.

"I have no doubt about one point," said Ray, as he drew a second arrow from the new, fancifully decorated quiver on his back. "What you heard from the medicine man was genuinely intended as a message for me. I take the message seriously. And I'd prefer that you tell no one else about it."

The two men were completely alone in the woods at the moment, there being probably no other human beings within a kilometer in any direction. Merit was at the hospital, where she was spending most of her time these days. The medical reports were good, and Vito was due soon to be released.

"I won't tell anyone else about it if you say so," Adam said. "But why not?"

"Humor me."

"All right. But the Space Force is going to hear about your message anyway, through the Tenoka."

"I suppose they will. But let's not confirm it." Ray nocked his second arrow on the bowstring and took quick aim. A moment later another shaft sank into the bullseye, close beside the first. At archery, as at everything else, he was superb.

"And the communication was from Alexander Golden," Adam said, meditatively. "Pierced Arms said that name very plainly. And I don't understand it at all."

"I don't believe the message really came from Alexander Golden, but through him," Ray answered calmly. "Or through what's left of him, more likely."

Adam paused in the act of reaching for one of his own arrows. "What?"

Ray was looking at him soberly. "Even before I left Sol System I was vaguely, distantly aware of very strong parapsych activity, here on this planet and around it. Yes, I know, the enormous distance. But the mind, the Jovian mind at least, is not entirely constrained to obey the laws of physics . . . and since I arrived on Golden I've been able to confirm the parapsych activity. There's more of it here than there is on Earth, or anywhere else I've been. It may be that there's something natural about the planet, that induces or promotes it. You never had a precognitive experience before you came here, did you?"

"No . . . but what is all this activity that you detect here? What's the source?"

"Some of it emanates from these native people. The Tenoka here and around the Stem area, and others of their species around the planet. But the preponderate amount of parapsych action on Golden comes from the beings you have called the Field-builders." Ray studied Adam's reaction, and added: "Oh yes, they're still around. Very much so."

It was Adam's turn to shoot, but he still stood with his bow forgotten in his hand, staring at Ray. "If that's so . . . then you're the first person from Earth to ever make contact with them."

Ray smiled faintly. "Except for the unfortunate Alex Golden, of course . . . but they don't want such contact, Adam. They prefer to hide from us, from both Jovian and Earth-descended humanity, and study us at their leisure. And more and more . . ." Ray came to a halt, gazing at Adam in an abstracted and unhappy way.

Adam had a premonition of fear. "What?"

"Just that they hate us, Adam." Ray's voice had fallen almost to a whisper. "I can see the sickness in them. I become gradually more and more aware of what they are capable of doing. I admit it's a touch frightening . . . more than a touch, I must confess. They try to bury the sickness and hatred deep in their minds but there it is. I don't think Merit is able to make contact with them at all, which is perhaps just as well."

"Frightening, yes," Adam muttered. He remembered Merit's scream in the medicine man's lodge. "And the Field-builders are still right here, on this planet? You're really sure of that? I mean if you can contact them at the distance of Earth . . ."

Ray nodded. "They're here, all right."

"But where?"

"That question was not so easy to answer." Ray had another arrow drawn now, as if automatically getting ready to shoot again, but once drawn the shaft rested in his hand ignored. "By the end of my first day on Golden I had determined that they were somewhere in the other hemisphere. And I was also sure that Alexander Golden does not exist any longer. Not as a human being, anyway."

"What?"

"No, he's not human any longer. I can sense what they're like, Adam, the Field-builders, I can tell it by the things they do. To people here and elsewhere. And by what they'd like to do to us. But they'e a little cautious. We're quite strong."

"Ray. Gods of all space, Ray."

"I know, I know. Most likely all that's left of Golden by now is a sort of telepathic frequency converter, a bridge over which messages can be forced from their minds to those of ordinary Earth-descended humans, or to the Tenoka."

Adam was listening in horror.

It was as if Ray were reluctant to speak, to reveal the horrifying things, but was able to see no other choice. "I've seen . . . sensed . . . the Field-builders' dungeons, Adam. The torture chambers, where Alexander Golden still exists—I can't really say that he still lives—along with other prisoners. By now I've determined more precisely where they are, over on the other side of the world from here. Not stone walls with chains hanging from them, no. And not physical torture, or not that parti-cularly. They—the ones you call the Field-builders—have solved somehow the old problem. How does a being, determinedly evil, use parapsych talents to inflict pain? And how can one maim and kill . . . with the mind alone . . ."

Ray's voice had grown grim, and now it almost quivered. His expression had darkened. Adam had never seen or heard him this way before. Now the huge man paused, staring into space. Suddenly Adam saw him as tired and strained, living under a burden that would have been too great for any ordinary human.

"Alex Golden was an Earthman," Ray said suddenly. "As I am." He looked at Adam suddenly. "Those who have done what has been done to him are on this planet. And I intend to call them to account."

"You—?"

Ray smiled at Adam. "General Lorsch thinks that we Jovians consider *her* our enemy."

"If you don't—and if you have some definite knowledge of the Field-builders—why not tell her the truth?"

"I've tried to do so, Adam. She and I once enjoyed a very private chat. More private than the lady realized, because I turned off the spy devices in her office. And then I even used what we call projection to present our case. That method gives me very considerable powers of persuasion." Ray grinned faintly, and Adam had no trouble believing him. "But she's a tough lady, Adam, and a stubborn one—and even if she could be persuaded to come to terms with us, she could not for very long deceive or disobey her superiors, and we would still have to deal with them."

"Look, Ray—even if she doesn't like you, I don't see why you can't tell her what you've found out about the Field-builders. About your contact with them. Did you try to tell her that? And why shouldn't we tell her about this message that purports to be from Golden?"

"No, Adam. I didn't try to tell her that." For the moment Ray sounded less like an old friend, and more like a patient schoolmaster. "Because there is nothing that she or the Space Force can do about Alexander Golden, or about the Field-builders either—at least not while the Field still covers the Ringwall, over on the other side of the planet."

"That's where they are, then." Adam almost whispered it.

"That's where they are ... what we must do with General Lorsch is get her to prepare for a fight—let her think, if necessary, that we are the ones who must be fought. Then we shall convincingly uncover the real enemy."

"Uncover them how?" Adam paused. "You mean you can control the Field?" If it were anyone else talking to him ... but it was not anyone else. He found himself ready to believe anything of Ray.

"Not yet," said Ray calmly. I don't expect to be able to control it from this side of the planet."

"From the other side, then ... the Ringwall again?"

"That's right."

"But how are you going to get there?"

It was as if Ray had been waiting for that question, as if everything he had said up to now had been calculated to lead up to it.

"Watch," the huge man said.

A moment later, Ray's heavy bow dropped to the muddy ground; the hand that had held it was gone, had winked out of sight along with the rest of Ray. Ray Kedro had vanished completely, as if he had never been.

Teleportation. It had to be that. One parapsych effect that Adam had never seen before, that no one he had heard of had ever seen. He had heard or read somewhere that not even the Jovians were capable of it. Some authorities went so far as to say that there was not a single properly authenticated case of teleportation in all of human history ...

But what else could it be? Now teleportation ... Adam looked to his left and right, and behind him, and he was still utterly alone.

He turned around. He called out, tentatively: "Ray?"

"I was slightly off target," said Ray's voice from behind him. Adam spun round again. The big man was standing near the far edge of the clearing, grinning wryly at his own condition. Ray's feet and legs were plastered with wet mud, up to above his knees.

Ray picked up a piece of dead bark and with a faint grimace began to scrape away some of the goo; there were still some human situations, it appeared, that no amount of intelligence, parapsych talent, or superb co-ordination were capable of dealing with gracefully.

Pointing with the defiled bark, Ray explained: "I was aiming for the top of that little hill over there; I was sort of curious about what was on the other side, which may be why I came down beyond it, in a mudhole." He raised his eyes to Adam's. "But the point is that the parapsych talent is not adversely affected by the Field."

Adam sat down on a handy log. After all that he had learned in the past few minutes, he felt he needed to sit down. "I thought the story was that all the Jovian parapsych talents were disappearing. That they've been fading steadily since you all passed adolescence."

"You're absolutely right, Ad. That's the story."

Ray's grin was, as of old, infectious. "You don't still believe all the stories you hear, do you?"

"You mean . . ." Adam let it trail off.

All he could think of for the moment was that Merit hadn't seen fit to enlighten him about the powerful talents that she, too, must still have at her disposal. But all he said was: "You're lucky you didn't land on one of those jagged stumps over there where I did my logging, for the cabin. Or come down right on top of a poison lizard in the swamp."

Ray shook his head. "That would be physical harm caused directly by the use of parapsych talent, within the meaning of the law—and that, leaving out minor bruises and such, is still a practical impossibility. Remember?"

"Still an impossibility for you. Not for the Field-builders. You were just telling me how they . . ."

"Yes . . . well, they may no longer enjoy a total monopoly on the ability to use parapsych as a weapon. We must develop, are developing, means of self defense. I can put it more precisely: violent harm from parapsych causes doesn't happen to us, to Jovians, by accident . . . teleportation is probably the safest form of transportation yet invented."

"If you say so . . . Ray, what's your plan? You said you were going to call the Field-builders to account."

"I am indeed," said Ray with calm confidence. He had now finished scraping most of the mud away, and he threw down the piece of bark and came to sit on the log beside Adam. "Our siblings have finished constructing a starship, at the old base on Ganymede where Doc—"

Adam held up a hand. "The Space Force knows about your ship. I was wondering if I should men-tion it to you, but then I assumed you already knew they did."

"Your assumption was quite correct. And General Lorsch I suppose is worried lest we be bringing our ship here, and planning to upset things for her somehow? Well, we are. Our ninety-eight siblings are bringing our ship along to Golden now. It'll be here when we need it."

Adam got to his feet. He walked a little distance and turned back. "Ray? I don't like this. I mean this between you and the Space Force. I know them, and I know Jovians, I suppose better than anyone else does."

"I'm sure you do, Adam. And what is it you don't like, precisely?"

"They don't understand you, Ray. And I'm not sure you understand them. As soon as that ship of yours arrives in normal space near Golden they're going to arrest whoever's operating it—or try to arrest them. They consider that kind of a ship illegal, and they take things like that seriously."

Ray threw back his head, and his laughter roared out, sudden and surprising. The log rocked under him. "No, Adam, we're not going to fight a battle against the Space Force—although we could. Sorry if I let you think that, even for a minute. We'll park our ship about six hundred kilometers above the Ringwall, and there they'll surround us with a large force—I hope—trying to arrest us as you say.

"We can keep them at arm's length, until events on the surface below have made it possible for them to join us in our endeavors, and convinced them that they should do so. Does that help to set your mind at ease?"

"No, Ray. No, not really. Events on the surface? What events? I don't understand. Look, I'm just a slow human. Take it easy and explain it all to me slowly."

"Adam, we're just going to have to show the Field-builders to the Space Force. It's a case where mere explaining and arguing won't do the job."

"Show them how?"

"Bring them out into the open, out of their dungeons into the light of day. Display them as they really are. I and a few others are going to teleport to the Ringwall from here—from in the Stem or somewhere near it. We ought to be able to reach the Ringwall in, I suppose, five or six jumps. We'll do that while our ship and the Space Force ships are above it. The enemy can be found there, at the Ringwall. And they have the key to the Field there with them, Adam. I've felt it. I've seen it in their minds. Once we arrive there, we'll be able to take that key into our possession. We'll turn the place upside down and inside out if need be."

It was all coming at Adam too fast, much too fast. "You, and a few others, are just going to walk in on the Field-Builders and do all this to them? How many of them are there?"

Ray strode over to where he had dropped his bow. He picked the weapon up and stood there gripping it. "I'm not sure, but we can do it. Numbers won't count for that much, not in our part of the struggle. A little later we will need the ships and weapons of the Space Force—that's why I'm taking steps to make sure they'll be on hand. There'll be plenty for our brothers and sisters of the normal Earth-descended strain to do; but basically, primarily, this is Jovian business. We are not going to submit to being laboratory animals for the Field-builders; we don't intend to sit here like rats in a cage, tapping our noses against the Field.''

Ray was obviously bitter, and deeply angry. Again, Adam thought that he had never seen Ray quite like this before.

Adam himself felt small and inadequate, as he rarely had since he had been a toddler. He asked Ray: "Why are you telling me all this?"

"Because you are a Jovian," Ray answered.

"Doc never knew about you," Ray was explaining, a little later, when Adam again felt capable of listening to explanations. "I was only two years old, myself, and a long way from being able to assume leadership, when the other children began trying to duplicate Doc's experiments. That Ganymede installation was and is a huge place. There were vast areas within it that Doc hardly ever entered, and we had a good deal of freedom. And we had abilities that Doc never imagined, at least until much later. He didn't miss a little genetic material from his stock.

"When you were decanted, Adam, one of the laboratory workers was bribed into seeing to it that you were transported to Earth safely. At that point, something about my colleagues' plan went wrong—they couldn't oversee the details from the distance of Ganymede, and you wound up in a public Home instead of a real one as they had intended. My elder siblings tell me they were sorry about that, and I believe them; but as events turned out, we all had to follow you into similar places, at least temporarily, as you know. By the time I was fourteen, I had learned about the experiment that produced you, and I was anxious to get a look at the result. I managed to get myself assigned to the Home that you were in, when it became necessary to go into one—the rest, as they say in stories, you know."

". . . but I never guessed . . ."

Ray grinned at him. "Oh, and one more thing, Ad—Merit has never known. She'll be as surprised as you are."

It was all too much. Adam sat down on the log again, making a helpless gesture.

"I haven't told you any of this before," Ray went on, "because there have been times, many times in fact, when it seemed a distinct disadvantage to anyone to be known as a Jovian. Also, I admit, my older siblings expressed some curiosity about how you would develop, living in an environment substantially different from ours. Whether you've gained or lost by now knowing your heritage—who can say?"

Adam continued just to sit there. He felt numbed, stunned, like part of the log himself. He looked at Ray for a while, then stared into space, then looked back at Ray again. He couldn't doubt any of this, basically, that Ray was telling him.

He, Adam Mann, was a Jovian. He wondered if the curious kids who had created him had given him some other name at first. If so, he didn't think he wanted to know what it was.

No wonder that all his life he had known a sense of being different from the people he lived among, a chronic sense of outrage at the surrounding human idiocy.

"I am telling you this now," said Ray, "because very soon I am going to need the willing help of every Jovian mind and body. And you have it all, Adam. Whatever talents we have are yours, at least in potential." Ray was calmly ready to resume his archery practice, and now the big man's bowstring thrummed again.

Adam raised his eyes just in time to see the arrow hit home. A perfect shot, as always. And now, for himself too, for Adam Mann . . .

Gradually the realization was growing in him. A foretaste of the new world that he was about to enter. A Jovian world, in which he might climb to heights that were now beyond even his imagination.

"This is what I call the right way to convalesce," said Vito Ling, pulling two rabbit-like hoppers out of his game bag, and dropping them on a rock beside the cooking fire. The biochemistry of Golden's native life ran so closely parallel with that of Earth that an inhabitant of either world could generally provide safe nourishment for an inhabitant of the other.

"Convalesce!" Ray laughed. "I think you've just been loafing for the past week. Like me."

"And I'm glad," said Merit, on her knees beside the fire and feeding it with kindling. "I'm not eager for you two to vanish back into Fieldedge, and find a way to spoil this planet. I've decided I like Golden just the way it is."

"We'll convert our scientists to Field-lovers yet," Adam said. Several days had passed since he heard Ray's revelations. Ray had said he hadn't yet told Merit much about the coming struggle, though she was certainly aware of his preceptions of the Field-builders' minds. And Vito had as yet been told nothing.

Merit had been informed, by Ray, of the truth of Adam's Jovian origin. And, as far as Adam could tell, she had been as astonished by the news as he was himself.

Immediately afterward she had come to Adam with a strange look in her face: "Ray just told me . . ."

"About me?"

"Yes."

And those were the only words the two of them had yet exchanged on the subject. There had been little chance for them to be alone, with Vito now out of the hospital. But ever since that moment Merit had looked at Adam in a different way. Exactly what the difference was he could not analyze.

At the moment, Adam was sitting with his back against a tree, feeling comfortably tired and at peace in a way that he had never really known before. Since the day of Ray's revelations, Adam had been spending the mornings trying to develop his latent parapsych talents, under Ray's tutelage, and the afternoons in teaching Ray, Merit, and Vito his own hard-won skills of the primitive life. Ray had warned Adam that probably he would never be able to teleport unaided, but he had already learned to achieve some intermittent telepathic contacts.

And now, relaxed, Adam felt a sudden quick touch against his mind. It came like a glimpse of monstrous black wings overhead, foreshadowing some danger.

If Merit perceived the dark passage, she gave no sign; she and Vito were now horseplaying like happy newlyweds beside the fire. But Ray stood up, and with a beckoning motion of his head got Adam to walk away from the fire with him.

Once out of sight of the clearing where the four of them had camped, on a supposed vacation, Ray stopped, looking Adam in the eye. "By this time tomorrow, we must be ready to move."

"As soon as that."

"As soon as that." Ray was brisk and business-like. "Are you with me?"

Adam shook his head. "I'm keeping up so far." His tone was almost plaintive.

Ray grinned and clapped him on the shoulder. *Like the old days, playing some game at Doc's.* The message came through plainly, without spoken words. "Good enough. Right now, jump with me into Stem City, okay? Let me guide."

Adam nodded and turned his back on Ray, who was standing just out of physical reach. They had taught him teleportation theory; they had held him back, so far, from the brink of actual movement. This would be the first time—if it worked—

Adam let the wall of trees before him slide out of focus in his eyes. His vision, his attention, came to be centered somewhere else—

—he felt the premonitory aura, stronger than it had ever been in practice—

—and then before his eyes there was a different wall, the interior surface of some building. They had arrived.

"A hotel room I use," said Ray. It was a cheap hotel, Adam decided; the small room was piled with loaded camping packs, canteens, axes, knives, arrows, enough to set up a small wilderness outfitting company. "Help me decide what to take to the Ringwall, Ad. We might be several days there, though I doubt it's going to take that long ... something wrong?"

Adam drew a deep breath. "Just that your confidence strikes me as a touch overwhelming—you know, if it was anyone else suggesting this kind of an expedition to me, what I would tell them?"

"It's not anyone else."

"Right . . . so who's going on this expedition? The two of us, and . . . ?"

"And Merit. I want every Jovian to be there, in the action. All one hundred and one." Ray winked lightly. "There'll be ninety-eight of our siblings aboard the ship above us. I've had confirmation of the number."

"And what about Vito?"

"What about him? Oh, I think I see what you mean. Well, he can find his way from here back to Stem City, he's essentially recovered now. Or, we can carry him along if he insists, and Merit insists, as they both probably will."

"You think they will?"

"I'm reasonably sure. Don't you think so?"

Adam sighed. "All right. Three of us, or four. And when we get there?"

"Yes? What about when we get there?"

Adam picked up a pack, and tossed it down again. Knowing that he himself was equipped with the genes for Jovian intelligence seemed to make no difference in the difficulty of understanding Ray, when Ray started explaining his plans, or rather started actively not explaining them. Adam said: "I don't know what I'm supposed to *do* when I get there, Ray. That's what about it. I won't know a Field-builder from a fencepost if I bump into one."

But Ray was not perturbed. "You'll know. And you'll know what to do, when the time comes."

PART FOUR

Chapter Sixteen

"If she does go on any such expedition, I'm going too," said Vito Ling, speaking very firmly. There was in Vito's attitude a strong mixture of you're-all-crazy-but-I'm-going-to-humor-you, along with a good measure of grudging respect: some of the three of you at least *might* be smarter than I am, you Jovians have been right before, and you could be right about this too. This was not Vito's very first reaction. Merit had only kept her husband from immediately informing the authorities of the plan to teleport to the Ringwall, by not telling him about it until the party of four were out in the wilderness, with no possibility of quick communication with anyone back in the Stem. Still, when Vito was finally informed, it had required all the persuasive abilities of the other three to keep him from starting a solo hike back to Stem City immediately.

For perhaps the fourth time in the last few minutes, Vito looked at his wife and asked her: "Why are you going, Merit? Maybe these two guys have lost their minds . . . but why you?"

She gave him a strange smile. "Jovians together, against the world."

"If the ninety-nine others all walked off a cliff . . . all right, Adam, the hundred others." One more item had been revealed.

"Ray might be wrong about the Field-builders," Merit admitted suddenly, and looked suddenly at Ray, who gazed back at her calmly and did not appear particularly upset by the suggestion.

Merit went on: "If he is . . . there's only one way to prove it." She looked at her husband again. "And, if he's not . . ."

"That's about the way I see it," Adam said. Not that he really thought Ray might be wrong, but it was a good way of putting the situation to Vito. And the fact that Adam was convinced and was going along with Ray's plan had from the start made Vito stop and think; he had considerable respect for Adam.

But the argument wasn't won yet. "Then the only basis you have for this whole thing," said Vito, "is Ray's word."

"That's right," said Adam. Merit nodded.

Vito and Ray looked at each other.

"I'd be skeptical too, in your place," Ray said to him mildly.

Vito looked at his wife again. "Then you've never seen these Field-builders, except, as I understand it, in Ray's mind."

"No," she answered. "I never have. There are a number of parapsych things I'm not strong enough or skilled enough, to do without Ray's help." Adam listening, couldn't tell whether she was getting angry with her husband or not.

"But you're convinced you have to do this." There was a new finality in Vito's voice.

"I am."

"To teleport," said Vito, as if to himself, and Adam could see how fascinated he was, as a scientist doubtless, but not only in that way.

"That's what we're talking about, yes." Ray's voice was quiet, but held a certain challenge.

"If you go," said Vito to his wife again, "I'm going with you."

Darkness was falling now at their camp, in the archery-practice clearing only a hundred meters or so from Adam's cabin. Ray had announced that they should be ready to start within about twenty-four hours. He explained that it would take them about an hour, with several rest stops included, to teleport halfway around the world, and he wanted to arrive in the vicinity of the Ringwall soon after dawn there.

"I've explained the dangers," said Ray to Vito calmly now. "If you insist on going, we can take you." Then Ray looked at Merit, as if the final decision in this matter should be hers.

"My husband makes his own decisions," she told Ray firmly, before the angered Vito could speak for himself. "He has said that he accepts the risks, on your word that they are necessary. I accept them on the same basis."

"I thank you. All of you." Ray glanced up briefly toward the stars. "Obviously our ninety-eight siblings have already agreed with me. If not unanimously—near enough."

"Not unanimously?" Adam asked.

Ray looked at him, as if fearing to be disappointed by what he saw. "Near enough. They'll have the ship in place over the Ringwall tomorrow."

Merit closed her eyes, and nodded. "So be it, then."

When the next day's sun dipped out of sight behind the trees just to the west of their campsite, the four from Earth stood in a circle, packs, weapons, and other equipment strapped to their bodies. They faced each other across a close circle, not quite touching each other.

"We may be temporarily separated after the first jump," Ray warned the others. "But we should still commence the second jump at the same time, if not from exactly the same place. And I guarantee we'll get back together when it becomes necessary. After four or five jumps we should arrive together in the vicinity of the Ringwall—not in it, but in sight of it. All you all ready? Then here we go—"

—and they were standing on another wooded hillside, a place Adam did not recognize; it was still dusk here, so they could not yet have traveled many kilometers toward their goal.

Vito was not with them. Merit, her sudden fear evident, looked around in all directions for her husband. But he was gone. She turned to Ray.

"It's all right," Ray told her, calmly, paternally. "The little feller isn't too scared—I've still got a touch on him."

Merit's eyes blazed briefly in anger, and Adam was glad they were not aimed at him.

The three of them waited, resting minds and bodies between jumps. They had warned Adam that teleportation could be physically draining, and he was learning that they were right. They walked about a little, restlessly, as individuals, but still kept close together. Dusk was deepening slowly. Limited conversation was exchanged. Ray had to keep reassuring Merit, or trying to do so. "I tell you he's all right."

"He'd better be. He'd better be."

"Time to go," Ray told the others presently. He was as calm as ever.

—and they were standing in the middle of an open space, a larger clearing surrounded by a different forest, and now it was deep moonless night. The group was still three strong; Vito had rejoined it somehow, but now Ray was nowhere to be seen.

Merit almost crushed her husband hugging him, crying out softly in her relief. Then the three exchanged whispered information. Vito had spent his time of separation from the others in almost total darkness. Except that he had been under trees somewhere, evidently in a forest, he could offer no intelligent opinion as to where he had been, or how far from the others.

Overhead, the Galaxy sprawled across a velvet sky. From the position of the constellations Adam estimated the local time at about two hours after sunset. That meant that they were well on their way around the planet, standing now on Golden's surface at a point much farther from Stem City than any other Earth visitors had ever reached.

Vito was fumbling with something in the dark. Then he announced: "We're still in the Field here. Just as I was on my solo side trip. I thought we might strike a pocket of normality under the Field somewhere. Theoretical possibility, but we haven't come to it yet."

Adam whispered to Merit: "How long will we wait here, do you think?"

"Maybe as long as half an hour. I don't think the next jump can be delayed more than that—Adam?"

"What?"

"Did Ray show you—anything of the Fieldbuilders, as he did me?"

"No. He evidently couldn't—I'm not able to see into his mind that clearly."

"He showed me. If he's right, well, what we're doing is more important than—almost more important than we can imagine."

"Great." Vito sounded more impatient than impressed. "Is that the sea I smell?"

They all sniffed the air. There was a certain alien tang; none of them could be sure if salt water was a component.

Adam said: "But we can't be far from the sea now, anyway. Do you think we'll make the other coast in one more jump, or will it be an island?"

"There's no way to be sure," said Merit.

Adam could feel an inner tide rising, an oncoming aura of teleportation. He opened his mouth to speak, but there was no time to speak. Then the ground dropped out from under Adam's feet, and he lost his surroundings in the darkness. He was aware, for just a moment, of a strong, cool wind blowing in his face from out of the continuing darkness, as he fell feet first through empty night.

And then he splashed into salt water, deep and rough.

He fought his way back to the surface, swimming desperately to keep afloat against the weight of pack and weapons. The pattern of the icy stars told his racing mind that the time here was near midnight, and that in turn meant that he must be somewhere near the middle of a great ocean.

Parapsych theory to the contrary, there seemed to be nothing to prevent his drowning here as a direct result of his teleportation. Adam slipped out of his pack straps, abandoned bow and quiver to the sea, and let the belt that held his knife and hatchet sink away from him. There was no choice.

The water was almost comfortably warm. At least it felt considerably warmer than the air, and now, relieved of his burden of equipment, Adam could swim quite easily. There was no need, at least as yet, to shed his boots. They were light-weight and non-absorbent, Space Force surplus like some of the rest of his clothing.

From moment to moment he expected to be rescued from the sea by another teleporting jump. But the usual premonitory sensation did not come to him, and no jump happened. Did that indicate that even in the middle of the ocean he was really not in serious danger? So Ray had reassured him. Adam wouldn't have cared to bet on it. But now he had no choice.

Adam bobbed about in moderate waves, turning to look and listen in every direction. He tried to keep a screen blank in his mind, ready for any telepathic message that might be sent his way. He called out vocally, but got no answer.

At first the night around him had appeared featureless. But as his eyes adjusted more fully to the dark, he thought he saw, in one direction, a dark mass at the horizon, blotting out stars in the lowest part of the sky. Having no other plan to follow, Adam paddled toward the blot. Still really expecting to be teleported away at any moment, he took his time, coasting relaxed face down in the water for long seconds, then coming up for a quick breath and a lunging stroke with arms and legs.

It was impossible to judge the distance of the land ahead. If indeed it was land—it still might be clouds, for all he knew. Whatever it was, Adam swam on toward it, through the alien sea and night, each moment half-expecting the next tele-portation jump to whisk him away.

The stars informed him that something like an hour of steady swimming had passed, before he felt completely sure that the dark mass was solid and that he was definitely closer to it. Then almost at once he heard the sound of gentle waves on a beach, and touched sand with his feet.

He had been in excellent physical shape and well rested when the teleporting started, and the swim had not really tired him. With hardly a pause for rest, Adam walked up out of the water onto a sand spit which curved away toward a greater land mass, his original dark target bulk. There were no lights to be seen ahead, nothing but featureless darkness. Staring through the darkness, Adam tried to formulate a plan.

He was beginning to grow worried. He should have been swept away many minutes ago, together with his fellow Jovians, in another teleporting jump. But he had not been swept away. Something might have gone wrong. The telepathic world was dark and cloudy too, as far as his own limited, half-developed powers could show it to him.

It was borne in on him how much he was dependent on the others, on Ray especially. Too dependent. There was no help for it now, but Adam didn't like it. He was going to have to develop his own powers.

But now was not the time to start on that. Still it was not in a planeteer's nature to just sit and wait and hope for the best—nor was it in a Jovian's nature, Adam told himself. He began to walk slowly and cautiously along the narrow curving spit of sand toward the dark amorphous mass ahead. He tried to probe ahead with his mind, willing to settle for a minimum, for the foreknowledge of a few meters of space, a few seconds of time. Even this modest effort failed.

Slowly the dark blur resolved itself. An island gradually grew and widened and took shape around Adam as he advanced. There were many trees, sheltering pools of deeper blackness. He could not guess at the island's size. For all that he could see, it might have been some portion of a mainland; but he was still sure that he was somewhere near midocean.

His steps slowed as the darkness thickened. The only artificial light he had with him was matches, and he feared they might only reveal him without letting him see much of his environment. He decided that it would after all be best to find some kind of hiding place in which to wait for daybreak. Then, when he could see, he would cope with the situation as best he could, assuming that teleportation had still not swept him on.

Adam was moving forward, one cautious step at a time, under a thick growth of trees, when the stench hit him. The overpoweringly evil smell came at him in a wave, as suddenly as if some huge beast with bad teeth had yawned in the midnight darkness immediately in front of him.

But it was not really the odor of rottenness, though it was just as bad. It was not only repugnant but totally strange. It stopped Adam in his tracks, and sent him centimetering his way cautiously backward.

And then there was a voice out of the darkness ahead, a kind of voice that formed words, though it was otherwise an utterly inhuman, belching sound.

"Earthman," it said, creating words in the common language of Earth, carving them out in a strange heavy accent. "Earthman, I like to think about your kind."

"Uh—uh—" Adam stuttered; he nearly fell. An impulse to giggle fought within him against an even stronger urge to turn and run. Planeteering training won out, and he neither ran nor fell into hysterics, but only backed away another step, his arms rising automatically to a defensive position.

Talk, his training urged him. If someone on a strange world spoke to a planeteer, the planeteer was supposed to answer.

Adam replied: "You like to think of us? Why?" He experienced a trivial satisfaction at the steadiness of his voice.

The voice came again. "Why? I marvel at your grasping of the small. And why do you kill each other with such enthusiasm?" The basso barking, belching at him out of the night had a tympanic sound, like the deepest roar of a lion. Still Adam was able to sense nothing else about the speaker, except the smell—the smell was gradually fading now, and perhaps it did not really belong to him, or her, or it.

"I'm not sure why we do these things," Adam temporized. "What do you want of me now?"

"You have come to an island where I am. Do you know why you have come here?" There was a pause, just long enough for Adam to have forced in an answer if he had had one ready. "Then follow me," the voice commanded.

There was a receding sound. Adam's imagination, trying to match that sound convincingly with something in the physical world, could picture nothing more likely than a hollow metal drum, being dragged away forcefully through dense thorny bushes.

Adam hesitated only briefly; then with a mental shrug he followed the sound, walking with slow lightless caution through the almost perfect darkness under the trees. Within a few strides, at approximately the location from which the voice had spoken to him, he stepped on something that quivered and scattered like small hard living creatures under his boots. A wave of the strange ugly odor rose overpoweringly about him, only to fade quickly as he moved on.

Under the trees Adam encountered neither thorn bushes nor metal drums, nor anything remotely like them. The ground was level and largely barren. The sound led him on steadily, at an easy pace. Adam paced cautiously after its maker through the darkness, sensing the treetrunks only just in time to avoid bumping into them.

Soon the source of the sound changed the direction of its movement sharply. Adam followed the change, and soon after that bumped up against a wall of something that felt like sandstone. His groping hands told him that the wall was no more than chest high, but thicker than he could reach across.

His guide seemed to be following the wall now, moving to the right.

After a few more turns, all made following the windings of the wall, Adam saw a yellowish light ahead. At about the same time, he and his guide emerged from under the trees. Now the starlight showed him the being he was following, but only as a vague shape, the size of a man perhaps. It was ten meters or so ahead of him and moving quite close to the ground. Whatever it might be, it was not a human of the primate theme.

The yellow glow ahead was coming from inside a one-story building. The structure was of a simple, flat-roofed design, with doorways and windows open to the tropic night. It appeared to be constructed of the same rough stone as the low wall. There was a gateway in the wall now, and they passed through it, Adam still following his guide, toward the building's largest doorway.

"Go inside," said the tympanic voice of Adam's guide, who had now stopped at a little distance to one side. "Go inside and look. I want to see what effect on your parapsych theories is had by the sight of a possible result. Did I phrase that correctly? I am not one who knows your speech behavior well. But go and look. Be my fellow scientist, hey?"

Adam walked toward the open doorway at the center of the low building. Inside he could see a large, plain, stone-walled room, illuminated by the bright yellow glow that was coming from no visible source. The room contained nothing but a large, open pit or tank sunk into the middle of the floor and defended by a circular low wall.

The sight of a possible result. The Field-builders' torture chamber, or one of them. Adam paused in the doorway, intuition whispering to him that in this room he was going to find the half-alive remains of Alexander Golden.

He didn't want to see that. He hoped more fiercely than ever that the next teleportation jump would quickly come, come now, and take him out of this. But he made himself cross the floor to the low wall around the tank, and look over the wall and down.

"They came in past the robot picket ships ten hours ago," said General Lorsch. For the first time in many days there was no tiredness in her voice. Her electronic pointer flashed as it marked the location of the sighting on the holographic model of the space around Golden. Around her the small,

dimly lighted briefing room on the command deck
of the flagship was quiet, the small group of people
who filled it listening intently.

"The pickets have been following them," the General went on, "and no doubt they are aware of that.
Now they're within fifteen hundred kilometers of
planet surface, and holding position there. We're
going to surround them as best we can with our
three manned ships, and then we're going to ask
them some questions. Yes, Colonel, what is it?"

Brazil stood up in the small group of senior
officers present. "Ma'am, is an arrest certain?"

Lorsch paused for just a second before answering.
"I'd say almost certain. This is the Jovian ship,
and it's illegal; we can't have people jaunting anywhere they like in starships, involving all humanity in God knows what.

"I don't know if the Jovians intend to resist
arrest. We don't know what weapons they may
have. Considering their abilities, maybe something
very new and very good." She looked around her
solemnly. "We'll be three ships to one, but, frankly,
this operation may develop into a battle. We must
be ready for that."

Another officer stood up. "Boarding parties,
ma'am, I presume?"

"Correct. Colonel Brazil is going to be in command of that part of the operation. Colonel, I want
you to me right after this meeting."

Me and my hotshot record, Boris thought, sitting
down again.

Adam stood looking down into the tank, feeling
a kind of strained, puzzled relief, an anticlimax.
Five meters below, an amphibious beast of a kind
that he had never seen before splashed and wal-

lowed in shallow water. There was nothing in the appearance of the beast to connect it with Alexander Golden, or indeed with humanity in any way; rather it looked vaguely like a seal. Assuming that the creature was native to Golden, it was hardly surprising that Adam had never encountered a member of its species before. Golden was after all an Earth-sized world, and he was now standing in a hemisphere of that world that had never before been explored by Earth-descended humans.

There was a tiny splash in the water, just beside the seal-like creature. And then another splash and then another. Something, a slow hail of small objects, was falling into the tank.

Adam looked up at a blank stone ceiling, close above. He could see the tiny objects materializing in the air now, a thin rain of them, looking like pebbles, coming out of the air under the low ceiling to fall and patter around the thing living in the tank. Suddenly, like an animated rubber toy, the creature stretched its body completely out of its old shape and into a new one, altering its form completely into something like that of an octopus. Still it never at any stage of the change looked anything like Alexander Golden, or any other human being of Earth.

"Observe classic symptom of falling stones," boomed the guide's voice, from somewhere in the darkness outside the building. "But do you not detect the sickness? I thought you were a sensitive, teleporting as you were."

Adam turned to face the wide dark open doorway. All he could think of was to try to change the subject. In his growing state of shock, ingrained planteering methods won out again. "Will you tell me your name?" he asked.

"I am studying you, not the other way around. Co-operation, please."

"I only want to—"

Afterward Adam could not remember just what he had meant to say he wanted. He found himself sitting on the stone floor, with his back against the low wall that guarded the tank, and with no idea of how long he had been sitting there. He felt no pain and had no memory of any, but the feeling that he had driven his will into some analog of a stone wall, so that his will had been bent back upon itself. The effect was disorganizing, like an electric shock to the central nervous system.

The guide's concussive voice, patiently curious, now repeated its question from the outer darkness. "Do you sense the sickness of the one in the tank? Answer, please."

It seemed wise to avoid further argument. Adam got to his feet and looked into the tank again. No further change in the occupant was observable. "No. This being looks—strange to me. But I can sense nothing wrong, in the sense of sickness." *Merit, Ray, where are you?*

They were nowhere, as far as he could tell.

Could he somehow have missed, been left out from, a teleportation jump?

If Adam's guide was aware of his efforts at telepathy, it did not comment on them. "That being in the tank has deformed itself," the creature outside in the night explained. "Crippled its mind and body, by using what you call parapsych forces in an attack upon another being. Such is the usual result of attempting such use—" The guide interrupted itself with a sudden skreeking noise. "Did you think he was one of your kind? Not so, he is one of mine, and this planet is his native world.

Such as he are brought to this island to reach for health, and I am here to help them. I think you came here because of that, and because I like to think about your kind."

Adam knew that straining anxiously for the teleporting jump would not help him to attain it. He strained anyway. He got nowhere.

Again he tried to contact Merit's mind, or Ray's, and again he had no success.

The guide asked him again, with patient interest: "Why do you of Earth destroy each other with such enthusiasm?"

Trying to think of a reasonable answer, Adam for the first time and without trying caught a flash of the guide's mind; a glimpse not of black threatening, foreshadowing wings, but of something incomprehensible but magnificent. Adam's mind supplied the image of a carven alien palace.

Was *this* a Field-Builder? But no, it couldn't be. Ray had been very vague in his physical descriptions of them, but he had said . . .

Now that Adam tried to think of it, he could not recall that Ray had given any physical description of his enemies at all. But their minds, their minds as Ray had pictured them, were vats of sickness.

Now the guide, with keen curiosity, was telepathically directing a question—Adam could not tell what question—to another of its kind. Adam sensed that other mind, too, for one instant, then both were gone from his perception. Through the open doorway he heard metallic scratching noises again, as his guide went moving away through darkness.

Adam was left alone with the thing, the creature in the tank. *But do you not detect the sickness?* He could not. Remembering his hallucination on the

Stem City slideway, he closed his eyes briefly; the low stone wall beneath his hands felt utterly and completely real.

Opening his eyes, he saw a light outside the building, and for an instant interpreted what he saw as the dawn. But this was a much closer fire, not far outside the doorway now and moving nearer still.

After another glance at the wallowing, stretching thing in the tank, Adam went to the doorway and looked out.

The fire came walking quietly around the corner of the building and toward him, in the shape of a tall man. A man being consumed steadily by flame, pacing toward Adam, who backed away mechanically, with almost no capacity left for astonishment. With dim horror Adam saw that the flesh was already charred away from the bones of the man's arms and fingers. The figure turned a blackened horror that was no longer a face toward Adam. Sound came from it, a parody of speech.

Only then was Adam able to react with some semblance of purpose. He dashed back into the building, with the vague thought of somehow getting water to throw on the burning man, or some flame-smothering thing to wrap him in. But there was no way to scoop up water from the tank, nothing within his reach but stone, no way to help. The seal-like creature in the tank still sloshed gently, in water far down out of Adam's reach.

Adam turned away from the tank and ran outside again. He was just in time to see the flaming figure collapse. There was no writhing in pain or shock; the body was simply too structurally damaged now to stand.

As Adam watched the body shrivel on the sand, the next teleporting jump swept him up unexpectedly.

Chapter Seventeen

Colonel Boris Brazil had just left a last briefing session with the General, and now he was conducting a similar meeting of his own, meanwhile wondering in odd moments how he had ever managed to get himself into this.

"We're about twenty-four thousand kilometers from them right now," he was telling the hundred potential space marines—most of them really planeteers—who sat in rows looking up at him. "We're keeping station. And they're just sitting there, eight hundred klicks directly above the Ringwall. They won't answer us, but they certainly know we're here. In a few hours we're going to start closing in on them from three directions, and do whatever we have to do to get their attention one way or another. If it does come to a fight, and the General does decide on a boarding action—well, you and I are elected."

The hundred faces arrayed before him were all sober, and the great majority of them were young.

They asked him silently: Are you going to be able to lead an operation like that? What do you know about it? How many of us are going to get killed?

Boris went on: "I don't need to tell you that a genuine battle would be something new for all of us. I've been in a little fight or two, here and there. And I did get a high score the last time I played at maneuvers with robot ships, if that kind of thing reassures anyone."

His audience relieved him somewhat at this point by managing a faint perfunctory laugh, and he went on. "All right—let's see who among you had the highest ratings in boarding techniques, last time you practiced. Anybody with A-one, raise your hands. Good. How about A-two?"

In a matter of minutes he had squad leaders chosen. Dismissing the rest temporarily, he called the handful of squad leaders, a much more manageable number, into a smaller meeting to sketch in a tentative battle plan.

"We have half a dozen yesmen available for what look like the dirtiest jobs. So I'm going to volunteer six people, I want you to suggest names, for the comparative safety of puppet chambers aboard this ship."

Wish I had Adam Mann here for this job, Brazil thought to himself. He was remembering that first geryon hunt here on Golden, with Mann in the puppet chamber then. That seemed now like so many years ago.

Adam came out of the last teleportation jump into broad daylight, standing almost upright at the bottom of a ravine overgrown with low vegetation. He staggered, off balance for an instant, crashing through bushes of unfamiliar types. The sky visible above the steep sides of the ravine was a clear blue, with a few clouds in it red-tinged by a sun quite low in the sky. The time was either shortly after dawn, or late in the afternoon.

There was a sound like steady thunder, coming from somewhere in the middle distance.

No one else was in sight.

Adam started up one side of the ravine. When he had climbed a few meters he could see drifting, mountainous clouds of spray in the lower sky ahead of him, and he knew that he was very near the Ringwall now. The thunder in the air must issue from the vast falls and rapids of its surrounding rivers.

He climbed all the way up the side of the ravine, and stopped. He could see now that he was standing about halfway up the side of a larger slope. All along the wide valley below him, a wild nameless river tore itself over kilometers of rocks. Above the river's opposite shoreline, rainbow-haunted clouds of mist climbed steadily, as if impelled by a rising wind. The clouds were ascending a steep, barren slope, kilometers long, to fog the morning sky above the Ringwall itself.

Built atop that long opposite slope, the outer cliff-face of the Ringwall went curving and angling away from Adam in both directions. It had a look of unreality, like a surrealist painting on a stage backdrop; yet it was real. Flying birds were distant specks between him and its bulk.

And it was not really a cliff face, or at least it was not completely natural. Looking at it this closely, from this angle, Earthly eyes could at last be sure of that. The Ringwall was at least in part deliberate construction, made according to some intelligent design.

There were outcroppings, along its top and upon its flanks, with lines as straight as those of any structure ever built on Earth, their shapes suggesting turrets and battlements. There were calculated niches, and true columns, and real buttresses, appearing here and there along the length and height of that awesome wall. In the blue-shadowed recesses between the larger projections there might be room for small villages—but Adam knew somehow that villages would not be there.

The Ringwall. Adam Mann looked down at the foot of its island, then looked up, up a kilometer and more, at the face of the wall itself. He could see now how a million niches and a million windows of various depths and shapes had been cut into the white or brown or gray rock. There were streaks of pure crimson, straight or in perfect curves, that ran among the openings and marked the joinings of stone blocks whose sides were measurable in hectares. Trees grew on the wall in places, miniature forests less like window-gardens than like moss upon a castle wall.

Adam thought of the thousands of pictures taken from Space Force scoutships, ships driving or floating six hundred kilometers or more above this scene. No telescopic camera had been able to see detail anything like this, not through the eternally rising mist and through whatever it was that fogged the films in infrared. Not simple heat, apparently. Adam, at his distance on the ground, could feel no radiant heat.

There were certainly structures on Earth at least as high as this one. There might be one or two as big, measured by volumes and distances. Measured by sight and feel, there was nothing to compare with it.

Adam tore his eyes away from the Ringwall at last. On his own side of the river he scanned the long bushy slope, cut with small winding ravines, that extended for a great distance to his right and left. He was looking for his companions, and once he began actively looking for them he quickly spotted Ray. The huge man, his body tiny against the backdrop of the river valley, was standing some distance below Adam, on a slittle rocky plateau directly above the river's edge. Ray had his back turned to Adam, and was gazing steadily across the river, up to where the giants' stonework waited.

Adam cupped his hands to his mouth, but the yell he had been about to utter died in his throat. When he looked at Ray more closely, he saw that Ray was standing firmly in midair, his feet half a meter above the rock.

It was no news to Adam that Ray Kedro had the power to do such things; but the sight of a parapsych trick now, here in the face of the enemy, gave Adam a sense of something indefinably wrong. Was the trick meant to impress someone? The Fieldbuilders? If not that, what?

Adam looked around again in all directions, but could see nothing of either Merit or Vito. He turned and scrambled back down to the bottom of his small ravine, then followed its sinuously eroded curve down the larger slope toward Ray. Adam had lost his weapons, his food, and his canteen, but such losses might not matter much. Not if they could quickly complete whatever job Ray had in mind . . .

Adam halted for a moment, closing his eyes. For the first time, doubt came over him with dizzying force. What job did Ray expect to do here, exactly? No one knew that but Ray.

And Adam hurried on. Yes, complete the job—or quickly abandon the attempt, Adam thought to himself—and jump out of here again within a few hours.

He wondered at himself, as he trotted down the ravine. Why had he ever agreed to come here? Three men, one woman, against . . .

Against what, exactly? Adam thought of the creature who had spoken to him on the island, and of the burning man he had encountered there.

If it had been anyone else but Ray who had suggested that four of them come here and attack the Field-builders, Adam would have called it madness. But because it was Ray . . .

And then I even used what we call projection to present our case, Ray had said to him once. *That method gives me very considerable powers of persuasion.*

Did Ray *actually* mean for only the four of them to—

Adam stopped again. Somewhere down the ravine ahead of him, a woman was wailing. It was a low sound, expressing terrible grief. Slowly Adam moved forward. A terrible buried suspicion was rising in his mind, and he could not yet let himself see exactly what the suspicion was.

He came in sight of the woman, and she was Merit, collapsed and weeping on the ground, huddled over a hiking pack. Adam knelt beside her, to lift and turn her gently. Her face was contorted, in agony of some kind, in an agony of grief, and her blank eyes seemed to look up through Adam to the sky.

He saw now that the pack Merit was crouching over was the one that Vito had been wearing. Adam saw also that the shoulder straps of the pack now ended abruptly, in short stumps, and that the very ends of the straps were burned black, as if a slow laser might have cut them away.

Still not really looking at him, Merit spoke to him suddenly, in a hurried and mumbling voice. It was as if she were hardly conscious of who she was speaking to or what she said.

". . . he said, the time has come for defiance—of something. He said that now was the time for a bold decisive step. He told me he was behind what they did to Vito in Stem City." Her eyes came to focus on Adam's face at last. "And he was the one who made Vito try to fight you, at Fieldedge. I thought so, then, I feared so, but I couldn't believe it."

"Who?" Adam asked her. As if he did not already know.

"Ray. Ray, Ray, Raymond Kedro. Then they burned my husband to death just now, he and the others."

"The others?" Adam whispered. He added dazedly: "I saw a burning man."

"The others. Most of our siblings, up in the ship. Most of them follow Ray. They have for years. I followed him too. I did everything he wanted, all these years. Almost everything. I had no children. But still he had to kill Vito. Vito, Vito!"

Merit bent again, swaying from side to side as if in physical agony, and a long keening moan, an almost animal sound, came from her.

Adam spoke to her. He petted her and stroked her hair. Then after a few moments he abandoned the effort and stood up. He could do nothing for Merit right now. He moved on down the ravine.

The raging water was near at hand, and the sound of it was loud, when Adam reached the foot of the rock that Ray was standing on, or rather standing above. Ray still gazed as if entranced across the river, at the Ringwall. Ray's right arm was now almost two meters long. The arm hung grotesquely out of its sleeve, the big hand trailing along the rock below Ray's feet like something Ray had forgotten. The arm was stretched out of all natural shape and proportion. It suggested the deformed members of the creature that Adam had seen on the island, confined in the sunken tank.

Ray, continuing to gaze at the Ringwall, paid no attention to his altered arm, or to Adam, calling up to him.

Adam climbed the rock, with difficulty. By the time he reached the flat top, Ray's feet were down on rock again, and his arm had regained a normal appearance. Adam noticed now that Ray was also missing his pack and weapons and canteen.

The huge man looked at Adam now, calmly and without surprise. "Ours," Ray said, raising an arm and pointing to the Ringwall. "Whenever we choose to take it. And after that, the Field. And, after that, the universe."

"Merit says you killed—"

Ray interrupted, his loud voice riding over Adam's as if he were not aware that anyone might be speaking. "I was wrong, before, when I thought that a greater race than ours might come after us. That would be impossible. I see now that we are the ultimate peak of evolution. I could have allowed pure-bred Jovian children to exist, for they could never have become our superiors. Never. But ... it's best after all that we've waited for them. All my decisions are for the best. When this little war is over, we will have a time of peace. There'll be time enough for children then."

Adam grabbed at Ray, seized the arm that a moment ago had been stretched. In his grasp it felt quite human and normal now, plain flesh and bone. "You and the others killed Vito? Why?"

"Easy, Ad. Take it easy." Ray pulled his arm roughly away. "We had to spank Merit, but she'll be all right in a little while. You don't know yet what it is to be a Jovian. So don't try to tell me what to do."

"Spank her?" Adam could hear panic in his own voice. "What are you talking about? Who do you mean, we?"

Had the Field-builders somehow managed to drive Ray mad?

"Our ship's up there, now." Ray pointed overhead; listened to word by word, he sounded rational, as firmly in control of himself and of events as always. "Merit fought us, over that human husband of hers, and so we had to discipline her. I should never have allowed her to have him, to begin with—but she'll get over it. She'll be all right, soon."

Adam backed up, getting as far from Ray as he could on the little plateau. The river roared at the rocks below, not caring what people did.

Why do you kill each other with such enthusiasm?

Ray was looking at him now with an expression of—well, of annoyance. And meanwhile one of Ray's legs was beginning to elongate, doubling up under the big man's massive body. Ray shifted his balance, putting his weight on the other leg, but otherwise he did not appear to notice the new change.

Ray said to Adam: "Don't look so shocked. Remember, Ling was only human."

"Only human."

"Yes." Ray nodded soberly, as if he considered

that he was making quite a serious point. "And he was keeping Merit away from us. Away from me especially. And what if she had become pregnant by him, and carried such a hybrid to term? That was a possibility, you know. Interbreeding is still possible, and the purity of the Jovian race must be preserved. She'll be glad, when she finally understands what it means to be a Jovian. Yes, the purity of the race must be preserved." A shadow crossed Ray's face, and he raised his voice. "I tell you, don't look that way at me! After all, we once did the same for you."

The river thundered in Adam's ears.

Alice.

Chapter Eighteen

For combat Brazil was buttoned into his boarding capsule, melded with the machine into a semi-robot that along with a swarm of others like it had been fired out of the flagship into the sunlit vacuum of six hundred kilometers altitude above the Ringwall, where it now clung, a leech among other leeches, to the huge hull of the Jovian ship. Instruments now reported to Boris Brazil, the man inside this particular semi-robot, that one of its metal arms was gone now, burned or blown away already, and that the temperature of the capsule's outer surface had risen well past the melting point of lead.

The heat inside the Colonel's capsule was still survivable. It was the hole in the armored hull of it, near his left foot, that might be going to finish him. Something had pierced the capsule at its foot, and had come through the leg of the armored suit the Colonel wore inside it, and clobbered his own left foot and ankle. The suit's hypos and torniquet had bitten him. Flesh and blood had no business, he thought, mixing into this kind of a fight.

The capsule had sealed itself again around him, and Brazil had no time to worry about his numbed leg. Now he was scrambling his boarding capsule, under semi-automatic control, over the surface of the Jovian's hull, probing for some weak spot where he could hang on successfully and start trying to dig in. At the same time he was trying to co-ordinate the similar activities of the rest of the boarding party, which was under his command.

Until about half an hour ago, the Jovians on their ship had behaved like relatively sane people, talking calmly if a bit unreasonably to the three Space Force ships confronting them, while the four of them rode together in formation around the planet, leaving the dawn terminator behind them and keeping the Ringwall below.

Then a disturbance had erupted inside the Jovian ship. It had begun, as far as the Space Force listeners could tell, suddenly. First there was the background noise of verbal wrangling, coming plain over the communications channel open between the ships. Then there were sounds of some more violent trouble.

It began with one voice, that was heard over the radio channel for the first time as it broke into a wrangle over space law and the rights of travelers, crying jubilantly: "We've done it, we've killed with our minds alone!"

Then protest, from other voices, equally fierce and sudden:

"It's wrong!"

"And what of the reaction, have you thought of that?"

But the protestors had been obviously a minority aboard the Jovian, for they were shouted down. Then pandemonium. They had forgotten to turn off their radio transmitter over there, or they had scorned to do so, or else they had deliberately wanted the human world to hear. To Boris and other outsiders listening, it was as if everyone aboard the Jovian ship had suddenly got drunk, or gone mad.

"For the purity of the race!" one voice, a woman's, had cried out from there, exultantly. And on that note the Jovians, or their prevailing majority, had started the firefight without warning, aiming what must have been everything they had at Lorsch's flagship. The flagship was hurled a hundred and fifty kilometers away, her outer hull punctured in spite of ready defenses, and three of her crew killed instantly.

Lorsch had driven her ship back as fast as possible to where the others were roasting each other, and her three ships had clamped on to the Jovian with forcefields, the flagship using all the power of her space-bending engines, so that the four ships hung locked together now, like atoms in some giant molecule.

While their computers fenced, striking at one another with their flickering hammers of weaponry, women and men huddled in their cocoons of metal and padding, waiting for computers to present them with the next decision that could be made slowly enough for humans to have competency.

General Lorsch made one such decision, and the boarding party was launched, led by yesmen in the first six capsules. The Jovians' smaller weapons picked out and destroyed the yesmen, and killed or wounded the first six human beings to launch, Brazil among them, before any of the boarders reached the enemy hull. And here and there, in a capsule-cocoon that had been penetrated by no apparent physical force, a Space Force man or woman burned silently and perhaps painlessly to death.

To Boris, the battle was experienced largely as electronic signals inside his capsule, and the movements he made with the capsule's inhuman limbs; the gabble of question and answer and noise inside his helmet, and heat and shock and pain. And the gradual conviction that his left foot and ankle were completely gone.

In his helmet a voice said, at intervals: "We're holding, we're holding." The Colonel understood what the voice meant: the engines of the Space Force ships, acting as generators now, were standing the overload of combat, resisting the enemy, and striking at him with weapons of heat and force and disruption, powers like something out of the heart of a sun.

And the enemy was still resisting too, and still hitting back hard, but it seemed that he could spare none of his incredible strength to pick the metal gnats of the boarding party from his armored surface.

Each metal gnat was protected from Space Force weapons by its own friend-or-foe radar beacon; the racing combat computers on the big ships picked the tiny voices of friendship out of the inferno of battle noise, and channeled their violence elsewhere—at least, so matters went in hopeful theory. Practice, to Boris, was being bounced off the hull time and again, when something heavy hit nearby, then getting back to the hull again with his capsule's jets, and scrambling again for a hold.

He was bounced off again, more violently than before, and coming back saw on his capsule's viewscreen a red-rimmed dark hole, a couple of meters in diameter, piercing the smooth bright Jovian hull just ahead of him.

"Breach! Breach!" someone else was shouting, having spotted the hole at the same time.

"Thor, this is Bee, we are entering a breach," Boris called back to the flagship, giving the machine called Fire Control the information that fragile friendly human flesh was about to do just that.

"We're gaining!" shouted the voice that usually said *We're holding*—the voice of someone who watched an indication of the total force being exerted by the Jovian. The enemy had been hurt now—either that or he was faking, pretending weakness, gathering his strength for an even greater effort to come.

Brazil led his boarding party into the torn-open hull, hoping to stay alive, trying to take the enemy alive. Weapons ready, he scrambled his capsule forward through a slick patch of still semi-molten metal, into the breach.

"You killed Alice. You were behind everything they did to her." Adam spoke as he stood facing Ray on the flat rock, with the wide river roaring below them and the Ringwall looking down.

Ray looked at him calmly, and made a slight dismissive gesture. "Oh yes. Your wife. But never mind that now. We knew best. You have to admit that we always know best." The answer was delivered almost absently, as if Ray were overwhelmingly distracted. Even before he finished speaking he had turned his face partly away from Adam, and was looking up at the Ringwall again.

Ray said: "The Field-builders are in there, with their victims—and they're aware of us out here. Aware at this moment of me here, looking in at them ... but our ship is overhead—did I tell you that?" He looked back at Adam, calmly and inquiringly.

Adam stared back. Even rage had to pause. "You've forgotten telling me that, two minutes ago?"

Ray blinked at him, as if Adam's question had no possible relevance. Then Ray, as if continuing with some subject already under discussion, said: "It was years ago when we first began to weed the human garden. For a time, a long time, we were too conservative. We removed only certain very objectionable people—the power-mad, the organizers of hate groups and of crime syndicates—obscene little creatures, unworthy even of our true human ancestors. Then gradually we began to feel more confident, and to do more.

"From now on, we will do more still. You of course were wrong to mate with a human female. But you didn't know then that you were Jovian. We can forgive you."

"You—can forgive me Alice."

Ray ignored the answer. "We were right, of course, to dispose of her. But I see now that we were in—can I call it error?" He shook his head, muttering for a moment to himself. "Of course I can call it error, I can say whatever I like ...."

He looked closely again at Adam, and for a moment Ray's old infectious grin was visible. Then the grin as gone, replaced by—something else. A look that would have gone better with a long, scaly neck. ". . . in error, in our choice of methods. Hired physical violence." Ray's voice expressed contempt, and he shook his head. "You foiled the attempt on Ling in Stem City, and I'm glad now that you did. The use of such means is really beneath us. *Now*, after we have killed with our minds alone, I understand that . . . I think my intellect is growing tremendously now, hour by hour, even minute by minute . . . now I understand that, and now I see the true glory of . . . of . . . what was I saying?"

A pebble fell, from out of the clear blue sky. Adam saw it clearly as it fell, as it struck Ray on the shoulder and bounced off to come to rest with minor clatter on the huge flat rock where they were standing.

Ray looked up, puzzling at the sky with slow, vague eyes.

The mighty intelligence was crumbling, the godlike powers falling in upon their center. Adam watched the collapse with cold rejoicing, violent hatred.

Adam said: "Damn you to hell, you deserve what you're getting!"

"Ohhh?" Ray again tore his gaze down from the Ringwall. And now, for the first time since Adam had climbed up on the rock with him, he gave Adam his full attention. Ray's body came jerkily back to normal shape, the elongated leg restoring itself as in some dream, or some conjuror's trick.

Ray said: "One thing you must remember, one thing about being a Jovian. It is that I am your leader, and I am always right. If you dispute that, you must and will be disciplined. We have begun with Merit. I think that it will be perferable to destroy her personality entirely, and then rebuild—"

A trigger pulled in Adam's brain, sending him two steps forward, left, right, and then the front snap kick with the left foot, snapped faster than the eye could follow.

Ray moved almost as fast, and very lightly for all his bulk, sidestepping perfectly. He smiled pityingly, and shook his head. "Adam, Adam, will I have to rebuild you too? How can you hope to fight a telepath physically? One who is bigger and stronger than you are?

"I think I will remove both you and Merit to the ship, and begin the process there, as soon as the difficulty with the human ships is over." Ray squinted up into the misty sky. "That should be soon now." He turned his back on Adam again to gaze up at the Ringwall. "Later I can return to deal with the—creatures—who live there." Without looking Ray dodged Adam's chop at the back of his neck. Then the huge man spun around, avoiding a driving knee, and swung.

Adam saw the enormous fist coming at him, and thought he had it ducked, but it seemed to swing lower, following the movement of his head. There was a flash in his head and his consciousness was gone—

—for what must have been only a second or two; he found himself rolling onto his back, hands and feet ready for defensive work. There was a numb fogging pressure on his mind, and his eyes were blurring.

Ray was standing back, calm and safe, talking and talking, delivering a lecture:

"—acting like a human—cannot condone—"

Ray, Ray, who was Ray? Alice's killer, Merit's tormentor, freely confessed, standing there in front of him. Adam rolled up into a catlike crouch, and

heard himself muttering the gutter words and
threats of his childhood. In a few seconds the cold
computer in his head was clear enough, the body
ready. He started forward in a half-crouch.

"You cannot fight a telepath in such a way."
Ray was leaning forward, speaking very distinctly,
as if to a child. Then a shade of alarm crossed his
face and he started his dodging motion in time to
avoid the first kick and the second. Then he par-
ried the smashing backfist strike with his forearm,
and launched a kick of his own that Adam was
expecting and easily avoided.

There was not much room on the little table of
rock for stalking, the cold computer commented
unhappily to Adam. He moved in again on Ray,
and saw knowledge of his own intentions in Ray's
eyes, knowledge disregarded by Ray's supreme
confidence.

Adam threw another combination of kicks and
blows. Again Ray could not totally avoid the final
impact, though he almost succeeded in dodging it,
so much of the force was lost. But the last kick
caught him just above the knee. This time Ray's
counterpunch went only halfway before he jerked
it back, just in time to keep from being grabbed by
arm and shoulder, levered off his feet, and slammed
down onto rock.

Adam and Ray moved hesitantly closer, then
alertly jerked away from each other. Now, whenever Ray's weight came on his right leg, he limped.

A purple welt from one of the exchanges was
now rising on Ray's hairy forearm. But he was
able to make himself stop limping. "You are a true
Jovian," he said, sounding like a proud father. "A
true—"

He got his guard up just barely in time. Again

the last phase of the attack damaged him; he could not move swiftly enough to escape entirely what he perceived was coming. Nor could he strike back with Adam's unthinking speed.

Adam made no conscious tactical plan. He moved in on Ray, and let the years of training and practice take over.

Adam was knocked down again. Then when Ray stepped close to kick at him, Adam blocked the kick with his own feet, tripped Ray and threw him back and down. Both men got to their feet, almost grappling, breaking apart at the last instant. Then they lunged and fell together, lungs sobbing for air, arms locking and twisting for advantage. Ray's greater strength began to tell. Adam got an arm free, and jabbed his enemy in the throat, and broke away.

Timeless and bloody, the fight wore on.

Adam stood watching Ray's head sway back and forth. It was an almost hypnotic movement against the background of the Ringwall, and Adam could not tell how much of the unsteadiness was Ray's and how much was his own. But Adam had to pause for a moment, to gasp for breath, he had to rest. He felt as if a gang had been beating him, though he could remember no details of the times that Ray had been able to get to him.

Ray's head swayed farther to one side; then all at once the huge man sank into a half-sitting, half-kneeling position. His hands lay down at his sides, his arms moving, quivering as if he were trying to lift them and could not. His throat made a choking whistle with each breath, and now before he could speak he had to spit out something bloody.

"I must conquer you." Ray could get out the words only a few at a time, with little sobbing breaths between. "Or I must kill you. Can't you see. I am the leader. I am. The greatest. Jovian of all."

Adam could still stand up. And he could still talk. "You killed Alice."

The blue eyes of the superman were filled with pain. Once before, long ago, Adam had seen those eyes look just like that. But now Adam bent and picked up a sharp piece of rock. Just the right size. His hard hands hurt, and a rock would be a handy thing with which to crush a skull.

Ray was trying to say something more. "I—I—if you *are* the leader, Adam—" He gasped, and shook his head. "Lead them well, Adam." He looked up, pleading. "Don't get them into trouble. I—I—sometimes I feel sick—"

Ray managed to lift his hands all the way up to his head. Then he rolled over sideways, writhing on the rock. From the clear sky there came a fall of pebbles to patter around him.

The rock in Adam's hand felt far too heavy now; his bruised hand was trembling under the weight of it. He turned and pitched it out into the river. Now there was nothing left.

No, one thing, one person. Merit. He had to get to her.

Climbing down from the little plateau of rock was painful. And after he had climbed down he could not rest, but had to go staggering back up the little ravine. Because Merit was there.

From across the river the Ringwall looked down on him, as indifferent as the sun. Someday, he told it, we'll learn what you really are. But now he had no emotion left for it.

Merit was sitting almost where he had left her. No more contortions of grief, but apathetic calm.

Adam sank down beside her, looked into her eyes that followed him gently, and reached out with his hand. Without meaning to, his fingers left blood on her cheek. Maybe it was the feel of the blood that pulled her up to full awareness.

"Adam, you're hurt." Gently she took him by the neck, and pulled his head down into her lap and held it there, her hands pressing and rubbing the back of his head tenderly. "I was afraid for a long time that they'd do something to Vito," she said softly. "Still when it happened I couldn't believe it."

Adam closed his eyes. His whole body trembled violently for a moment, then was able to let go in utter relaxation. "I fought with Ray," he told her. As if he were a child hoping for an explanation from Merit, for reassurance, for something that would make sense. "He's still alive, sitting up there."

"I know, I know." Her fingers soothed him. "Later we'll worry about him. Rest now. Heal."

Time passed. Adam felt the strengthening morning sun on his back. Suddenly he became aware of two things: he was intensely thirsty, and his cheek was resting on the thigh of a very desirable woman.

He raised his head and opened his eyes, and saw a geryon looking at him, from only thirty meters up the ravine.

Chapter Nineteen

They had one knife between the two of them, one small blade with which to try to defend themselves. Looking over the upper edge of their little ravine, Adam spotted four more geryons, higher on the broad slope, and working their way slowly down. The hides of these animals were darker than those of the geryons of the Stem area, and these were perhaps on the average a little larger; but from what Adam could see of them so far, their hunting formation appeared to be the same. He had no doubt that they were hunting now, and little doubt of what they had selected as their prey.

He held a quick discussion with Merit, and they began to make their way down toward the river; no other direction appeared to offer any chance at all of avoiding the animals.

When they came in sight of the high rock on the shoreline, Ray was no longer there. He was nowhere to be seen.

"Adam."

He paused. They were almost at the shoreline now. "What?"

Merit was holding both hands to her head. Then she looked up, as Ray had, squinting toward the few high clouds that trailed through the calm silent sky above the endlessly rising mist. She said: "Something terrible is happening—there's killing and killing, out there."

"The Field-builders?"

"No. I don't know if they even exist. All I know about them is what Ray . . . I mean our people, and . . . our people. We can't expect any help, down here, from anyone."

"You teleport," said Adam. "Jump out of here. Try to get back to the Stem, or up to a ship, whatever. We'll forget about the Field-builders, they don't seem to be bothering us. I'll be all right, until you can get some kind of help back to me."

"No." She looked at him. "I wouldn't leave you."

"Go, I tell you. I'm used to this kind of thing. I enjoy it. I'll be all right."

"No. Anyway, you don't understand. I can't teleport alone. Not now."

Adam had no breath or strength left in him for argument. He looked back. The things with human faces were getting closer, coming slowly and methodically down the slope in their fan-shaped formation. A couple more of them had appeared from somewhere. They were able to smell the blood on him, of course, Ray's blood and some of his own; they could tell a kilometer away when something was hurt and weakened.

Should he separate from Merit? Not yet, anyway; there were advantages for her as well as for him in the two of them being together. He would try to get away with her down the river, or across it; the water ought to wash him clean of blood and that might help.

They forced their way through a shoreline row of tall bushes, and emerged from it with the river right at their feet. They were in full view now of the Ringwall, towering distantly atop the rocky slope that went up from the far shore. The river here was swift foaming water a hundred meters wide, everywhere shallow and dotted with small rocky islets. Not far from where Adam and Merit were standing, a fallen tree made a bridge from shore out to the nearest of these islands.

The geryons were closing in on the two humans quickly now, their hunting formation only fifty meters away. Adam urged Merit out onto the fallen tree.

It was sturdy enough to bear them, and they both reached the nearest island easily. But the island promised no safety. Within a minute there were seven geryons gathered only a log's length away, on the shore that the two people had just left. The animals began cautiously testing the water with massive feet.

"They're going to come after us," said Adam.

"Then we'll have to cross the river."

"All right. Let's go." It did not look absolutely impossible—and there really was no other choice.

Gripping hands, they slid into the water, that was here about waist deep.

Behind them, the animals were entering the water together, beginning a slow swimming and wading progress toward the first island.

The crossing would have been a perilous one, even starting fresh and with no danger in pursuit. Wherever the water was deep, the man and woman swam and were swept downstream. When a sand-bar or one of the small islands came within reach, or the stream shallowed sufficiently, they would brace their feet on the bottom and wade again, or grip and climb on rock.

Their lead over the cautious animals steadily lengthened.

There were periods of time, some of them lasting for many seconds, when Adam found that his mind and Merit's were in contact, when without using precious breath they could trade exact pictures of grips and footing and the distance of the pursuing animals. Perhaps it was this mental contact that tipped the scales, and brought them across the river alive.

Adam crawled out upon the shore of the Ringwall's vast island feeling that another three meters of river to cross might have been too much. Now he could imagine no experience in life finer than just to lie on firm ground, without moving, and concentrate upon the enormous job of breathing that there was to be done.

The geryons were still following them, so far as inexorably as death. But they had made the crossing with their usual prudence, and without the help of human hands to cling to island rock. Therefore they had been swept well downstream, and were now visible only as a scattered cluster of small dots in the distance, still in the water. The animals' crossing of the river was not yet finished; it might well be half an hour before they reached this spot. But their presence downstream killed any idea of escape by simply drifting or floating in that direction.

Merit had recovered enough to sit up. But all

was not well with her. "Damn it. I've done something to my ankle."

Adam raised himself on his elbows. "Teleport.
Get out of here. Bring back help. Do it for me. I'd
do it if I could."

"I tried, Adam. A moment ago. I tried to teleport
to a spot just in front of the geryons. I thought it
might scare them off. But I couldn't jump. Anywhere. Not even ten meters." Merit gave a little
watersoaked smile that quickly faded. "When Vito
died, and the others who were burned like him, up
in their ships, there was some kind of terrible—
backlash. A parapsych reaction. None of the talents are working properly any more."

Adam grunted. Finding himself able to move
again, he got over to where Merit was sitting and
started to examine her ankle.

From behind him, a familiar voice said: "I plan
to rebuild your minds. Both of you."

Ray was there, seated crosslegged in the air, two
meters above the ground. His eyes looked vacantly
out at them from his battered face. Ray's arms
both hung limply at his sides; one of them was
elongating and shortening again, over and over,
bone and flesh and even the sleeve included. Ray
did not appear to notice the varying deformity at
all.

"*I* crossed the river easily," said Ray. He spoke
in a cheery voice that made the rest of him infi-
nitely more horrible. "I can still teleport. I am the
unique leader. The Field-builders won't be able to
hide from me now. What do you suppose they
think of that? Watch."

And he flickered out of sight.

Merit buried her face in her hands.

Adam stood up, and took her by the hand, and

tried to get her up on her feet. "Never mind about Ray. Don't think about Vito. Those animals haven't given up. We've got to keep ahead of them, till we get somewhere they can't follow."

Merit managed to stand up. She even found a laugh from somewhere, though the sound of her laugh was far from reassuring. "At least we've had a good drink now," she said, and hobbled to refill their single canteen from the river. Their course now was going to take them uphill, away from water.

Adam asked: "How's the ankle?"

"I can block that kind of pain. And I think there's no great damage. I can walk."

Adam's beaten body had already stiffened from the short rest. he straightened up fully, with a grunt, and looked up the long rock-strewn slope toward the Ringwall's overwhelming pile.

"Then let's start up the hill," he said. "Who knows, if there's anyone home, we might even get some help."

From a rich supply of shoreline driftwood they chose two broken, dead branches to serve as staffs. They started up the slope, svaing strength at the start by going slowly. Not that they were capable of much speed anyway. The pursuing geryons were still only distantly in sight.

Ahead of them, Ray sat on a rock, waiting.

Merit cried out to him: "Ray, do you know me? Can you understand me? We need help."

"I know you, both of you." Ray nodded wisely. "I understand you better than you understand yourselves."

"Ray, we need help."

"Against the Field-builders—yes, of course. And it's only right, only proper, that you should pray to a superior being for the help you need. Yes. Only right." Ray's face still showed some effects of the battering Adam had given him, but Ray no longer appeared dazed. Rather there was a look of profound wisdom in the blue eyes.

Adam glanced back over his shoulder. The geryon pack was completely across the river now, and were coming along the shore at a loping pace. Already they had gained a hundred meters or more. He said: "Ray, what do you want from us? Either do something to help us, or go away."

Ray looked at him keenly. "Adam, I want . . ."

"What?"

"I want you . . . I want you to come and visit our school when you can . . . Doc and Regina will be glad."

Ray still looked wise and confident. He presented the image of a leader that any human might be glad to follow.

In Adam's memory rose the events he had witnessed during the night on the ocean island. He let the picture rise, and pushed it forward in his thoughts; he could see in Merit's eyes, turned now to him in desperation, that she was reading it, and he could see that the implications of it hit her hard.

Adam took her by the arm. "Never mind. No time to think about all that now. Come along."

There was still only one way to go; animals and fate were driving them up to the Ringwall itself.

They walked around Ray, and in the moment of their passage he disappeared again.

The sun rose higher as they climbed. It burned down on them through the high rolling clouds of mist that here went up eternally from the great confluence of rivers. The rocks nearby, the great angled pile of the Ringwall ahead, the methodical animals steadily gaining in their pursuit, all shimmered faintly in the heat. Merit and Adam alternately drank from the canteen, a swallow at a time, and climbed on, not daring now to pause for even a moment's rest. Not when each backward glance showed the unhurried geryons a few meters closer.

We'll make it, Adam thought, trying to project encouragement to Merit. With his imagination at least he reached forward, trying to anchor himself on that approaching moment when they would stagger into the shadow of one of the Ringwall's mighty buttresses. There was no use trying now to look beyond that moment, to see what form safety was going to take.

But they were not going to win the race. There was no moment when the hope of escape vanished; it faded away slowly. The geryons were closing in more rapidly now, still without appearing to exert themselves. One of their commoner tactics was to let prey exhaust itself in flight, thus weakening the final resistance.

Merit stumbled suddenly—Adam had forgotten about her injured ankle—and he caught her by the arm. "Teleport out of here," he told her. "If you love me, go."

She shook her head, her body swaying in exhaustion. "I can't." She clung to him briefly, then pushed herself away, standing on her own feet. "I won't."

He took a last drink from the canteen and handed it to Merit. "Finish it," he ordered. Then he bent and picked up a small rock and threw it thirty meters downhill at the nearest animal. The stone missed the arrogant, handsome face, and bounced harmlessly off the dark hide of one shoulder. The animal stopped for a moment, then took another hesitant step forward.

Adam screamed at it, a brief volley of obscenities. "We didn't come all this way to finish in your rotten guts!" Now all of the geryons paused briefly in their patient climbing, to watch and listen to him.

His throwing arm possessed no yesman power now, so it was unlikely that he could damage the animals seriously with rocks. He climbed again with Merit. He had not thought, looking at this slope from the other side of the river, that the way up would be so long, the Ringwall so remote. The very size of it had fooled him. Now human strength was failing, draining from their trembling legs and sliding feet.

As always, the pack followed. Now suddenly one animal pulled out of it, and ran past Adam and Merit up the slope, grunting and wheezing in its brief effort for speed. It got ahead of them easily cutting them off from the foot of the Ringwall. Blocking them from the towering mass of shimmering convoluted stone, laced with shadows whose foot Adam now estimated was only a hundred meters ahead.

"There must be something there," Merit croaked to him. "There must be some kind of help there, if they trouble to cut us off from it." She was hardly able to stand, and her hands were bleeding from the sharp rocks that she had gripped and fallen on. It would be of no help to Merit if he were to separate himself from her now.

"Come on." And Adam led her on, climbing straight toward the waiting geryon. The beast weighed ten times what they weighed together and its yellowed teeth were the size of human hands. Yet it shook its head nervously when they moved straight at it. Adam pulled out the knife from Merit's belt, and used it to slash a rough point on the end of his driftwood staff. His legs kept working under him, somehow still driving him upward, slow step after slow step.

"Give me that." Merit took the pointed staff from him. "I can't throw as well as you can. You keep the others off."

Adam picked up rocks. There was always some chance, with geryons, if you could fight back enough to hurt them at all. Geryons waited and watched, and followed, and waited some more. They always waited, if they could, until you were too weak to hurt them. Adam hurled rocks downslope at the following pack, and kept on climbing.

Now he diverged slightly from Merit's course, hoping that the animal ahead of them would be more likely to retreat if they came at it from two different directions. He still had the hunting knife, and he held it ready, out where the geryon could see it. Adam was sure that the damned things were able to recognize a weapon.

Merit climbed straight toward the waiting beast, leveling the pointed stick at its head.

"Wait!" Adam staggered closer. "Let me get—"

She jabbed the spear at the geryon's face, just a second too soon, before the animal might have backed away. Adam heard its teeth bite through the foolish stick as he lurched forward, stabbing the hunting knife into the beast's leathery neck, trying to turn it away from Merit. The geryon's lunge at her became panicky flight the instant it felt the knife. It trampled Merit blindly and galloped downhill, seeking the safety of the pack; and again the rest of the pack hung back briefly, startled.

Merit lay on the rocky ground. For a moment Adam could touch the blurred confusion of her mind. He put the knife between his teeth, tasting geryon blood, picked up Merit and slung her across his shoulders.

He staggered up the hill again. The pursuing geryons still delayed, watching the wounded one as it leaped and twisted, trying to bend its long neck enough to snap at its own wound. Adam ceased looking back; before the animals got near enough to attack, he would be able to hear them coming on the loose rock.

He climbed. Merit on his back was still breathing, and was not bleeding very much. He would stop when he could, and do what he could to help her.

He climbed. Until a time came when there was deep, cool shade around him . . .

. . . then he was aware that more time had passed, and he was lying on his back, after someone or something had just rolled him over. His eyes opened to the sight of a geryon face half a meter from his own, and he slashed up at it instantly with the knife that was still in his hand, carving the human nose.

The animal screamed and reared up like a horse. As it spun around to flee, its foreleg struck Adam's right arm. The knife flew away, and he thought for a long instant that his arm had been torn off. But the limb still hung from his shoulder, bleeding, and with a heavy numb pressure inside it that was soon going to turn into pain.

The pack of animals had backed away again, and were content now to sit in the sunshine twenty meters away, and wait. Merit was lying close beside him, but just out of reach.

He called to her, but she did not move or answer. She was still breathing. Her eyes were closed, her face was drawn, but there were no geryon teeth marks on her yet. Adam looked for the knife but could not see it anywhere. That was almost a relief; if he could see the knife he would have to try to crawl to it and get it back.

Sitting up, he got his back against cool stone. Slowly he realized just where he was. They had reached the shadowed base of the Ringwall. He knew the great smooth stones around him towered on up into the sky, but he could see neither the stones nor the sky very well just now, nor think about them clearly.

Now Adam saw that one of the waiting geryons had caught a little animal of some kind. And now the pack found some amusement in killing the creature as slowly as they could. They never allowed themselves to become completely distracted by the lesser game. Always one of the pack was watching Adam. *Soon, now, you will be weak enough,* the patient yellow eyes informed him. *We can make you last much longer than this little animal.*

Adam got to his feet, without thinking about whether such movement might still be possible. The packs were long gone, food and medicine gone with them. Canteen still here—Merit had it clipped to her belt—but Adam knew that the canteen was empty. Water gone, then. And now the knife gone too.

He got himself over to Merit somehow, and got his one operational arm around her, and picked her up. Then he half carried, half dragged her deeper into the cool shadow. There was a doorway waiting for them there, within a recess and then another recess of the towering stone, or at least they came upon an opening of the proper size to be a door. Adam looked at it as calmly as he would have looked now at blank hopeless walls. Holding Merit, keeping her from falling, he limped forward into a passage that was large enough to let the geryons follow.

Adam followed the passage. He knew without looking that the geryons still pursued. There were no branches, no agonizing choices of which way to go. There was light enough to see the way, daylight, he supposed, filtering in somehow from overhead. He wasted no effort in trying to fix the source of light. Merit moaned as she walked, leaning on him. She said nothing, and half the time her eyes were closed. There were odd blocks of stone, projecting from the floor and the walls. Adam bumped into them and fell on them frequently.

He thanked whoever might be responsible that his injured arm had not yet begun to hurt. Or maybe it was hurting, and he was just too far gone to know the difference.

There were many turns in the passage, all of them with sharp, right-angled corners. Sometimes at a corner Adam looked back, and when he looked there was always a geryon head sticking around the last corner, watching him carefully. Here the animals could follow only in single file, and they were being very cautious. The thing for prey to do was to get into a smaller passage, where geryons could not follow. But there was only this one wide passage, filled with light enough to see, when Adam's eyes could see, and stone blocks on which to fall.

Adam stumbled into a pool of water a few inches deep, formed by a small stream that came gurgling merrily and for no apparent reason from a plain fount in the wall. He drank and wallowed in the pool, and took the canteen from Merit's belt and filled it up again. He waved his useful arm, and shouted echoes at the geryons when they dared creep closer. He splashed Merit, and thought he got her to swallow a little water from his cupped hand. He himself felt shivering and sick and unreal after his drink; he didn't want to revive, didn't want to know what was happening to him.

He was moving on again, somehow, holding Merit up with his good left arm. They came upon Ray, sitting crosslegged in the passage.

"I've thought about the geryone," said Ray, in conversational greeting. Now it was Ray's face that was changing in and out of its proper shape, altering, bulging, sagging like wet plaster. But Ray did not mind. He said: "They're not just animals, you know. They're something more."

"They're after us now, Ray. They're right behind us." Adam slumped down, unwillingly, his legs just giving out beneath him.

"I know what they are," said Ray.

"They're animals and they want to kill us and eat us. Ray. Can you—"

"No, not mere animals, Adam. I am considering, evaluating, the possibility that the geryons are really the Field-builders themselves. They are the ones who really built . . ."

Ray paused. His face, handsome once again, frowned lightly. "What was it that they really built?"

"Ray. Listen. Can you get Merit out of here somehow? Teleport with her?"

"You see, Adam. First, at the bottom of the scale, there are vegetables . . . no, start with viruses. Or perhaps one should really start with rocks . . ."

"Ray."

". . . and vegetables, and then there are animals, and then comes good old Earth-descended Homo. Sap. And then at the top are Jovians."

"Ray, I'll listen to it all some other—"

"The ladder of created being," said Ray in a loud firm voice. "That's what C.S. Lewis—do you know him?—wrote somewhere . . . but he was wrong. Very wrong. Because that is all there are . . ."

"Ray."

"Rock, vegetable, animal, human, Jovian. We're at the top. Now I am considering the possi—the possi—I am thinking about . . ."

"Ray."

"Lemme think. I—can't—think—" Ray's body distorted into new frightfulness; a moment later he once more flickered away out of sight.

Adam stared stupidly; had Ray really been there at all, this time? Adam's arm was throbbing violently now. He must be feverish. He looked around and saw a geryon watching him, from the last bend in the passage, watching with those yellow eyes, like those of a dead thing. The geryons were real enough.

The animal stretched its neck forward, the human face as always lacking any expression except for the illusion of pride. Was it at long last impatient, ready to charge? Adam got to his feet.

Merit's mind touched his again; now it was as if he could hear her calling to him, out of a foggy distance. *Adam, leave me, go on, look for help.*

It took no courage to say no to that. There was no place in the world for him to go, if he left her.

Some time later, they were again limping along in glaring sunlight. Adam realized that they were now inside the Ringwall, because now the daylight was much brighter, and around him there were tall trees and tall stones, and towering, unentifiable shapes that he had not seen outside. But it didn't matter. Soon everything would be over. He kept expecting to feel teeth.

At one point he realized clearly that he was crawling up a little slope, moving on his knees and his one good hand, and that Merit was standing beside him, trying to pull him along. Then they were sitting together, side by side, backs propped against a wall, looking down a little slope to where the familiar geryons—almost old friends by now— peered from among tall rocks to see if their victims were yet weak enough. Merit looked as if she had passed out again. Good. That was good. She might never feel the teeth.

Chapter Twenty

A frightening thought came to disturb Adam's calm. It was that he might be able to get up and go on farther if he really tried. It would be much easier just to sit here and be chewed to death. But he couldn't just sit here, that was impossible. There welled up in Adam a terrible puny rage, a fury like that of a sick old man, against the animals. He would not them defeat him, destroy him and his woman. He could not. He groped with his left hand for something, anything, to use as a weapon. Like an animal, he growled at the other animals that menaced him.

They cringed away uneasily. But not from Adam. They looked around, raising their leathery ears beside their human faces. They turned and looked behind them, aiming their tails in his direction. Then they retreated prudently between tall rocks, to watch and wait. Someone was approaching from that direction. Or something was.

A figure wearing heavy Space Force ground armor emerged from among the tall rocks, a little distance beyond the geryons. The figure came walking, with steady powerful strides, straight toward Adam and Merit.

"Our plan has succeeded," said a voice at Adam's side. Ray's voice. Ray sat there on the ground. His face still showed what Adam's hands had done to him, but his shape was normal again, as he sat watching the walking figure approach.

The newcomer halted a few meters in front of them. Through the transparent front of the ground-suit's helmet a man's face was plainly visible ... and Adam thought that he had seen that face somewhere before. Somewhere, somewhere.

"You're not real," Adam accused him suddenly. "We're in the Field here. Your groundsuit wouldn't work if you were real."

"But my suit does work," the stranger's air-speaker replied calmly, in what sounded like a native Earthman's voice. "Therefore we are not in the Field. Not right here."

Ray stood up, towering taller than the other. "Now I have you," Ray said to him majestically. "Your race is in my power. I am the supreme being of the universe, do you realize that? I have come to harrow your dungeons, release your prisoners, destroy your power."

Merit was still passed out.

Ray's mad rambling voice seemed to be reaching Adam's ears from a distance. *Not in the Field*, the man in the groundsuit had said. *Not right here.* What did that mean? Adam couldn't think. His mind was running itself to death in a little circle of animals and rocks.

The man in the suit had said something to Ray, and now Ray was speaking again, arguing with him: "—no, I am not human. I am much more than that."

"But you *are* human," the stranger answered. "And so are we. Did you think that we who built the Field were more than that? You have a small idea of what being human means."

"I am not human."

"I have never understood you Earth-descended, though I know you better than most of my kind know you. Because I have lived among you."

"Alex Golden," Adam croaked, suddenly remembering. Both of the other men turned to look at him. Merit did not turn her head. She was still out cold.

Ray only seemed annoyed by the interruption, but Golden—yes, it was he all right—gave Adam interested attention.

"Yeah, that's me," the man in the suit said, in a different, more ordinary voice. "The only Alex Golden that ever was. This is my planeteering outfit." He raised a gauntleted hand and gestured at himself; whether he meant the suit alone, or suit and body both, Adam could not tell.

Ray's annoyance had grown. "Lived among us, did you? That's nothing! I can change my shape, too!" He demonstrated. "I can get free your prisoners."

"We have no prisoners. Your mind has torn itself on its own weapons," Golden told him, watching bizarre alterations with little apparent interest.

Adam could feel a wave of faintness coming over him. "Help us," he asked, of anyone who would listen.

Golden turned back to him. "Most of my kind would not take notice of you here. It's not that we're your enemies; Kedro here sees our minds only through his own hate, he fills our images with his own sickness. There are no torture chambers here, except the ones he has imagined. But most of us would simply not take notice. Our minds and yours *are* vastly different. I think it's only because I lived so long on Earth that I realized you were here now."

"I am no human. And I can do more than you can do! I am going to turn you into a telepathic frequency converter." Ray stood beside Golden, grabbing at the smaller man's armored sleeve. But even Ray was not going to be able to push around someone wearing heavy ground armor, and Golden was not perturbed. The Jovian towered beside him like a giant child, fretting and plucking, demanding more attention.

"Help, then," Adam whispered.

"I've already told you," said Golden. "All you need to know. You can do the rest."

There was a silence. Ray stood clenching his hands and staring helplessly at Golden. But Ray was being ignored.

Adam suddenly pushed himself almost erect, leaning against the rock behind him. Every time he blinked his eyes, the figure in armor wavered, like everything else in his field of vision. But it did not disappear.

"Your suit works," Adam croaked. "So there's no Field here, inside the Ringwall."

Golden regarded him calmly, but gave no other answer.

"So seven years ago your scoutship had room enough, altitude enough under the Field, to pull out of its fall. It landed here, as you knew it would."

Maybe Golden smiled, just a little, inside the helmet.

Ray sank down on his knees, suddenly, with a loud cry. "No! I must be more than human!"

Golden immediately crouched down too, as if he wanted to keep on a level with Ray to speak to him. He waved at the skulking geryons. "Those are only animals, no more than animals now, no matter what their faces say. Once—they were more. Consider that. We are above them, you and I. Above the human, there is nothing, or one life-form only. Is there not pride enough for anyone in that?"

"One life-form only . . ."

"Not you, my sick man, no, not you. Those sane beings who say they see it call it God."

Ray shook his head slowly, slowly. "I am more than a man. More than a man."

"There is much pain, too, in being human," Golden said. "But there is only one way we can turn to rid ourselves of that. And that is backward."

"I defy you, Field-builder, torturer." It came out as a mad scream. "I will destroy you yet!"

Now Adam could no longer see Ray anywhere. The big man had disappeared again. But Adam could spare no time or strength for Ray, wherever he might be. Adam was thinking, and thinking now was as hard a climbing a cliff. He dared not slacken his grip for a moment.

"The scoutship is still here, then," he said aloud, staring at Alexander Golden. Adam could feel the throbbing in his arm, going faster and faster. The sun shone down on him. He was awake, he must be. "Even if you're not real, it's still here, crashed or landed. A lot of it would survive a crash. At least there'll be a first aid kit."

Golden stood erect again. Now his head turned to one side, so that his eyes looked toward the open space, the vast unroofed center of the Ring-wall. Then he too was gone.

Adam stood up straight with a gasp, lurching away from the rock that had supported him. Only Merit was still with him now. He bent over her and slapped her, trying to wake her up; she only moaned. With his one good arm he dragged her to her feet. His bad arm had started to hurt like hell now. Good. It would keep him awake.

He laughed aloud, and there was a mad horrible echo from the laugh, and the geryons who had started to come out shrank back again among the rocks. Maybe he had been keeping the pack at bay for an hour with the loud sounds of delirium, maybe this time neither Ray nor Golden had been any more than fever dreams. But it didn't matter. Because, somewhere near here, landed or crashed, the scoutship had to be real.

He shook Merit by the hair. "C'mon, get moving, kid! We've got to travel!"

He got her walking down the slope, angling away from the geryons, taking the direction in which Golden had turned his head.

In the middle of a grassy meadow the scoutship waited undamaged, in perfect landing position. As Adam finished the last dragging step, he could hear the geryons moaning behind him, still not quite daring to charge and kill the beings who had fought them for so long.

If an illusion cast a long shadow in the after-noon sun, if it felt like solid smooth metal when you leaned against it, then an illusion was enough, no one could ask for more. Adam was gathering his strength to knock on the ground level hatch,

when it swung open. The standard model planeteering robot stepped out and caught him as he
started to fall.

He was aware of not hurting anywhere—not until he tried to move. Even then, a blanket of protective numbness enfolded his body, thickly enough
to constitute a vast improvement. He tried the
fingers of his right hand and thought that he could
feel them rub against each other. Not bad, then. It
wasn't bad at all.

Adam opened his eyes to find himself in the
familiar setting of a scoutship's small control room,
strapped into the right seat. Maybe the last seven
years had been all a dream, and when he turned
his head he would see Boris—but no, the robot
was bending over him.

"How do you feel, sir?" the robot asked.

"The woman who was with me—"

The robot pointed, and Adam turned his head,
heavy skull swiveling on neck muscles that cried
out with pain when forced to work again. There
was Merit, securely tucked into a bunk.

"She is asleep now, sir, and seems to be in no
immediate danger from her injuries, though she
needs further medical attention as you doubtless
know. I have administered first aid treatment to
both of you. Now, will you please identify yourself
to me, sir?"

"My name is Adam Mann." It sounded strange,
it even tasted strange as he pronounced it. "I used
to be a planeteer. Oh, one thing, very important.
I'm a human being, nothing more."

"Certainly, sir," said the robot, unperturbed. It
knew a human when it saw one, or it thought it
did. Probably its programming included instruc-

tions to humor crazed wanderers, or accident victims, when they said strange things.

But the robot wasn't going to let his identification go at that. "Please answer this question," it requested, and then queried him on a technical detail of scoutship operation. Not one civilian in ten thousand would know the answer, but not one planeteer, or former planeteer, in ten thousand would have forgotten it.

Adam consulted his memory, and gave the correct reply.

"I accept that you have had planeteering training," said the machine. "I place myself, within limits, under your orders."

Adam took thought. Thinking, at least, was not painful. "What were your last orders?"

"My last orders were given me more than seven years ago, by Chief Planeteer Alexander Golden." As the robot quoted, it reproduced the tones of Golden's voice: " 'Stay with the ship and keep it in good shape until another Earth-descended human comes.' The type of order is unique in my experience, as are the conditions under which this scoutship landed here."

"You fell, through a condition we have named the Field, which surrounds this planet almost completely."

"I was inoperative through the fall," said the robot, "but since landing I have observed this Field, as you term it, on the radar screens."

"What happened to Golden, after the landing?"

"Immediately after giving me the order I have just quoted, he walked away. I have had no contact with him, or any other human, since then."

"So." Adam drew a deep breath; his ribs hurt

too. "Can we take off from here, and get back into space?"

"Yes. I have computed that there is room enough under the Field for the necessary acceleration. The scoutship can be made to coast upward through the Field, on a ballistic path, if it is assumed that control and power can be re-established above six hundred kilometers altitude."

"They can be." Adam let his eyes close; a robot could make the takeoff, if it could be made. "Let's go, then. You'll probably see some Space Force ships when we get above the Field. There may be fighting in progress."

"Fighting, sir? In space?"

"Yes. If you see any, avoid the fighting ships and drive around the planet to the antipodal point—there's a shuttle port there now."

"First there is another matter."

Adam opened his eyes again.

"It requires human judgment to decide," said the machine. "Since shortly after your arrival, a creature I cannot identify has been outside the ship, moving among the large animals that pursued you. I cannot decide whether or not it is human."

The robot switched on a viewscreen in front of Adam, showing the meadow outside the scout. Adam watched, for long, long seconds.

"Did you say 'no'?" the robot asked.

"Yes," said Adam. "Yes, he's human. Go out and bring him in. Lock him in the alien room. You must stun him if he resists; I order that, and take responsibility. He is mentally and physically ill."

"I will obey. Then we must leave the surface and obtain medical help."

"Yes." Adam let himself slump back in his seat

He could let go, now. Drifting toward a pleasant stupor, he watched the screen, where a somewhat smaller animal cavorted among the geryons. It had a scaly body and furred legs, like one of their young, but it lacked the true geryon shape. It lacked true shape of any kind. Suddenly the creature went down, as if hit by a stun beam; a second later the robot appeared in the viewscreen's picture, to drive off the larger beasts and lift the small one carefully.

Its head swung loosely, dangling on the long geryon neck, and it had the wide powerful geryon jaws. But he nose and eyes and forehead were those of Raymond Kedro.

Adam realized that he was lying in a bed. He blinked his eyes open and shut a couple of times, without really comprehending anything they saw. He rolled over, and grunted when his arm twinged fiercely.

"The beauty sleepeth," said a familiar male voice, quite near at hand. "And where in all the realm can be found a maiden desperate enough to awakeneth him with a kiss?"

Adam opened his eyes again. "Boris."

Brazil sat bathrobed in a wheelchair, his left leg sealed into a cabled mold. "Howdy, bub. Anything nteresting happen to you lately?"

They were in the sick bay of some big Space Force ship, Adam realized. The place was crowded, with casualties overflowing into extra beds. The background feeling and faint sounds suggested hat they were in space.

"Yeah, she's all right," Brazil said. "No need to train your neck looking. She's up and walking round already."

Adam lay back. "You lanky ape," he said. "Looks like you had a fight and won."

"You looked like you had one and lost, when that robot flew you in. In Golden's scoutship, yet . . . yeah, we had quite a scrap here. We took about fifty people alive out of that hundred. We might even have come out on the short end, but they started fighting among themselves. About someone being burned, whether it was right or not—maybe you can enlighten us on that."

"Yeah—but it's a long story."

"That fellow we took out of the alien room of that scoutship—he's Kedro?"

"Yes."

"Some of the other people were pretty sick, in the same way. I wonder what got into them? All we wanted to do here was hand 'em a parking ticket, so to speak. And they opened up on us with everything at once. And they kept talking about burning this fellow Ling. And a couple of my people got burned to death too, in a most peculiar way."

Maybe this is my first official interrogation, Adam realized suddenly. Just Boris sitting there in his bathrobe, talking things over. He thought about the question.

"It started a long time ago," Adam answered after a while. "They had a plan—Ray Kedro had a plan—that didn't work. As I say, it's a long story."

"Yeah. Well, not all of 'em thought that way."

Adam looked at him.

"I mean your girl Merit, among others."

"If you think that she—"

"At ease! Calm down. Nobody wants to hang her. Unless some evidence comes up that I don't know about yet. It's no crime to have had you chromosomes manipulated. I merely remarked that she seems like a nice kid."

Adam let out a long sigh. "One part of the long story I'll tell you now. Ray Kedro told me that I was one of them too. Maybe he was lying; maybe not. I don't think he was, about that."

Brazil thought that over with raised eyebrows. Then he shrugged. "Well, I can stand it if you can. I expect it'll be a long time before Raymond Kedro can tell us a straight story now, assuming that he wants to. The medics have him in a deep freeze. Do you know what shape he was in when they took him out of that scout?"

"I know what shape he was in when we left the planet," said Adam. *I can stand it if you can*, Brazil had said. To hell with it. *I'm a man whether or not I came out of Doc Nowell's lab. I am what I am.*

And another voice, remembered but already fading: *You have a small idea of what being human means.*

"I assume I'm not under arrest for anything?" he asked. "Unauthorized exploration, maybe?"

Boris shrugged. "We asked your help in the situation, if you remember. I assume you were doing what you could to help. We've got enough prisoners, what do we need with one more?"

"And Merit?"

"I told you, no. Be reasonable, what would we charge her with? Teasing the geryons? Unless something new shows up when we get your stories in detail. Hey, now, about that scoutship—"

"Later." Adam relaxed, closing his eyes in peaceful weariness. He opened them again to see Brazil wheeling away. Adam called after him: "Hey. When we're both in one piece again, I just may be calling on you. To look for a job."

Boris nodded, his long craggy face solemn, and turned away again. He wheeled a little distance, suddenly roared with laughter, and turned back. "I don't know—look what we started the last time we worked together."

Adam groped with his good hand for something suitable to throw, but could find nothing. Never mind. He began to doze off, smiling. He could hear Boris's muttering, receding into the distance: "The sleeping beauty sleepeth again, and where in all the realm can be found a maiden of such courage as to—oh. Beg your pardon, ma'am."

Then there followed a silence. It took no exercise of parapsych talent for Adam to feel her approaching his bed. The aura of her mind was subtle and sweet as fine perfume. He opened his eyes and stretched out his good left arm.

THE END

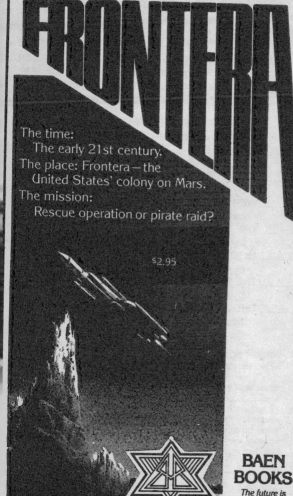